I0614164

# Beyond the Door

## by

## Iona Morrison

*A Blue Cove Mystery, Book 11*

**Beyond the Door**

Cover Art by *The Wild Rose Press, Inc.*

The Wild Rose Press, Inc.
PO Box 708
Adams Basin, NY 14410-0708
Visit us at www.thewildrosepress.com

Publishing History
First Edition, 2022
Trade Paperback ISBN 978-1-5092-4446-1
Digital ISBN 978-1-5092-4447-8

*A Blue Cove Mystery, Book 11*
Published in the United States of America

Peyton took the journal from her cousin. Wrapping it in the fabric, she placed the book back into the box. When she went to place the lid on the hatbox, that's when the battle began.

The lid flew through the space between them like a Frisbee only to be snatched out the air by Jessie's quick motion before she got smacked in the face. "Are you kidding me?" Jessie shook her head. "I don't think it matters what we decide. We didn't choose the book—it chose us."

"Looks that way. You know what they say about the power of books to change a person, don't you?" Peyton asked.

"Of course, that's why I bought a bookstore. All those words, great thoughts, and stories are life-altering as well as entertaining."

"Books seem to have been at the center of our problems and life changes more than once lately. I think we're about to test the theory again." Peyton placed the open box on the table, leaving the lid off.

"Here we go again." Jessie buttoned her coat and pulled her gloves from the pocket.

"At least this time it's about Cara's journey. How that is important to us I'm sure I have no idea."

# Dedication

Dedicated to my five grandchildren, Dylan, Jade, Noah, Liam, and Fiona who are the bright, shining rays of hope in my world. How I love each of them.

## Acknowledgments

I would like to acknowledge the work of my great editor Dianne Rich, RJ Morris for my awesome cover, and the staff of The Wild Rose Press who made the production of this book possible. A special thank you goes to a Twitter friend from Ireland, Brian Mulholland who helped with my research on Ireland during the Potato Famine. Thank you.

Chapter 1

Peyton awakened with a start, taking deep breaths to calm her racing heart. Turning on the lamp, she glanced around the room as the light slowly chased the dark shadows away. The nightmare always started the same, a prone figure lying still on the glistening white snow with a red pool spreading shockingly from a fatal head wound. Out of the reach of the bright moonlight stood a shadowy figure that she couldn't quite make out before the dream would suddenly end. Lately, the dream seemed more vivid, taking on a sinister feel that left her restless and troubled.

Someone had been murdered, and it was only a matter of time until the body was discovered. Where or when, male or female, Peyton Reynolds had no idea. But she knew the murder was real, all the same.

The dream served as her motivation as once again she found herself trudging through the snow on her way to the inn. She would be happy when winter left, taking the frigid air with it. The snow was pretty, but she missed the flowers, green grass, and the gardens humming with life. Walking in the back door at the inn, she waved at Katie standing near the stove in the process of reaching for her potholders.

"Yum, something smells delicious." Peyton sniffed the wonderful aroma. "I'll be in the attic if you need me." She paused for a moment to take off her heavy coat.

"I hope you find what you're looking for. You've been up there often enough." Katie took the freshly baked bread out of the oven and placed the pans on the rack to cool. "You can have a slice on your way out. This loaf should be cool enough to cut by then. There's nothing as good as a slice of homemade bread with butter and honey or jelly if you prefer."

"I'll hold you to your offer. The bread smells delicious." Peyton placed her coat across the kitchen chair. "Do you mind if I leave this here? The attic is a bit dusty."

"Be my guest." Katie motioned at her. "I'll miss seeing you when you get tired of going through all that junk." Katie chuckled.

"Never," Peyton told her. "I enjoy poking around up there. The space is filled with lots of wonderful books and boxes brimming with memorabilia. It's a treat. Besides I'm not sure what I'm looking for. I just have this grand idea that I will know it when I find it." She shook her head at the absurdity of what she had said.

"If this newfound treasure is worth money, let me know. I get first dibs. I wouldn't mind being rich." Katie laughed as she buttered the tops of the hot loaves and put two more into the oven.

"Of course, any riches rightfully belong to you." Peyton grinned and headed toward the stairs that led to the attic.

The minute her hand reached for the door at the top of the stairs, memories flooded her mind. Would this strange feeling always be with her? Impressions and sensations that kept the events of the past year traipsing through her thoughts at the strangest times. "No time for lollygagging," she muttered. "Time to focus on the task at hand." She opened the door. Today was the day; she could feel it in her bones. Whatever that meant.

Peyton got right to work, going through the stacks of old books and magazines first. Then she moved on to several of the boxes where she had left off on her last visit. She had carefully marked the ones she had already searched. Sorting through one box after another, she found some interesting items but nothing that reached out and grabbed her. Of course, it would help if she knew what she was looking for.

On a self-imposed mission, she searched for clues that she knew had to be hidden somewhere in one of the books, letters, or magazines that filled the shelves and boxes. Every chance she got she was either here or at the library looking for hints as to why the supernatural activity around the inn and in town always seemed extremely high. Not to mention her recurring dream. No details, other than the body lying in the snow surrounded by trees. Lots of trees, which didn't narrow down the locations. Trees and wooded areas were plentiful in Blue Cove.

As far as she was concerned, there had to be a good reason that the cove was a hotbed of activity. When she traveled back in time, she found out why she had the gift of sight, and the revelation made perfect sense to her. Peyton knew there had to be a reason for the town too.

One of her many foibles was once an idea took hold of her, there was no stopping her until she found the answer. Another way in which she and her cousin Jessie were similar. Although Jessie wouldn't own up to that tidbit. Or at the very least, Jessie would make the flaw sound like an asset.

"Nothing here," she muttered, pushing another heavy box off to the side and stacking it with the others after placing a strip of orange tape on the top.

How many boxes had she searched through? She had lost count of the amount several days ago. With no clues and no success to this point, it left her rethinking her bright idea. "Achoo." She reached for the tissue in her pocket. The dust swirling through the air had caused her to sneeze more than once in the last hour. The way the light hit the particles made them look almost golden and sparkly at times.

A lot had happened in her life since her jaunt back to the year nineteen-eighteen. Thankfully no more time travel, although it had been rad. No, the changes were in her real-life in the here and now. She had learned to feel more at home in her skin. The gift of sight that had passed down to her and her cousin Jessie from their great-great-grandmother no longer shocked her. She had simply learned to live with the idea. Not to say that the premonitions and ghost sightings still didn't shake up her life from time to time because they did. She never knew if or when she would see a vision or a ghost that pulled her off the sidelines and into the center of another strange adventure. It made life hard to plan. At least for a while, things had been quiet in that regard. Almost too quiet until the dream. She rubbed her arms where the goosebumps were now forming.

After testifying at the trial in Arizona about the drug ring she helped to break up, she had helped her boyfriend Jaxon finish packing his things before flying home to her cottage next door to Jessie's. Jaxon's new position landed him in the FBI field office in Hanover with Tom Maxwell as his superior officer. Although he spent most of his time during the week moving between DC at the FBI headquarters, and Quantico, Virginia, at the Academy going through agency training and learning the ropes of his new job. Maxwell had his training fast-tracked because of his experience. Thankfully, on the weekends he was all hers except for when she had to share him with Jessie's boyfriend Matt and their new project.

Another box to stack with the others. She would go through one or two more at the tops, and that's it. She pulled off a strip of orange tape, marked the box, and moved it out of the way. *There has to be something.* She glanced toward the books on the shelves. "I'm coming your way soon, but you can forget another portal. I'm not going anywhere." She opened another box and sorted through the contents.

Recently, Jaxon had bought a house overlooking the cove. A fixer-upper that Matt was helping him to transform whenever they got extra time, which wasn't often. Peyton had to admit she was anxious to see how they were progressing, but Jaxon wouldn't let her near the house yet. His excuse was they were in the demolition process which would shock her. She had a feeling he was holding out on her. Seeing ghosts and having dreams seemed easier than knowing what made Jaxon tick. Her experience with men could fill a thimble. She didn't have any, and getting to know him was a lot like learning to ride her bike. Exciting, but a bit awkward.

But at least she had found her dream job working in a special education class at the Blue Cove elementary school. Love was the word she often used to describe her job to anybody who would listen to her. Talking about how wonderful her students were was one of her favorite pastimes. Which reminded her—she needed to keep her eye out for the two young kids she saw being bullied from her classroom window. She didn't get out to the playground fast enough. There was something about them that tugged at her heartstrings.

Hopefully, she wasn't borrowing trouble taking on this challenge to find answers, but she couldn't seem to help herself. Something was about to go down, and she didn't want to be blindsided.

Almost all her free time was limited, between working at the school, editing, and helping Jessie in the bookstore. She managed to stay busy and out of trouble. Add in dates with Jaxon whenever she got the chance, and her life was surprisingly good. Jaxon's heavy schedule kept them apart more than they liked, but such was life.

After another box came up empty, she was ready to give up her search for the day when an unusual-shaped box perched precariously on the edge of a treadle sewing machine in the corner caught her attention. She couldn't remember seeing the box there before.

"That's odd. Where did you come from, my little pretty?" she asked, pushing her hair behind her ears. "I know I would've remembered seeing you." The shape reminded her of an old hatbox. Drawn to its pattern and design, she had to peek inside.

"Call me nosey, but I can't help myself," she muttered, swatting the dust off her pants as she stood. Excitement got her moving toward the spot followed by her hand automatically reaching for the box. The minute she touched the lid, a strange feeling came over her.

"What have we here?" she whispered. Wrapped in several layers of a gossamer material, a small leather book tied with a fraying pink ribbon rested. Her hands trembled as she touched it. Carefully, she untied the ribbon and opened to the first page. Handwritten in beautiful penmanship were the words, *Cara Cassidy's Journey in the year of our Lord, 1845.*

****

Watching unseen from the opposite side of the attic, anticipation rose within the tiny creature. At last, the dear girl finally saw the precious gem where she had artfully placed it. Several days had come and gone before Mila had figured out the perfect spot and the right way to display the journal for the young woman to discover it. Peyton had passed by the book so many times that Mila was losing hope. She even doubted what she knew to be true—that Peyton Reynolds was a uniquely talented young woman.

It was too soon for Mila to use her magic in the open, but she had to find a way to draw the girl's interest. Remembering what she had been taught and the motto she loved to live by, she searched for the perfect spot.

"Attention to detail is everything," Mila mused. How she had arranged the colorful hatbox was genius on her part. For it was the lovely box that finally caught the girl's eye. "Perfect," she sighed. Golden sparkles and misty kisses she could use liberally.

As soon as Peyton touched the box, excitement shot through Mila from her tiny shoes to her wings. She flittered about the attic, her heart dancing. Finally, the whole story would be told. Years had moved swiftly by while she had waited for the right person. Not that she had remained idle the whole time. No, she had been busy doing her job. Few people rarely came up into this world, but Peyton had come many times. She would do quite nicely. After observing her for weeks, intuition told Mila that this young woman would pursue the truth. Mila told her sister that in the end, the book had chosen the girl.

Chapter 2

Peyton's hand shook when she leafed through the book. A presence could be felt with the turn of each page. She rewrapped the journal and clutched it to her chest. "I promise to take good care of this for you," she whispered to whoever was watching her. Was it Cara or another? Maybe the answer was written in the pages.

Jessie had to see her discovery, and they could read the diary together. If nothing else this was Cara's history, and she couldn't wait to read her words. Thankfully, Katie had told her she could borrow anything she found. She would return the hatbox when she was finished reading the diary. It bugged her that she hadn't noticed it before. Another mystery to think about. In all her trips to the attic, why now? Destiny?

She held the box tightly and started down the stairs, closing the door to the attic. She made her way to the kitchen and her coat.

"Did you find anything of interest?" Katie turned to ask, lifting the spoon from the pan she was stirring on the stove.

"I found an old diary that looks promising. I'll bring it back when I'm finished." Peyton reached for her coat and slid her arms into the sleeves as they talked. "Did you ever see this cute box in the attic before?" She held the box out so Katie could see what she was talking about.

"No, I'd remember if I had. Did you find the journal inside?" Katie took a step closer to look at the box. "It almost looks like it's hand-painted."

"That's what I thought too. The journal was tucked inside, and I can't wait to start reading it." Peyton smiled wistfully. "There's something special about this book."

"Now you sound like Jessie. I don't understand either of you, but that's okay. I don't need to." Katie squeezed her lips together. "Let me know if it's any good. My uncle told me there might be some items that belong to some of our Irish ancestors up there. I'm too busy to take the time to search, but if you find anything out about them, you can tell me. The Donovans originally came from County Limerick in Southwestern Ireland. Some of them migrated here during the Great Potato Famine. Wouldn't it be crazy if they settled around this area?"

"Nothing would surprise me. I'll tell you if I find anything interesting. Hey, do you know what might be fun? We could do your family tree." Peyton answered her own question as she walked to the door.

"I would love that." Katie smiled at her. "Marriage limits my free time unless Dylan is working in the evenings. I still love being with my man. I'll let you know when I have a free evening, and you can bring Jessie too. A girl's night would be perfect. I could use one."

"Sounds good to me." Peyton wrapped her scarf around her neck.

"Don't forget your bread. I buttered the top and wrapped the yummy goodness in foil. Enjoy the small taste of heaven with a cup of tea. The temperature has dropped out there." She handed the package to Peyton.

"This is too heavy to be one slice of bread." Peyton's brows rose.

"I gave you extra. I have to take care of my single friends. Take this one to Jessie. You'll see her before I will." Katie handed her another package.

"We both thank you. See you later." Peyton opened the back door and made her way through the snow-covered gardens toward the cottage. The chilly wind sent shivers racing through her body. As far as she was concerned, the snow could go away and take the cold air with it the day after the Christmas tree came down.

"Hey, cousin, what are you carrying?" Jessie's boots crunched through the snow as she ran to catch up with her.

"This is yours from Katie. Fresh bread, and it smells delicious." She handed the package to her.

"Thank you. I love Katie's bread. What else do you have?" Jessie asked.

"Let's get inside, and I'll show you. The air is too cold to stand out here talking." She unlocked the door to her cottage. Every time she walked inside, she fell in love with her place all over again. The new feeling hadn't worn off yet. Jessie followed her inside. Peyton took off her boots and left them at the door. Her coat came off next, and she carried the box over to the couch and waited for Jessie to get settled.

"Something tells me you've found a treasure." Jessie plopped down in the chair across from her while unbuttoning her jacket. "By the way, I love all the new touches you've added. The pillows and throws are perfect with the window coverings. All the creamy and bright whites with the pops of yellow and turquoise are the perfect colors in this room. It's totally you, cousin."

"Thanks, it's coming together. How do you like being back in your newly remodeled place?" Peyton placed the hatbox on her lap.

"I'm happy to be in my cottage, but there are times when I miss you not being there. Especially when I'm awake at night and in one of my strange cleaning moods when I move furniture or canned goods." Jessie laughed, her dimples on full display.

"I don't miss those times at all." Peyton pictured the time she ran into an out-of-place chair at full speed during one of those moments. "I do miss our chats and fun though." She took the lid off the box. "Look what I found. I thought we could read it together." She slipped the journal from the material wrapped around it.

"Wow." Jessie stood and moved closer to get a better look at the book.

"This is the journal of Cara Cassidy. It's dated 1845. I have no idea who she was, but I knew the minute I touched this box there's something important for us to find written somewhere in the pages of her journal." She placed the book into Jessie's hand. "Have you heard of her?"

"I have no idea who she is, but there's a strong presence around the book. What's the plan?" Jessie clutched the book to her chest. "I may be wrong, but we need to read this together whenever we get the chance. Cara Cassidy has something to do with the inn or the cove in some way or maybe both. I can't wait to find out how."

"That's exactly what I thought. Our two heads working together are much better than one of us alone." Peyton leaned forward in the chair.

"The only question I have is, what are the unseen things that will involve us the minute we start down this path?" Jessie said softly. "May I suggest we think long and hard before we read these pages and that we prepare ourselves for the strange and the unusual which is bound to happen." She pressed her lips together. "Matt told me that someone discovered a body in the woods outside of town a couple of days ago." Jessie sat on the edge sofa facing Peyton. "He seemed troubled by the find and evasive."

"Male or female? Were they murdered?" Peyton asked. "I've had a dream several times about a body lying in the snow. I know they were murdered, but other than that I have no other details."

"You need to call him. Matt hasn't said much to me, but he keeps asking me if I know anything. He is tightlipped and won't give me any details. Believe me, I've tried to get him to talk. He's waiting on the forensics is all he will say. From what I've overheard, there was something unusual about the victim or the location. None of the guys at the station are saying much." Jessie stood, clasping the diary in her hand. "Call him."

"I will." Peyton paused when she saw Jessie looking at her like she didn't believe her. "I promise. Is that good enough?"

"Don't talk yourself out of it the minute I leave," Jessie told her. "I should go, and you need to call Matt." Jessie started to pace. "You don't suppose that somehow this is all connected, do you? No, how could it be?" She turned the journal over in her hands.

"May I suggest something else to consider?" Peyton stood beside her cousin when she nodded. "We should sleep on this tonight. And after work tomorrow we can discuss what we want to do. For now, I'll put this little gem away for safekeeping." Peyton took the journal from her cousin. Wrapping it in the fabric, she placed the book back into the box. When she went to place the lid on the hatbox, that's when the battle began.

The lid flew through the space between them like a Frisbee only to be snatched out the air by Jessie's quick motion before she got smacked in the face. "Are you kidding me?" Jessie shook her head. "I don't think it matters what we decide. We didn't choose the book—it chose us."

"Looks that way. You know what they say about the power of books to change a person, don't you?" Peyton asked.

"Of course, that's why I bought a bookstore. All those words, great thoughts, and stories are life-altering as well as entertaining."

"Books seem to have been at the center of our problems and life changes more than once lately. I think we're about to test the theory again." Peyton placed the open box on the table, leaving the lid off.

"Here we go again." Jessie buttoned her coat and pulled her gloves from the pocket.

"At least this time it's about Cara's journey. How that is important to us I'm sure I have no idea." Peyton handed Jessie the bread she was about to forget. "Cara, we have no idea what you want, but we are open for you to show us," she whispered under her breath.

"Any ideas?" Jessie wrapped her scarf, pulling it up near her face.

"None whatsoever. We're talking about a long time

ago. How that plays out today who knows." She stood beside her cousin. "I can't wait to find out, though. I keep thinking about your friend Sally Mansfield's experience at Christmas. She even had a fairy helping her through her problems. I believe the inn has more going on than we know."

"I've often thought that but haven't had the time to take on anything extra. Tomorrow is soon enough to think about it though. I've had a long day. Matt is coming over and bringing dinner. Is Jaxon in town?" Jessie walked to the door.

"Not until the weekend." Peyton followed her cousin to the door. "Hey, cous, are we running at the gym in the morning?"

"It would have to be early-early before work or later after work. Early doesn't sound good to me. I suggest after." Jessie opened the door. "I can meet you at four. That's when my help arrives."

"Sounds good, four it is. I can't believe you turned me into a runner." Peyton laughed. "See you after work. Don't worry, I'll call Matt as soon as you leave." She closed the door behind Jessie and locked it. Jaxon would be proud of her. She picked up her phone and told Matt about her dream. Her takeaway from the conversation was his one consistent statement. "Damn, here we go again." She smiled all six times he said it. She hung up after he made her promise to tell him everything new that came up.

She walked by the journal on the coffee table and resisted the temptation to pick it up and begin reading. Moving past the table, she walked into the kitchen to answer her ringing phone.

"Hi, just checking to see if you could hold out, or

has curiosity got the best of you?" Jessie laughed.

"I haven't even peeked inside, but it will be a long night." Peyton sighed, glancing at the journal. Her cousin knew her too well. "And before you ask, I called Matt."

"What did he say?" Jessie asked.

"Do you want the exact version?" Peyton leaned her hip against the doorframe, smiling.

"Of course."

"Let's see. He said six times, damn, here we go again."

"That sounds like him." Jessie chuckled. "Go ahead and start reading. We can read together tomorrow. I could never resist," Jessie told her. "If you don't want to, then I will come and get the darn thing because it's driving me crazy. Read it, please. I'm doing my best impression of my puppy dog eyes. I'll call you after Matt leaves, and we'll talk."

"You don't have to tell me twice. It's a tough job, but someone has to do it," she said as she ended the call.

Peyton made dinner and ate it slowly and deliberately, letting her anticipation build. When the dishes were finished and the kitchen cleaned, she went to sit on the sofa. Propping a pillow under her arm, she curled her legs under her and covered them with the throw. She had prolonged the anticipation long enough. She couldn't take it another second.

Chapter 3

The image of the body prone in the snow flashed through her mind, but Peyton wouldn't let it deter her. She fiddled with the two pillows behind her before they felt right. She leaned back against the softness and sipped from the hot tea placed conveniently on the table beside her. Finally comfortable, she adjusted the throw one more time, picked up the journal, and turned to the first page. From Cara's first words on the weathered page, Peyton found herself pulled into her story.

*Wind-whipped rain is falling from the sky by the inches, and my mama has placed pots strategically around the room to catch the constant drips coming from the leaking roof. Da moved our bed to the driest place in our small room. Nothing more than a small attic space really, but it is our place to escape to. Mine more than Brenna's. She likes to be near the action while I prefer to be alone with my thoughts and doodle them on paper.*

*On this night, like so many others before, we huddle together under the warmth of the thick quilts that our mother made us out of the clothes we've outgrown. Whispering, we conspire together in our usual manner until Brenna drifts off to sleep. Our nightly sister ritual is dear to my heart. I can't imagine growing up and leaving these special moments behind.*

Cara's memories seemed idyllic to Peyton as she

remembered how different her childhood was. No warm quilts made by her mother's hands, only endless nights of yelling and hiding from the sounds. Wiping at the tears forming in her eyes, she began reading where she left off.

*I don't mind the rain. Something is comforting about the sound of the drops against the thatched roofing, the musty smell, and the fresh rain scent all wrapped together in our little room. But it's the constant drip-drip and pinging against the metal buckets that makes it impossible for me to sleep tonight. Even Brenna's snoring can't drown out the noise of the rain and the wind. The same wind whistling through the small openings that Da must patch again. It makes the fire on the candle dance and flicker about more than usual, casting eerie shadows on the wall. It fuels my imagination, and so I write by candlelight when I'm supposed to be sleeping.*

Peyton could almost see the little room in her mind and the rain dripping through the roof. She couldn't help but wonder what Cara looked like. The first pages confirmed Cara was Irish. Did she have red hair? In Peyton's mind, red hair was synonymous with being Irish. A stereotype for sure. Before she continued to read, she looked up the style of clothes that young girls were wearing in Ireland in Cara's time on the internet. Not wanting to read the diary too quickly, Peyton let her mind visualize each passage she read. She wanted to savor Cara's words from the past and try to figure out how they fit into the present.

*I have this strange and restless feeling that my life is about to change. It comes over me now and then. But the last few days the feeling vibrates through me until it's almost smothering me with a strange longing. For what? I don't know.*

*My grandmother tells me I have the sense as she likes to call it. She married one of the Campbells from Ulster when she was only a wee bit older than I am right now. Marriage is the farthest thing from my mind. I have other dreams, inspired by my grandmother's stories. My mama doesn't like us to talk about Nana, much less, to visit where she lives. As far back as I can remember I've heard the rumors about a group of mystic travelers and the strange tales that surround them. I often wondered if people are only afraid of what they don't understand. I've sneaked to the village where my grandmother lives a few times to see her anyway and to listen to her tales. I find her interesting. She sees things that others can't, and she understands that I'm different too.*

Was Cara another with the gift of sight? The idea intrigued Peyton. Hopefully, before she finished the diary, Cara would describe more clearly what her gift was and more about the travelers. Travelers through time she understood a little about, but she wasn't sure if that was what Cara was talking about. It would be amazing if she were. How did her diary come to be at the inn? Maybe Peyton would find the answers in her writings. She took another sip of tea.

*Every night for the past few weeks, I've felt the disquiet grow inside me. Watching my da who seems too tired and walks with a heavy heart, rarely smiling while a worried expression creeps across Mother's face every time he comes in from the fields. Gone are the nights of Da playing his fiddle or telling his tales of the little people. Laughter has gone from our house, replaced with a smothering, stifling sadness that never seems to lift.*

*I'm old enough to understand something is wrong, but they carry the trouble alone. I've heard the hushed tones of their talking into the wee hours of the night. Even now with the storm raging, I can hear the muted sound of their voices through the cracks in the old floorboards. Tonight, I know I must hear what they are saying. How can I help if I don't know what's going on? Slipping carefully out of bed, not wanting to wake Brenna, I put my ear to the floor to listen.*

*"They confiscated more of our land," I heard my da say. I may not understand what's happening or who they are. I only know it isn't good because his voice sounds lifeless to me.*

*"What was their reasoning this time?" My mother's soft soothing voice spoke to him.*

*I can picture her standing behind him as he sits with her hands lightly rubbing his shoulders. I have seen her do the same on many occasions. Those wonderful rough, dry, overworked hands have such a gentle touch. I felt them squeeze my troubles away more times than I can count.*

*"I couldn't stop them, who could? I had no money for the extra rent. There were no crops to sell because something is killing them. My hands are tied. I have failed you and the children."*

*Tears filled my eyes, and it seemed in that moment, at least as I write this now, my carefree childhood ended right there.*

Peyton wiped the tears in her eyes once again. It was the perfect place to stop reading. Peyton had questions as she read Cara's words through the second time. Did Cara have the gift of sight, and did her grandmother? Peyton wanted to read more, but she also wanted to think about what she had read. At this point, she had more questions than answers. The sound of her phone ringing was a welcome reprieve. Cara's mother was a Campbell before marrying a Cassidy. It looked like she needed to do some research.

"Hi, you called at the perfect moment," Peyton said, answering the call.

"Good to know. Does that mean you miss me?" Jaxon chuckled.

"Always. You know I do. Wait until I tell you what happened today." Peyton told him about finding the journal, about her conversation with Jessie earlier, and what she had read. "I don't know how, but I'm sure the body and this journal are linked in some strange way."

"Dare I ask how?" Jaxon asked.

"You can ask, but I have no ideas yet." Peyton walked into her room, changing the subject abruptly. "You'd be proud of me. I'm learning to lock the doors like you've told me."

"That's good." He sounded distracted. "What aren't you telling me?"

"I'm not sure what you mean. Other than a few strange sensations, a lid that refuses to fit back on the box without taking flight, and a strange sense that there's more to come, everything seems all right." She sat on the edge of the bed.

"Remember we have a date Friday night." He changed the subject.

"I won't forget. I'm looking forward to it." She paused. "Why are you telling me this?"

"With you, I'm not sure what to expect." She heard

the weariness in his voice.

"Jaxon, I'm not planning on going anywhere. I'll be ready and waiting for you on Friday." She smiled to herself, finding his concern a bit cute the way he tiptoed around the subject. "Believe me I'm not up for any more jaunts through time. It's Jessie's turn if someone has to go."

"Thanks for the reassurance, but do you have any say in the matter?" he asked.

"Probably not, but I'm not raising my hand. For now, I'm only reading a journal written a long time ago. You would love it since you like history. Think about it, Ireland in the year eighteen forty-five. What's not to like about that?"

"History is one thing, but what comes with it in your life is what worries me." Jaxon paused. "Do your best to be there on Friday will you?" he muttered.

"You know I will. I miss you." She grimaced. "I hope you can live with the baggage that comes with me. It seems to be here to stay. Not to change the subject, but Grams said my dad is working hard in rehab. Part of his therapy is to have to face me and my sister—with supervision, of course."

"How do you feel about it?" he asked.

"Truthfully, I have mixed emotions. Every time I think of seeing them, it conjures up bad memories. They promised not to bring us together until all parties are ready. At this point, I'm not ready, and neither is Madison." She groaned. "I guess we'll clear that hurdle when it's time."

"Don't rule it out altogether. You might feel differently in time," Jaxon told her.

"I'll try to be open. I've accepted a lot of change in

my life lately. I guess you could say I'm learning to be flexible." She laughed.

"Or, as my mom would call it, acting like a responsible adult. I used to walk out of the room when she used that phrase because it always meant I had to do something I didn't want to do." His deep chuckle made her smile. "Either that or a lecture that I didn't want to listen to."

"I hear you. Being an adult isn't always fun."

"Before we hang up, I have a question. I know you well enough to know that if you think something is connected, then it probably is. What is your heart telling you about this journal?"

"It's not only the journal that has me thinking. There's so much supernatural activity in the area, and now a body. I've had several dreams of a body in the snow, and Jessie told me that one was discovered." She rubbed her head. "I've noticed a few things that have bothered me at the school. It's probably nothing, but then again it might be something major." She took a deep breath and continued. "I can't point at anything particular and say this is the reason, and yet I feel it. Sorry, I know I'm not making any sense."

"Peyton, you're making more sense than you realize. I've seen you in action twice. I'll prepare myself for what's ahead. See you Friday night, and we'll talk more."

"Okay. I miss you and wish you were here." She turned back the covers on the bed.

"It's good to know you're not sick of me."

"Not by a long shot. Sweet dreams, and may they all be about me," she said softly.

"You occupy a lot of my thoughts. Don't go

anywhere without me." He yawned.

"I don't plan on it. Get some rest; you sound tired." She sat on the edge of the bed.

After they said goodbye, Peyton got ready for bed. She had no idea how to lessen his concerns about her disappearing. Jessie told her it took Matt time. Her problem as she saw it was, it's hard to convince someone you're not going anywhere if you have no idea if it's true or not.

Chapter 4

Jaxon's body wanted to sleep, but his mind wouldn't cooperate. The last couple of weeks had been brutal. Thankfully, he was almost finished with the training. The last few days of tests were enough to last him a lifetime. He had to study twice as hard as when he was in college, which meant many late nights with his nose in the books. His experience as a lawman in Arizona helped some but not when it came to FBI protocol. Book time was his only recourse. He stretched out on the bed, folding his arms behind his head. He groaned when he moved his leg wrong. Somehow, he had managed to do quite well on the written exams, but the physical training kicked his backside even though he thought he was in decent shape. Every muscle in his body screamed with the knowledge they had been working overtime. The hot tub at the gym soothed his tired muscles but did nothing for his energy level. He eyed the half-eaten sandwich on the table from his unfinished dinner. He should probably finish eating. Maybe with a full stomach his mind would cooperate with his need for sleep. All he had to do was muster up the energy to get up and get it. He stared at the bag, willing the sandwich to come to him, but it did no good. He moaned as he stood.

A few big bites later and he was ready to try his hand at sleeping again. His conversation with Peyton earlier wouldn't let go of him. What seemed to bother him the most was he could see his quiet weekend with no complications slipping away. He had heard the excitement in her voice. She was already invested in what she was learning. Naturally, his mind wouldn't let go of the details she had shared with him and the ones she discreetly kept to herself. If what she had seen concerned her, then those details concerned him too.

Tired or not, that was the way commitment worked. He loved her. Though it might be too soon to tell her, he had decided to stop lying to himself about how he felt. With his feelings settled in his mind, he still hadn't come to terms with the weird baggage that came with her. Accepting might be possible, but understanding her unusual gifts might take him time. Hell, Matt was still trying to come to terms with Jessie's abilities. At least he enjoyed watching Jaxon deal with the same struggle and ragged on him from time to time. He would remember to return the favor when Matt grappled with Jessie at the heart of a case once again.

When it came to the subject of ghosts and premonitions, the two cousins were similar enough to be scary. What one didn't think of the other one did and so on. They played off one another in an effective way. Pretty awesome if you asked him. The last couple of cases taught him there was a lot more going on than can be seen or understood.

All he needed to figure out at this point was how a young girl living in Ireland in eighteen-forty-five could have anything to do with a body found near Blue Cove. Not good for his logical brain to try and grasp, but his gut told him that he was about to find out. Peyton informed him that the diary had chosen her. Why not? A fairly simple beginning to another wild ride. His life would never be boring with Peyton. She excited him in more ways than he cared to analyze. At least his boss Tom Maxwell understood where not many would because he had seen Jessie in action working with Matt.

Jaxon rolled onto his side, pulled up the cover, and closed his eyes. Even his eyelids hurt tonight. Thankfully, his time at the academy and training was ending. He couldn't help but wonder what all his instructors would think if they could spend a few days solving crimes with the Reynolds girls. Only a fleeting thought went through his mind before he promptly fell asleep with a smile on his face.

****

Peyton hoped Jaxon slept well last night. He had sounded tired when she talked to him. She had a busy day scheduled, along with a workout at the gym with Jessie later on. There were so many things she wanted to run past her cousin. Her mind was active as usual, and she needed to talk to someone who might understand. The classroom clock seemed to move at a snail's pace, ticking away the minutes ever so slowly all morning.

Her kids were more rambunctious than usual, and she had so many interruptions in her classroom that she couldn't keep track of them all. The morning had been a frustrating one, and the afternoon didn't get much better. After her class was over, she helped another teacher whose aide was out sick. The students in her class had a combined energy level that was through the roof, which made teaching next to impossible. Happy to leave the school behind, Peyton walked out the door and drove to the gym. A hard workout would be a piece of cake in comparison to teaching those squirming, giggling little people. They were maddening but lovable even on the worst days.

She grabbed her bag when she got out of the car and went into the locker room to change her clothes. Jessie arrived not long after she did and met her on the indoor track. For the first few minutes, neither of them spoke until they got into the rhythm of their pace.

By halfway around the track the third time, Peyton started telling Jessie all about what she read in the diary. "I need to find out more about the travelers. Cara's grandmother sounded like quite a character, and I've only read the first few pages. I can't wait to read more." She stopped running, bringing them both to a halt.

"What? I know that look." Jessie jogged in place.

"Sorry." Peyton started running again, thankful for the inside track. It was still too cold to run outside. "Cara mentioned she had the sense which piqued my interest. I hope she explains in the next pages what that means."

"I guess we have to at least entertain the idea that there are and were more of us strange folks around. Don't forget to keep reading. I will call you after Matt leaves to get the skinny."

After they finished their workout, they went their separate ways. Not wanting to cook, Peyton went by Sally's diner to get takeout. Carrying her treat into the house, she placed her dinner on the table. A cheeseburger, fries, and a chocolate shake that would undo all her hard work but sounded like the perfect comfort food to read by. She had enough salads and chicken this week to last her for several days. "Splurge today and run it off tomorrow, and the next day too probably," she muttered to herself. Her one consolation was she rarely overindulged at all. When she did, it was in a big way. *Go big or go home, isn't that what they say.* She simply chose to go big at home.

Grabbing the diary, she sat at the kitchen table. Not wanting to spill anything on the pages of the old book, she ate first, letting her mind free to imagine a young Cara Cassidy whose childhood ended abruptly. Cara, who might be more like her and Jessie than they realized.

\*\*\*\*

*I went to see my grandmother Alanna. Each time I go, I have to do more to get away from my mother's watchful eyes without causing suspicion. I did my chores without grumbling and even did extra chores, but I still had to lie before I could sneak off. I'm ashamed every time I tell my mother an untruth, but deception is the only way I can see my nana.*

*How I love the village where she lives. The sights, the smells, and sounds are all part of its charm and are written indelibly in my memory. I love the melodic sound of her voice as she tells the stories of our ancient ways and what her eyes have seen firsthand. Knowledge of the wild herbs and healing potions flow freely from her lips, and I strive to remember and write them down. I'm richer for my visits but conflicted too. Each time I raise my hand to knock at her door, I know a new adventure awaits me but am afraid I will be caught too.*

*"Come sit by me, my sweet Cara. You are carrying the weight of the world upon your young shoulders,*

*little one." She stooped, took the kettle from the fire, and poured the hot liquid into a cup. "Drink, it will soothe you. Tell me your troubles, my girl."*

*I told her about my worries, starting with what I had overheard the night before.*

*" 'Tis true that our world is changing, and the times are troubling, indeed." She patted my hand. "Your da and mama are trying to figure things out. They wouldn't want you to worry."*

*"How can I not? Their hearts are heavy, and there's no laughter anymore." I sipped the hot liquid. Each sip soothed my stomach and warmed me from the inside out.*

*"Many folks are in the same place, Cara. Many are choosing to leave the country and traveling to land far away by ship."*

*"But how could they ever leave? This is our home." I swatted at the tears forming in my eyes.*

*"Home, my dear Cara, is wherever your mama and da are." She reached across the table and pushed one of my stray curls behind my ear. "We Irish are a strong people and have suffered much. We have our beliefs and folklore to keep us company no matter where we roam."*

*"I don't understand."*

*"You are so young, my Creena, my heart. You have one who will always guard you no matter where you are. The fairies are always watching. They can appear as a person to help you or as themselves. You, my sweet Cara, may not have seen yours yet, but you will when you need them most."*

*I left the village feeling lighter than when arrived. I sensed I wouldn't have all that many days left to visit her, but I couldn't imagine why. All the way home I sifted through her words about the fairies. Had I ever seen one? She told me they lived under the mounds of the earth where they were ruled by a queen or a king. I tried to imagine what a fairy would look like. Her stories of fairies and leprechauns were among my favorites. Our legends say the little people roamed Ireland even before humans arrived. With their unique hats and red hair, they could be mischief-makers. From my grandmother, I also learned about the pooka or shape changers, some of the most feared creatures in our stories. I wished I understood more. Maybe I could help my parents if only I did.*

****

Peyton pondered what she had just read. Was it possible that's why Jessie's friend Sally Mansfield could see Elida, who she described as a fairy-like creature, at the inn this past December? Had Cara lived somewhere in the area? Nothing seemed impossible to her anymore. Sally had told her after she moved back to the cove all about the magic she had experienced at Christmas. One new piece got added to the puzzle to think about. Taking a big sip of her shake, she clutched the diary to her chest. *Tell us your story, Cara. You are tied somehow to this area, and I wouldn't be surprised if your grandmother is too. I'm hooked and can't wait to see why.*

She continued to read well into the night, pondering over a few of the passages several times. The journal described Cara's travel to America with her family and other emigrants on ships that became appropriately known as coffin ships. Cara's words painted a vivid picture of why they were given that awful name. Those who sailed from Ireland during the famine were often on ships overcrowded and sometimes unseaworthy. Cara described the weeks of being cooped up in terrible conditions together. Disease and death were often the final results with their lifeless bodies cast into the endless water of the vast seas. The fact that Cara and her family along with many others survived the journey was in itself a miracle. Peyton couldn't imagine the hardships they faced on their journey and all they left behind. The thought was almost depressing, and she was glad that her phone interrupted her spiraling thoughts.

"Hi, cous, what's up?" Peyton answered after checking the caller ID.

"Hi back at you. Matt just left, and I couldn't wait to hear what you read tonight," Jessie said.

Peyton filled her in on what the pages had revealed. "Cara talked about her grandmother as a traveler. I want to know more about the stories surrounding them. I might need your friend Jeremy's research ability with that. And get this, she talked about the fairies and other Irish legends. I tell you there's more to this story than we know."

"I remember reading a story about the travelers a long time ago. The mystics were supposed to see the future. If I remember correctly, they were often considered to be healers."

"Oh, that's interesting. I can see a lot of research in my future." Peyton leaned her head back against the couch. "It's like I can see everything she is writing in my mind. How awesome it is to be reading words written long ago and yet they seem relevant now. I'm excited to find out how."

"Great, now I'm hooked too." Jessie sighed.

"Did Matt tell you any more about the body they found?" Peyton asked.

"No, he's still waiting on forensics." She huffed. "Like I believe that excuse. He's holding out, and I don't know why. I get the feeling he's trying to shield me in some odd way. Anyway, we ended up talking about your dream and our theory about the book that chose us. He said the same thing to me that he said to you. The poor dear man. How I love him. After he did a facepalm and shook his head, he told me the body was well preserved, but he told me little else. Although he did keep looking at me with an odd look on his face all night, followed by another damn, here we go again." Jessie laughed, and Peyton joined in.

"I wonder why. He knows we're completely strange by now, dear cousin. I question what he knows that we don't or vice versa." Peyton pulled her hair into a ponytail and out of her face.

"Got me, I have no idea. Bring the diary with you to the store when you come tomorrow. We can read some of it together. If I know Matt, he'll be calling you soon to ask you more. If not, it's time we invite ourselves into the case. He knows he can't keep me out for long. His need to shield me doesn't work for my curiosity."

"Sounds good. Nighty night." After ending the call, Peyton made her way to the bedroom and got ready for bed. Once between the covers, she let Cara's words roll over her while she thought about what she had read. Another mystery to solve. Where would this one take her? Turning over onto her side, she closed her eyes and found herself in a whole new world.

****

Mila smiled at the sleeping figure. Placing her tiny fingers on the girl's forehead, she tapped lightly three times to awaken the images in her mind. Celeste had told her and her sister to come. Soon enough they would put into action the details of their assignment. In the meantime, the girl's dreams would be filled with the magic of her world. Images of lush green valleys, of heather growing wild, and of rocky hills that lead to the seas all intertwined with the amazing wonder of possibilities the girl had never seen would fill her. Of course, a dose of sadness had to be mixed in. Both were needed to move her in the right direction. Not able to contain the joy she felt, the unseen visitor blew a misty kiss and left the room.

Chapter 5

Peyton stood outside a cottage, the description of which she had come to know well through Cara's writings. From its whitewashed exterior and tidy yard to its thatched roof, Cara's home looked like Peyton imagined it would. Wild heather grew in the lush emerald-green fields surrounding the house in all directions, and lovely purple flowers framed both sides of the front door. The scene took her breath away with its beauty. She could almost see the family who lived inside busy with their daily work. Peyton exhaled when the door slowly opened, and a young girl stepped outside into the sunshine. The girl had to be Cara Cassidy. At least she hoped it was her. Peyton crossed her fingers behind her back as she watched the scene playing through her dream. The girl bent over to pick one of the purple flowers, sniffed its fragrance, and then tucked it in her hair.

Dressed in brown tights, a long skirt, and sturdy walking shoes, she looked perfect standing in her surroundings. Her red curly hair was tossed over her shoulders in a messy, carefree fashion. In one deft motion, she pulled the plaid from her shoulders up to cover her hair. The air still had a slight chill even though the sun was high in the sky and shining brightly. Not a cloud could be seen to mar the perfect day without even a hint of rain. Peyton smiled, seeing the joy written on the girl's face. She lifted her skirt slightly and did a merry jig as she hummed a lively tune.

"Cara Cassidy, where are you off to? Did you get your work done, girl?" A woman stood in the open doorway and called out. A slightly older version of Cara. Her red curly hair was tinged with strands of gray, but her eyes and smile were the same.

"Aye, it's all done. I'm going for a walkabout. It's the first sunshine to be seen in days." She smiled. "Isn't it glorious, Mama?" She motioned toward the sky with her hands.

"It is indeed." Her mother nodded. "Don't go too far. I know how you are when your mind is woolgathering. You be back in time to help with dinner." The woman made a wistful sigh as she swept around the door. "I mean it, Cara, and don't you be going to the village, you hear me."

"I hear you," Cara called over her shoulder as she began walking slowly at first and then took off running. She hummed another song, twirling and leaping through the air as she rushed away from the house.

Cara's mother watched her and smiled. Leaning against the broom, her eyes took on a wistful look. "Oh, to be young again. If only to believe that the sunshine could ease my cares." She grabbed the broom, carried it inside with her, and closed the door.

Listening to Cara's musings, Peyton couldn't help but smile too. Cara's carefree joy washed over her. Suddenly the beauty of the landscape had several magical onlookers. Out from under the mounds of dirt and from among the heather came the fairies. They flittered around Cara, dashing and darting and spreading their golden sparkles through the lush red curls of her hair. The air filled with the laughter of the little people as they peeked at her from behind the rocks, tipping their hats as she passed by unaware. Cara didn't seem to be conscious of their presence. Her steps slowed as she wrestled with her actions. She didn't like lying. The struggle around the girl became real enough for Peyton to sense as she listened to Cara reason it out.

"In all fairness, I didn't tell her that I wouldn't go to the village exactly," she said looking around. "Mama wouldn't see my action that way though," she continued. "I love my nana and wish to see her, but I don't want to disappoint Mama either. I wished someone could tell me what to do? Better yet, I wish Mama would visit Alanna herself." She sighed, walking slower with a heavy heart.

Peyton followed the girl through the lush green fields for what seemed like endless miles. Cara's demeanor changed once again when she came to the edge of a small community bustling with activity. She paused before she walked into the village. Cara walked past several small homes that were little more than shacks, a disheartening view among the rich backdrop of the green countryside. A sad almost depressing view of gray, mud, and gloominess. The sounds and smells at times were overpowering. And yet on closer observation, the people seemed happy even though they possessed little. A group of children played tag, and for a moment, Cara joined in and then continued on her way. She waved at those who called out to her. Determined, she walked through the village to a small hovel at the edge of the settlement. Pausing, she looked around and lifted her hand to knock at the door.

Peyton's anticipation built. Was she about to see Alanna? The door slowly opened, but Cara moved inside. For now, Alanna would remain a mystery.

One sight blended into another until the scene changed once again. A dark mist circled Peyton's ankles until it covered her completely, taking the village from her view. Gone were the green fields, replaced with brownfields and dying crops. No fairies or talk of the little people could be heard. The laughter and songs were replaced with sadness and darkness. Graves and mourning popped up everywhere her eyes looked, followed by a multitude of people surrounding her with thin, drawn faces and weeping. In a short amount of time, change had come to Ireland. Pain and hunger replaced the sound of music. In place of the legends of the little people, the screams of the banshee could be heard across the land. Cara's family had been impacted by what many others in the country had suffered too.

Peyton awakened while it was still dark. Propping the pillows behind her back, she sat up and tried to make sense of the dream. Seeing the children at the village where Alanna lived brought to mind something that she had tucked in the back of her mind. She remembered she wanted to check up on the three children—they stood out among all the kids at the school. Their clothing seemed different, and so did their mannerisms. They almost looked like they were from a different era. A thought she had chalked up to more of her fanciful thinking at the time, but now she wanted to investigate the situation more. Turning on the lamp, she grabbed her notebook and pen. She wrote a note to herself to find out who the children were, if they were real, and where they lived. She might need to run by the home to make sure they were all right. Maybe if she were lucky, she could see who their parents were when they dropped them off at school. Were they real or otherworldly? That was the question. Maybe they were simply shadows from the past. Peyton reached for Cara's diary. She started reading where she had left off. She found herself reading about some of what she had seen in her dream.

\*\*\*\*

As tired as he was, Jaxon couldn't shut down his mind. After his talk with Peyton the other day, he had to call Matt. What he had learned about the victim recently found in the woods didn't settle his apprehension. It grew stronger talking to Peyton earlier, especially now that he knew Matt hadn't told Jessie any details, and Peyton's speculations weren't far off the mark.

He'd like to say it didn't surprise him, but it still did. Not able to fully grasp the ability that came easily to her had the power to stop him in his tracks. It would take him hours and days of investigation to link events together. But with a diary from years ago and a slim knowledge of a murder, Peyton already was seeing the possibility of thinking outside of the norm. Her mind connected dots that others couldn't even begin to fathom. He found it fascinating. Reaching for his phone, he sent her a quick text.

Before he could close his eyes, his phone rang. "What are you doing awake?" he asked when he answered.

"I could ask you the same question." She paused. "Did you mean it when you said we should read the diary together?"

"I did. Read me a bedtime story, sweetheart." He stretched out stacking his hands behind his head.

"Where do you want to start?" she asked.

"At the beginning if you don't mind. I need to get the whole experience along with you." He loved the sound of her voice as she read the first few pages. She would pause now and then to tell him how Cara's words impacted her. He asked her to read one portion a second time and listened. There was a clue hidden in there somewhere.

*The first time I searched for Alanna and saw where she lived, it made me angry. Her house looked abandoned except for the curl of gray smoke that rose from its chimney. I paused before knocking to bring my emotions under control. The door slowly creaked open. The minute I saw her, I knew her, and she knew me. Her eyes lit up, and in that moment, she looked ten years younger. I could see my mother in her, and she could see my mother in me.*

*"My lovely Cara. You have come to me." She turned me around, touched my hair with her rough hands, and kissed my cheek. "You'll do. There's intelligence in your beautiful green eyes and a zest for life too I'm convinced. Come in, my girl, and warm yourself by the fire. I have tea to soothe you, my dearest child. Does your mama know you've come to see me?"*

*I didn't answer her directly. "She has told me I shouldn't come here alone, but I had to see you." I sat in the wooden chair by the table. "Couldn't you please come to our house and see her? She's your daughter. Brenna and I need our grandmother and grandfather in our lives."*

*"I can try, but she wouldn't want me to."* She turned her face away, but I could see the tears forming in her eyes.

*"What happened? I don't understand."*

*"Cara, that is for your mother to tell you. It's enough to know that she has always thought me odd, but I love her. I think you have the same senses growing inside of you that I did at your age. Your mother will not like it, but I fear there is nothing to be done but for you to grow into them. You are too young to worry about such things now. In time you will understand."*

*Looking back now, I can say she was right.*

"For tonight we should end there. Did I put you to sleep?" Her soft voice came across the line.

"No, but you have given me something to think about. What happened in Ireland brought many emigrants to our country. It's obvious from her journal that many of them settled in this area and became productive members of communities. A few were my ancestors." He yawned. "Maybe now I can go to sleep. How about you read to me tomorrow night too? I'll be back in a couple of days, and we can read together. In the meantime, let me know any ideas that come to your mind, and I'll do the same," Jaxon told her.

"Sounds good. Sleep well, and sweet dreams," she replied.

"As long as you're in them, they're sweet enough. Talk to you tomorrow, or should I say today." He looked at the clock when he hung up. Hearing her voice soothed him. In a matter of minutes after he had disconnected the call, he was asleep.

## Chapter 6

Peyton determined to look for those kids today at the school and for any bullying in the schoolyard. Had she seen them for real, or were they spirits? The line seemed blurred sometimes. Her dream last night seemed real enough, but it was a dream. She hadn't gone to Ireland in the year eighteen-forty-five. Jaxon would have flipped out.

Reading Cara's journal to him had been nice, and she enjoyed every minute of the call. He seemed genuinely interested in what she read. "Tell me a bedtime story," he had said. She would happily tell him a story every night if he were next to her. *I wonder what he would think if I told him that.* She grinned as she finished dressing for work. Her boldness when it came to Jaxon astonished her. What had happened to the reluctant girl who spent a lot of time running from him? The problem was she hadn't seen him enough in the past several weeks to satisfy herself. She would like to do something special for him this weekend. He had been working hard. Making a mental note to plan a few special times for her guy, she ran the brush through her hair one more time and rushed to the kitchen for a quick bite to eat.

Jessie walked out of her cottage at the same time she did. "Don't forget we'll run again after work, and you need to bring me up to speed on the diary," she called out and waited for Peyton as she locked the door.

"I remember." They walked the path together to their cars. "I'll see you later. I have a little sleuthing to do at school today. I'll tell you about it later. Wish me success." Peyton opened the car door and started the engine. With a scraper in hand, she got back out to clear the ice off the windows. Boy, did she wish she had a garage to park in. This was one of her least favorite jobs. She watched Jessie pull her window cover off her windshield.

"You need to buy one of these covers for frost." Jessie folded the cloth and put the covering in the backseat. "This small cover saves you a lot of work. It took me one winter of scraping the window to break down and buy one." Jessie got in her car and drove away honking and waving as she passed the inn, one of her cousin's many rituals that made Peyton smile.

The cover went on Peyton's to-buy list. Anything she could do to make her job on cold mornings outside of building a garage would be welcome. Although a garage would be mighty nice. She might even be willing to consider marriage to Jaxon if his house came with a garage. She chuckled. Not desperate enough to give up her freedom quite yet, she would start with the frost guard for her windshield.

Peyton pulled into a parking space at the school. No way would she wait outside this morning for the kids' arrival. She could keep an eye on them coming into the building from the inside. Pulling her briefcase out of the backseat with all her lesson plans, she walked in the doors to the welcoming warmth of the building. Between here and New York she should be used to the cold winters, but at heart she was a warm-weather girl.

She opened her classroom and got ready for the morning. A project with finger paints and a music lesson was the main part of her plans for the morning. The finger paints meant she would be busy alongside her aides to clean up the students' hands. She placed the box of paint shirts and a box of musical instruments on the counter. Pouring the paint into several bowls in all the bright primary colors of red, blue, and yellow was easier than when she had to mix them. Other colors would emerge as soon as they swirled all the paint together with their hands.

Reaching inside the box of noisemakers, as she liked to call them, she placed several instruments on the counter for the kids to pick from. Peyton loved to let each child choose their favorite instrument to play. They would shake the maracas, jingle the wrist bells, or beat on the tambourine with wild abandonment to one of the rhythmic songs she chose. Add in a few castanets, small cymbals, and sand blocks, and the children could create their version of the song they were listening to. Music time made for a noisy but happy moment for the kids. They loved playing the instruments, and she loved watching them.

With classroom preparations finished, she went to stand in the hall to watch the arriving children. This was one of her favorite times of the day. Their happy smiles were the reason she loved working with all her special kids. Amid the commotion of the students entering the building, Peyton caught sight of an apparition standing in the center of the hall watching each child as they passed by. Agitated, she searched as more kids walked through the halls. The more children moved through the hallways the more frantic she became. With the arrival of Peyton's first student, she could no longer watch the ghost. Peyton wheeled the little girl into the classroom, helping her take off her coat. Was the ghost new today, or had she been there before?

"Good morning," she said to each child as they came into the room.

Maybe next year the position would work into a full-time job if the budget was approved. Either way, she was happy to be here. As soon as the paint shirts were on, Peyton placed a piece of paper on the table in front of each child. One by one their hands were dipped into the paint, and her morning took off to a frantic and messy start.

****

Talking to Peyton last night convinced Jaxon he needed to speak with Matt again. After the call, he almost wished he hadn't. He had enough on his mind. What he had learned gave him something else to think about at an inopportune time. He was looking at one more test, and another murder with a few unusual elements that left him with too many things to think about in a head that was already crammed full of info.

The last few weeks of training had reiterated the fact that no crimes are as they seem at first glance. He had investigated enough murders in his career to know that you had to dig deep to solve some of the worst. Hell. He rubbed his temple. Hanging with Peyton taught him there could be elements involved that were outside the realm of all logical thinking. The FBI had a few stories of open investigations that were in the same category of the strange and unusual. Jaxon had to be ready for anything. The journal Peyton read from already had him doing a bit of research. He picked up his phone on his way out the door.

"Hey, Jaxon. How's it going?" Jeremy asked.

"Not bad. How about you?" Jaxon got into his car.

"Slow right now. I could use the excitement of another strange case with the Reynolds' touch to it." Jeremy chuckled. "Are you nearing the end of your training?"

"I am. I finish this week and will start in the field office next week. Peyton doesn't know it yet. I'm going to surprise her with the news on Friday."

"I bet she'll be happy. You haven't seen much of each other the last few months."

"I'm down with not having to travel back and forth every weekend. Hey, speaking of excitement, I have a favor to ask of you." Jaxon told him about Cara's diary. He asked Jeremy to research the Cassidys and especially the grandmother Alanna.

"You know I've read some of the legends built around the travelers. I'll get right on this. The whole story has great possibilities for some fun research. Leave it to Peyton and Jessie. I'm excited to delve into this."

"Thanks, Jeremy. Let me know what you find." Jaxon started his car and flipped on the heat.

"I will. Congrats on finishing your training. We'll talk again soon."

"Sounds good." Jaxon turned onto the street and drove the familiar few miles from where he was staying to FBI headquarters. He wouldn't miss the morning traffic or evening rush hour. There was a lot to be said about living in a small town.

He pulled into a parking spot. Afterward, he

stopped to talk to one of the agents as he walked into the building. Happy this phase was almost over for him, he was ready to get settled into his new job. Closer to home and extra time with Peyton would be nice too. He wondered if his idea of additional free time was only a pipe dream. Everyone told him he would be busy with more than he could handle as an agent.

Matt had been an agent, and the stress of the job made him rethink his career choice and become Chief of Police of Blue Cove. Jaxon would have to wait and see. Only time would tell. Being a homicide investigator wasn't easy either. He had seen some of the seedier sides of life in the past several years. But meeting Peyton had brought some balance into his life in an odd sort of way.

He loved being with her, but she challenged his well-ordered thought processes and his way of doing his job. And she was challenging his ways again. He couldn't wait to see where this took them. Peyton was a handful and exciting in more ways than one.

Chapter 7

Peyton went for a drive on her way to Jessie's store. She had no idea where she was going or why. Compelled might be too strong of a word, and yet that's how she would describe the sensation that kept her driving in the opposite direction than she should be driving. She found herself turning off the main road and driving through a wooded area she had never seen before. She passed what looked like an abandoned homestead off to the right of the main road. It seemed impossible that anyone could live there, and yet a curl of smoke rose steadily from the chimney. She circled back and pulled onto the shoulder of the road. Something pulled at her to check it out.

The blast of chilly air hit her, sending chills running through her the minute she opened the car door. Thankfully, she had worn her winter boots. She didn't relish a trek through the snow in a pair of regular shoes. Knocking on the door, she waited for a response. None came. Carefully, she opened the door enough to peek inside. What she saw stunned her, but it didn't stop her from entering the small house.

Once inside, the door closed behind her with a bang, and no amount of coaxing would open it again. Though a small space, the cabin was filled with warmth from the fire roaring in the fireplace to the homey touches found around the room. Peyton had an odd sense that none of it was real, but that she was viewing a moment in time. Someone had lived in those tidy rooms once. Who, she wondered. Maybe soon she would understand the reason for her being here. Besides, the door still wouldn't budge when she tried the handle. Her shoulders tensed. She would be here until the door opened.

As she stood there, the room slowly came to life. A young girl began to set the table while a woman buttered the top of a freshly baked loaf of bread. When she had finished that task, she grabbed a long-handled spoon and stirred the pot cooking on the wood-fed stove. An older gentleman with thinning gray hair walked in from the other room.

"Alanna, you need to send Brenna on her way. Her mother will be home and won't be happy if she finds her not there. With all the youngsters missing these days, we don't want to worry your daughter."

"I know." She cut a large piece of soda bread, slathered it with butter and honey. "Here, my dear girl, I'm glad you stopped by. Tell Cara thank you for showing you the way. Your grandpa is right though; your parents will worry over you, and your mama won't be happy you came here."

"Why, Nana?" She plopped down in the chair in frustration.

"The next time you come to me, I will explain it to you. It's enough to say that I'm different, and that difference can be scary to those who don't understand. My Cara gets it, and I'm thinking you might too." Alanna stroked her hand through Brenna's soft hair. "Now get on your way because I want to see you again, my lovely girl. Cara reminds me of your mama when she was young with her red curls and fiery spirit. But you, my sweet one, make me think of my lovely mother with her kind heart and beautiful eyes. I know she often wondered how she had a daughter like me, but her love was bigger than her questions about where I came from. It took me a while to find my way to myself, but now I wouldn't want to be any different. Stay true to yourself, Brenna. Be a good daughter and go home. Don't dawdle." She handed Brenna her coat, helped her button up, and wrapped her colorful scarf around her neck. Alanna kissed her cheek and opened the door. "Hurry, on the way with you now."

"I hope for her sake she makes it home on time. Our little girl would never lie to her mama. I'm sorry, Alanna."

"Why?" Alanna turned to look at her husband.

"I know how your heart would be broken not to see your granddaughters anymore. Whether we agree with her or see her reasoning, your daughter simply cannot accept who and what we are."

"It's not your fault or even my daughter's either. As you know, neither could my mother." With a faraway look in her eyes, she stirred the pot one last time. "Sit yourself down, Ronan. It's time for dinner. My greatest worry is the pooka who roams the area freely. The girls' safety is more important than them visiting me."

As the scene ended, Peyton found herself standing alone in the empty, cold cabin long since abandoned. How the small house was still standing was beyond her. Had she seen Alanna? Was it possible she had once lived in this house? She couldn't wait to read further in the diary to see if she could find out if any of what she saw had happened in the past. Had Alanna and her husband moved to America during the famine in Ireland too? Alanna mentioned the pooka as though he was in the area. What was a pooka, and why was that something for her to worry about?

When he called, Peyton would be reading to Jaxon from Cara's journal tonight. She had to find out more. She left the small homestead, closing the door behind her. She walked across the rickety porch, down the loose steps, and through the snow back to her car. She couldn't wait to tell Jessie about her discovery. Turning to look at the old cabin one more time, she noted there were no signs of life, only a dilapidated building barely standing. One thing she knew for sure: this small space had once been filled with love and laughter.

Peyton drove to her cousin's store and pulled around back where she went in the door. "Have you been busy?" she asked, taking off her coat and hanging it up.

"Not too bad. Although, I don't mind being busy this time of year. Things generally slow down after the holidays. So far, the store is holding its own with the folks here for the winter activities. Especially on the weekends." Jessie placed Peyton's purse behind the counter beside hers.

"You'll never guess what happened to me." Peyton rested her elbows on the countertop.

"I'm sure I'll probably regret asking this. What?" Jessie grabbed one of Peyton's hands, rubbing her cold fingertips. "When it comes to us, it always means something more is to follow."

"I took a small drive out of my way after work." Peyton squeezed her cousin's hand. "I guess I should start my tale at the beginning."

"I wondered why you were late." Jessie pursed her lips.

"Focus, would you. I'm trying to tell you something important. Besides, I'm not that late." She scrunched her face. "Now where was I?" She stroked her chin and smiled.

"Start at the beginning, at least that's what you said you were going to do."

"I saw a ghost at school today." Peyton went on to tell her about the sighting.

"Have you ever seen one there before?" Jessie asked.

"No. She seemed to be searching among the kids for someone. I couldn't watch for long because my students started to arrive, and I had to go into the classroom. I have no idea what her visit was all about, but I'm sure at some point I'll find out."

"What else happened? There's more to your story, isn't there? I mean to see a ghost doesn't seem all that earth-shattering anymore. It's sad to say, but it's kind of old hat." Jessie shook her head as she said the words aloud. "That sounds weird even to me. Please save me from my wayward mind and tell the rest of the story." Jessie laughed.

"This is where it gets interesting." Peyton told her about her drive, the abandoned homestead, and the vision she saw while standing inside. "The smoke curling from the chimney seemed strange enough, but then to walk inside and see the house furnished made me think for a moment that the vision was happening now…" She paused. "And yet it wasn't. Afterward, I saw how the place actually looked. Believe me, there wasn't a fire in the fireplace and no homey touches only an old cabin with cracks in the walls and ceiling. It was cold." Peyton leaned her hip against the counter.

"How is that even possible?" Jessie asked.

"I have no idea how any of what has happened to us is possible. We live in the realm of the impossible every day." Peyton straightened the bookmarks in the basket as she stood there. "I read something last night to Jaxon from Cara's journal that makes about as much sense as anything."

"Tell me. I need something to hold on to." Jessie pinched Peyton's arm. "Give me something."

"Ouch. You were never one to be patient." Peyton took a deep breath. "Cara made the statement that there is an unseen world and one that is seen. Her grandmother told her that people like her had simply become mindful of what most others were too busy to see. Seeing in either world may make you seem different, but it shouldn't. And some people could travel between them. What do you think?"

"That sounds similar to what Pastor John once told me. He said I was what happened when people became attentive to what is going on around them, even when others can't see or hear anything. I remember his words helped me at the time."

"Oh, I like his explanation." Peyton nodded.

"Ever since you told me about our great-great-grandmother and great-grandmother, it relieved the pressure I felt that I was somehow an odd bird until that moment. Of course, you being equally strange helped a lot too." Jessie laughed, making an absurd facial expression.

Peyton rolled her eyes. "Stop it!" She paused to get

control of her giggles. "Naturally, you would like me to suffer too. I mean misery does desire company. Isn't that what Matt told Jaxon? Speaking of Matt, did he ever tell you any more about the body they found?" Peyton's fingers tapped lightly on the countertop. "I already told you what he told me."

"He's been quiet, which is unlike him. I'm telling you there is something strange about his investigation. I'll see him tonight, and I'm going to try to wheedle more info out of him."

"In the meantime, we'll have to keep reading the journal. Something is going on at the school, at the inn, and with the body that was found, and somehow they all tie together. And there is something more, and I have no idea what it is, but it may be even worse," Peyton told her.

"Dang, Peyton, you could have gone all day without saying that. Let's get to work. Something may come to us. The truth is I'm not sure I want to know."

"I don't want to know either, and yet I do. Once I start to see things, I can't seem to unsee them, and I find myself caught up. Then I want to solve it because I'm involved." Peyton stepped behind the counter to get her phone from her purse. She stuck it in her pocket.

"I'm the same way, as you know. I was pulled through a mirror, and you went through a book into another era. We are quite a pair. You'd think we were twins instead of cousins." Jessie waved at her grandmother's friend Reba waving at her from the front window.

"Besides all the weird stuff, we're a lot of fun even if a bit quirky." Peyton smiled. With the words hanging between them, they tried to act busy.

## Chapter 8

The first words Reba said when she walked into the store made both Peyton's and Jessie's mouths drop open.

"I would have to agree you girls are fun. You've brought a lot of happiness to this old lady." Reba took off her coat and placed it over a chair.

"Where's your car? I didn't see you drive up." Jessie wrapped her in a hug.

"Thank you, dear. My friend dropped me off. I'm meeting Lawrence for dinner tonight at Angelo's." She patted Peyton's hand. "I came early to browse and catch up on the latest cove news."

"Is that all?" Jessie looked skeptical.

"You know me well, my dear. I give as much as I take, don't I? Not to worry, my dears, everything has a way of working out. Now first things first, I need a good cup of strong tea and after that a little shopping. Then we'll talk." Reba walked through the open doors into Joe's coffee shop.

"Well, cousin, there's your proof that something is up." Jessie shook her head. "She always knows."

"So it would seem." Peyton watched Reba talking to Molly. "We're bound to learn something we don't know."

"We always do." Jessie walked closer to the open doors to eavesdrop, which was quickly interrupted.

The bell above the door rang, and an older couple walked into the store. Hand in hand, they stopped to look at the front display table. The woman turned her head to smile at Peyton. Her faded red hair was streaked with silver, but her lovely green eyes were full of life. She lifted a book from the table and showed the cover to Peyton. The woman whispered something in the man's ear, and he turned to look at Peyton. She had a strange sensation akin to her hair standing on end when she saw their faces. Not possible. She shook her head and rubbed her eyes. Her imagination had to be playing tricks on her. Jessie walked toward the pair and asked if she could help.

The two of them were the spitting image of the people Peyton saw earlier in the vision at the abandoned cabin. It was official; she was losing all sense of rational thought. She observed as Jessie talked with them. If the woman wasn't Alanna, she was one of her descendants for sure. As soon as Reba came back with her tea, the couple abruptly left. Peyton rushed to the table to take a closer look at the book cover. A ferocious wolf stared at her, sending shivers down her back. Peyton was compelled to buy the book.

"Something happened while I was away, my dears. Would one of you care to explain?" Reba placed her tea on the table. Sitting in the chair that Jessie pulled out for her, she arranged her napkin on her lap. "Now then, I'm ready."

Peyton looked at Jessie who was staring at her. "Be my guest, Peyton. I'm at a loss."

Sitting across from Reba, Peyton began to tell her about her vision at the cabin and the couple who walked into the store. "I have no idea how any of this is possible." She pushed the book over for Reba to see.

"He's evil-looking, isn't he?" Reba shook her head. "It seems we'll have to put our heads together to figure this one out. To me, this isn't any stranger than you going back in time and living for a moment your great-great-grandmother's life." She grasped Jessie's hand. "Or you either, little missy, going through a mirror into another dimension."

"You're right as usual, my friend." Jessie clasped Reba's hand.

"One important question I need you to answer, Peyton. Were they real or ghosts?" Reba asked.

"They seemed real enough, but they could only be a shadow from their time if that makes any sense. You know, like all the people who I saw in my time travel." Peyton's face creased in thought.

"If that were true, then how do you explain Mary Ballard coming forward in time with you from your great-great-grandmother's time?" Reba asked. "She's doing well and fitting in. I hope she'll meet someone to share her life with. I think Mary must get lonely."

"Good question. I have nothing," Jessie said.

"I can't explain her any more than I can explain Mary's husband John. We'll put them in the category of the strange and unexplainable. I can say that this couple seemed real to me. What do you think, cous?"

"I thought they were an ordinary couple until you told me about seeing them earlier in your vision. Now I have no idea. They didn't seem out of place. They looked through the books normally until they found this one and showed you the cover. We can only go on what we have. We'll have to wait and see how this plays out."

"That's my cue." Reba smiled at them. "One question will lead to another. Some will lead down rabbit holes, but a few will lead you to more questions. In the end, you'll uncover a few surprises and probably be left with a few unanswered questions that will find answers another day." Reba patted her hair.

"How will we know what questions to ask?" Peyton frowned.

"Don't frown, dear, you'll wrinkle." She pointed at Peyton's face. "You've asked the right ones before. You will this time too." Reba glanced at her.

"How do we avoid getting off the trail?" Peyton shook her head. "Rabbit holes seem like such a waste of time."

"You know better than that, my dear girl. Wherever any case takes you, there is a clue that either leads forward or in reverse. No question is ever wasted because it either reveals the truth to be found or something to be changed in you. Helping others is as much about changing your life as it is about changing theirs."

"Okay, no more serious talk. I need to close up shop, and you have to meet your husband." Jessie stood. "Speaking of Lawrence, he's standing outside waving at you now." She motioned him in.

He placed his hand on his wife's shoulder. "It's cold and icy out. I thought I should come and walk you over."

"You're the best, Lawrence. You should have a class to teach some of the younger guys, although Jaxon is pretty great himself." Peyton smiled when she thought of Jaxon's manners. He didn't want to disappoint his mama.

"Matt is too," Jessie told him. "Still, it's reassuring to see your love on display after being married for so many years. It gives me hope that not all marriages lose the romance."

"Hear, hear!" Peyton cheered. "Enjoy your dinner, you two lovebirds." She waved as they left. She glanced at her cousin. "Looks like we'll have to run another day."

****

All his classes were finished, and his tests were done. Happy didn't adequately describe how he felt at the moment. He glanced at the clock and ordered room service. Jaxon wanted to hear Peyton's voice reading to him more pages from the journal. After hearing about the new security warnings on ransom cyber-attacks and domestic terrorist threats, what he needed now was the sound of her voice reading Cara Cassidy's words about her family.

He used some of his spare moments to do some research of his own. Between a blight on the potato crops and governmental greed, many Irish landowners were pushed from their homes, and their lands were confiscated. Starvation and dreams of a safer and better place to raise their families sent them on ships heading for America. Limited by funds, many families were forced into the lower part of the ship into stuffy and close quarters. Sickness took its toll, causing too many of them to die before reaching their destination. How many dreams had died on those ships? He couldn't imagine, but he bet there were a lot. How many more were broken when they weren't welcomed with open arms in their new country? People were usually afraid of strangers and often would take advantage of them.

From the sounds of it, Cara's family was one of the lucky ones that survived the trip. The question that plagued him was what happened to them after their arrival. With any luck, the journal would reveal more tonight. Matt had filled him in on the murder and strange circumstances surrounding the girl's death. He wondered if Peyton had seen any more in her dreams.

In only a couple of days, Jaxon watched as the mystery began to gather momentum even from where he sat. Frustrated to be out of town and not right in the thick of it, he wanted to hear the details and not be caught flat-footed. Tomorrow couldn't come soon enough. Glancing at the clock, he picked up his phone to call.

"Hey, sweetheart, I'm ready for my bedtime story," Jaxon said when she answered the call. "What's new?" He was taken by surprise by what she told him had happened to her earlier at the cottage. "How is that even possible?"

"We aren't sure, but hey, maybe that's what being a traveler is all about. You know how it works. I'm in the dark until I'm not." She laughed, causing him to smile.

"Which means we'll be surprised a few times." Jaxon raked his hand through his hair. "I heard enough today to turn my hair gray."

"Like what?" she asked.

"Oh, you know, your basic domestic terror threats and cybercrimes which are happening at a more rapid clip and impacting more of our day-to-day life. I can't give you any details, but I can say it's getting heated out there. I know you've had to hear about companies in the news whose systems are hacked, and they have to pay a ransom to become operational again. It's crazy what criminals are thinking up." He folded his arms behind his head. "What I need now is a little history. Words from another time would be nice. Read me to sleep."

****

Peyton picked up the journal and carefully turned to the page where she had left off the last time they read.

*Da told us tonight he had booked passage upon a ship to leave for America in a few days. I'm scared, for I've heard sad tales about those ships. Both Brenna and I cried. Da assured us that all would be well, but how can he know? I'm afraid of the water, and we will spend many weeks crossing the turbulent seas. What happens if I get seasick? Many do, and I could be one.*

*"Pack only what you need." He had looked at us with sadness in his eyes. "The ship will be crowded, and there will be no room to store your possessions and no way to protect your belongings. I will sell everything else."*

*I climbed the stairs to our small room which seemed like a palace to me at that moment. Glancing around the room to my desk where I spent hours writing in my books, I cried. My da had made it for me. I didn't want to leave any of my possessions behind. Especially those made by my parents' hands.*

*How can I choose what to take from among my treasures? Their importance to me is tied to a memory that I hold dear. I ran my hands lovingly over all the articles that made up my days and nights in our room. Each would be missed and dreamed about over the next few weeks more than I could imagine as my heart took stock of them. The tears came easy to me that day and would flow many times over the next many months.*

*I watched in sadness days later as one by one my treasures left the house and it was no longer our home. Life would never quite be the same. At that moment, I felt deep despair that was stirred with a sense of adventure for something I could sense out of sight and yet close enough to touch. The closing of one door was the opening of something new, and I was both sad and strangely excited.*

Peyton went on to read about Cara and Brenna's surprise when her mama took them to the village to see Alanna the next day. Cara had a hard time believing her mother would take them. She seemed to enjoy being with Alanna, which made little sense. After they had said their goodbyes, they had more questions than answers about their mother and grandmother.

*"Thank you, Mama, for taking us," Brenna said.*

*"I thought it only fair for you to see her and say your goodbyes in person, but this is the last time you'll go to the village, girls. You're never to go there without me. Do I make myself clear?" We nodded, but I wanted to say more. I found it hard to keep my anger in check.*

*"Why?" Brenna asked. "I don't understand; she's our grandmother and your mother."*

*"Yes, dear, but there is much you don't know, and you're both too young to understand. Someday I'll explain it all. For now, you'll have to trust me it's for the best."*

*"I don't see how it can be. I think you're wrong, and I want to visit her again before we leave," I chimed in.*

*The look my mother gave me told me I had better*

*not say anything more or she would know I had disobeyed her many times. And since I planned to continue to see my grandmother until we left, I shut my mouth.*

*I had no idea that day it would be many long months before I saw her again in person. She did visit me in my dreams on many occasions which kept me from losing my way.*

"Are you still listening, Jaxon?"

"I'm here." He yawned.

"What are your thoughts?" Peyton leaned her head back against the chair.

"I can't help wondering what happened between Alanna and her daughter. It seems like there's a lot more to the story than we understand now."

"I'm sure that's true. I have a strong feeling that the next few days will teach us more. And besides, you'll be here tomorrow night, and I can do more when you're here to investigate with me. We work well together. I don't relish doing this without you." She rubbed her temple. "Get some sleep. You sound tired. This case won't go anywhere if you're not here."

"Is that right? How can you be so sure?" He yawned again.

"We're a team, and I need you to bounce my crazy ideas off. See you soon." She crossed her fingers as she said the last sentence. She wanted to believe she wouldn't be going anywhere without him. At least Jaxon needed her to believe what she told him. Who knew where this investigation would take her if anywhere besides a history lesson? She might need to convince herself before she tried to tackle Jaxon.

Peyton got ready for bed. Tomorrow would be

another demanding day at school, and she wanted to wake early and be ready to go. Those precious kids kept her on her toes. Her reward tomorrow would be a date with her handsome guy and all the magic that came when she was with him. How could she surprise him? Ideas flooded her mind. Now all she had to do was come up with the right one. She stretched out on the bed. Wow did this feel good!

Chapter 9

All thoughts of a surprise for Jaxon were put on hold when her phone rang. Peyton wanted to sleep, but Jessie wanted to talk. They ended up reading more of the diary and talking into the wee hours of the morning. What Cara wrote about the place in town where many girls went to work after they first arrived kept them trying to guess what business she could be talking about. It meant research and, of course, getting Jeremy involved. Many of the young girls ended up disappearing. The rumors were abundant about what happened to them. A few of the circulating stories included murders and runaways. No one knew for sure, which added to the heightened fear among the townspeople.

The warnings that greeted each new ship were plentiful. Immigrants learned fast who in the town were accepting of new arrivals and who wasn't. More than once Cara's dad received caveats about a certain man that was hiring the Irish. The man was described as powerful with friends in high places. He often refused to pay people their wages and made false charges against them so he didn't have to. The law never sided against him.

"I wonder what the name of the business was. Hopefully, she'll tell us at some point," Jessie said.

"I do too. A powerful man certainly adds to the

mystery of the story. It must have been hard for those folks to come all this way and not have people welcome them."

"Can you imagine going to work and having to fear for your life?" Jessie asked.

"I guess there's nothing new. People still have to worry about being safe in the workplace. Only now it's a mass shooter." Peyton went on to tell Jessie about the kids she had seen being bullied in the schoolyard. "The sad thing is with all the school shootings, schools don't feel that safe for kids anymore." She sighed. "School was my sanctuary. I still remember the day I had to do my first active shooter drill with my kids during the first week of school. We locked the doors, pushed desks against them, and moved the kids to a safe place in the room away from the windows in the doors. My kids thought it was a game, but it shook me. Other teachers told me they had students cry and who didn't want to come back to school. I understand we have to do the drills, but it's tough on the kids."

"How sad. I can see how some kids would panic. Especially kids who know what's going on. There's always been crime, but now we have a splashier news version that can be seen quickly around the world." Jessie paused. "Matt needs to hear about what we read tonight. This has more to do with what's happening today than we realize. Bring the diary to the store tomorrow, and I will scan it into my computer. Something tells me this is one of those all-hands-on-deck moments. I know I'll be thinking about it tonight," Jessie muttered. "Young girls who disappeared, a cruel boss who didn't pay his employees, and a couple from the past coming into the store to show you a book.

What's to be alarmed about? All everyday occurrences in the life of the Reynolds girls. We should sleep peacefully and not think at all," Jessie said, sounding satirical.

"I'm not sure I like the idea of resting in peace." Peyton chuckled. "Sleep well, cousin, if you can." She smiled, picturing how her cousin would react. The visual of Jessie with her hands on her hips popped into her mind. She waited for her cousin's comeback.

"Are you trying to be funny? Not! Goodnight." Jessie hung up.

Peyton pulled the blanket up to cover her shoulders. She would pay for this late night in the morning. Reaching for the journal, she opened it once again.

Rereading the same section over, she looked for a clue they might have missed the first time. Living, intermingled with sadness and joy, was described on the pages. Different times—life had changed, and yet it hadn't.

"Enough is enough." Peyton made herself close the book and turn off the light. Yawning, she tossed and turned, trying to get comfortable. A racing mind made it next to impossible to relax. Boy, how she hated nights like this. Closing her eyes, she forced herself to lie still.

**** 

Blowing a misty kiss, Mila watched Peyton wrestling from the other side of the room. "Sleep, my darling girl, and dream my dreams. There is a world of truth awaiting you." She flittered about the room, waiting for sleep to overtake her. The journal had been kept for this moment.

Magic was her forte. And as she knew all too well,

magic was delightful and could be wonderful but sometimes dark when the wrong person was involved. Aelfric, once a friend but now a sworn enemy, proved the theory that even the good can turn bad. From a beloved fairy to a cruel pooka, his transformation happened over time. This town had known both, and the secrets were buried deep in its psyche and the soil on which it grew. It was time for some light to come to Blue Cove, and she was just the one to make it happen.

At moments like this, she loved her job. How she loved this small corner of the world. It was still a part of her after all these years. She enjoyed the times when she could spend an interval among the lovely memories she had made here. Who knew any place could replace Ireland in her heart? Her mission had been to follow Alanna and Cara so long ago. When the right moment presented itself, she revealed herself to Cara. Now, at last, she was here again along with her sister to help her dear Cara once again. It had been a long time coming. Alanna knew the stories well and passed on her abilities to Cara. Brenna was destined for them too, but alas Brenna's life was altered.

The world was filled with sadness and heartbreak. Mila had seen many humans suffer, and any time she was allowed to make something good happen was a wonderful day indeed. Permission to interfere was rare but a treat when consent was granted. Not that there wouldn't be hard days ahead for the Reynolds girls, but it would end quite nicely. A little magic here and a few dreams along the way and lives held captive for many years would suddenly be free. Their voices once silenced and cut off would finally be heard. What happened to their lives was the real story to be discovered and told. Her dainty fingers tapped against her forehead. Happy to be back at the inn, Peyton and her cousin Jessie would do quite nicely. Tenacious, smart, and kind—they would do the job, creating another opportunity for an inch or two to her and her sister's stature along the way.

****

The dream had come again with an added twist this time. Voices coming from deep within the earth called out to her for help. They were followed by faces and names. One face faded only to have another replace its haunted profile. The dream progressed as the clock ticked, as the days turned into weeks and years. With each passing year, the voices grew in volume until their noise became deafening.

Peyton awakened with a start. Her eyes strained to focus in the darkness. What did the dream mean? Were there more bodies close to where they found the girl's body? Maybe she should have stopped searching weeks ago for answers. But once a thought took hold of her, she could be tenacious. Were the voices those of the missing girls that Cara wrote about?

"Stop it, Peyton," she chastened herself. "Must you complicate everything?" Hopefully, Jaxon loved complicated, because his life wouldn't be normal as long as she was a part of it. All she needed to do was convince him and herself, of course, that normal was highly overrated.

Peyton turned on her bedside lamp and reached for the journal. There would be no sleep after that dream. Her hands trembled when she opened to the last page she had read. "Cara, what are you trying to tell us?"

She read ahead to the next break in Cara's story.

Jessie would need to write the news article, but she would draft the novel based on what she was reading. An early morning conclusion she arrived at after too much thinking. She glanced at the clock. Darn, she would be too tired to go out with Jaxon much less surprise him if she didn't stop this nonsense. What she needed was sleep and a charm or two to make it feel like eight hours.

****

"I can help with that, dear." A small hand reached up to her mouth and blew a kiss. Mila watched from her corner until she slept. She stroked the sleeping girl's forehead lovingly. "See only what is necessary for you to do the job you have to do. Many have been waiting a long time for their story to be told. You'll awaken refreshed and ready to go, my dear, with a new sense of direction."

Time was something she had plenty of until Celeste, her superior, would allow her and her sister to be revealed. Mila hadn't determined how she would do that quite yet. Her sister was keeping it a secret too. No matter how she showed herself to Peyton, it was bound to be an adventure for her. Another one of the many reasons she loved her job.

****

The next morning Jaxon loaded his suitcase in the car along with his books and the items he had managed to acquire during the last few weeks. "Blue Cove, here I come." Happy not to see this place again anytime soon, he checked out. He wanted to eat a leisurely breakfast and drop by the Academy on his way out of town. Peyton was waiting for him, and he was eager to see her. The fact she would be at work most of the day meant he didn't need to hurry. He had rushed too many times the past several weeks. Starting at this moment and for the next few days, he would be happy to go at a slower pace. Soon enough he would be back to rushing again. Tom Maxwell, an FBI field agent and his boss, had made sure to inform him how busy he would be. As of yet, he had no idea what case he would be working on, but he was looking forward to getting started. If the past few months held any clues, Peyton would somehow get him involved in what was going on with her too. Another ghost, perhaps, to go along with another murder.

## Chapter 10

Peyton told her cousin that the dream last night had seemed different. Yes, she had seen a body and a ghost at the school which wasn't anything new, but this had a distinctive feel to it. There seemed to be a war going on. If she was truthful, that wasn't new either. What felt new was the sweet voice in her head and a dark shadow roaming around the edges getting closer.

To this point, that shadow's voice had remained silent. On some level, the quiet bothered her. What could it mean? Peyton didn't like surprises. They made her feel like she was losing control. The idea of being in charge was important, even if it wasn't true. With one last glance in the mirror, she headed to the kitchen. How would she ever surprise Jaxon if she didn't stop long enough to think of one? It seemed she constantly raced from one place to another, and she was about to do it again.

After breakfast, she rushed out the door with her briefcase in hand. The sun shone on the snow blinding her with its brightness. What a beautiful but nippy morning. Glancing at the inn on her way to the car, she suddenly had a perfect idea. She couldn't wait to see Jaxon. Talking on the phone was okay, but being with him was even better. Thinking over the details of how to execute her surprise kept her mind busy as she drove to the school. Another day was off to a running start, but the atmosphere in the school when she arrived seemed off.

With a quick glance over her shoulder, she walked down the hall, stopping first to check in at the office. By the time she strode into her classroom five minutes later, the sensation had grown in intensity. What was going on? Placing her briefcase on her desk, she tried to occupy her mind with preparations for her students' arrival. But the unnatural chills creeping up and down her spine forced her to stop and wrap her arms around herself. The shadow she had known was around the edges of her vision seemed to be slithering closer. Would whoever it was show their hand soon? They weren't in the school but close enough to let her know that they were watching.

After a pep talk, she arranged the classroom for the morning's story hour. She loved the book she had found about a happy penguin. But staying busy wasn't helping. "Get ahold of yourself," she muttered to no one in particular. Back and forth she argued with herself, but it seemed to be a lost cause.

Why would anyone be watching her? She hadn't seen the murder, only a dream of one. Besides, the softer, sweeter voice was still stronger. As she readied the room, she stood near the window to keep an eye on the kids arriving at school. They came in various states, dragging their feet or waving at friends, making her smile. She loved watching them from the littlest to the oldest, and of course her special needs kids too. Life seemed happier with their shining happy faces in it. A glance at the clock told her the bell would soon signal the beginning of another school day, and she didn't have time to waste on someone she couldn't see.

She greeted each of her kids and got them situated in the area for story time. It was always the highlight of the day to watch their faces light up when they saw the pictures in the book as she showed them. Soon the shadow was forgotten in the morning rush. Peyton got caught up in the children and a story about a happy penguin who loved the snow.

After all the kids' parents had picked them up, her day was finished, and the weekend began for her. She needed to stop by the grocery store and swing by Jessie's store. Jessie wanted to scan the journal into her computer. Peyton wanted her cousin to be involved and to have time to explore the diary at her leisure. Each clue seemed to be hanging on its own with no links to connect them into anything else. The words that came to mind to describe the odd sensation were "stuck in slow motion." Like being bogged down in thick mud, unable to lift her foot without her shoe being left behind. Maybe that was all there was to her intuitive process for now. Nothing to see here to keep moving. She could live with that. But why did the book choose them? And why all the dreams?

"Where are you?" Jessie asked when Peyton answered her phone. "I thought you were coming."

"I am. I stopped off at the grocery store. I'm planning a surprise for Jaxon, and I needed a few things. I'm in the checkout line and should be there in a few."

"I've been thinking about what you told me last night. I have a few ideas that I want to run by you, but I'll wait until you get here."

"Sounds good. I've been thinking too. I'm not sure I have any ideas. At this point, I can use all the help I can get. Should I run my groceries home first?" Peyton asked.

"Are you kidding me? It's cold enough outside to keep them chilled for hours. This time of year makes me want to live in Florida or Southern California. I'm not a fan of the cold after Christmas until spring."

"We think alike on that subject. I'll be there in a few. The cashier has started to ring up my groceries." Peyton unloaded her cart, hung up, and chatted with the cashier.

Placing the bags in the backseat, she got in her car and drove to Jessie's store. She pulled into an open spot right in front of the bookstore. Jessie was right about the chill in the air. Another car pulled in front of hers. "Hi, dear girl," Reba said as she got out of her car. "Wait for me, and I'll walk in with you."

"Sounds good." She met Reba and latched her arm through hers. "It's always icy right here. This spot must not get enough sunlight."

"How is your day going?" Reba asked as she walked through the door that Jessie held open.

"A bit slow, but with you here it's bound to get more interesting." Jessie smiled at Reba.

"I was just thinking the same thing." Peyton rubbed her hands together and took off her gloves.

"Why don't you get comfortable, and I'll have Molly bring some tea and goodies. I'm sure you've come for a reason." Jessie walked through the open doors into Joe's. "I'll be right back."

Reba took off her coat and folded it neatly across the chair. "Make sure Molly includes a lemon bar." She sat and crossed her ankles primly.

"Of course, I could never forget your favorite

treat," Jessie called over her shoulder.

Reba gestured to Peyton. "Won't you join me, dear? It's time we do a bit of catching up. I may be wrong, although I rarely am, that we have a visitor among us. We'll wait until Jessie returns to discuss her. I'm sure your cousin talked to her a few times."

"I'm sure we have more than one visitor," Peyton mumbled under her breath.

"Molly will bring the tea in a minute. Here's your lemon bar, ma'am." She placed the small plate in front of Reba. "Now, why are you here, Ms. Reba? No, I'm not being rude, but I know the look you get when you're a woman on a mission."

"I'm sure you do. We've been doing this for a while, haven't we? Aww, there's our sweet Molly now bringing our tea. Tea makes everything better." Reba placed a napkin neatly on her lap. "Thank you, Molly dear." She slipped a few bills into Molly's pocket.

"Of course. You're one of my best and definitely my sweetest customer." Molly smiled. "Enjoy your tea."

"Molly, could you box me six of your wonderful cupcakes? Your favorites will be fine as long as one or two of them is chocolate," Peyton told her. "I'll be in to pay for them before I leave."

"I have the perfect combination, and I promise you'll have plenty of chocolate," Molly told her.

"Thanks."

"Shall we start?" Reba glanced at Jessie and Peyton. "Do you remember at Christmas when the inn had that dear little visitor? I know you talked to her several times, Jessie."

"How could I ever forget Holly? She had such a

lovely personality. Poor Chad was completely confused by her more than once. I had to rescue him a few times. Why?" Jessie asked.

"Holly, if that was even her name, or someone like her is in the area again. There is someone else too not as nice, but the light is stronger than the darkness. Not that this balance changes the situation at the moment. Although it will in time." Reba shook her head. "I'm not sure I'm making much sense. You girls have been looking for the cause and roots to why so many things have happened in our beautiful community. The darkness has been here for a while but has been left unexposed to the light. That's what this is all about."

"Voices silenced by the years will finally have their stories told or something like that." Peyton took a sip of her tea. "I understand what you're saying. I would describe it this way. There is a shadow around the edges, but there's a magic or light that can expose his crime."

"Okay, suppose you're both right. What are we looking at?" Jessie reached for the bag that Molly had placed on the table with the tea.

"Cara mentioned women who went missing, the ghost at the school seemed to be looking for a child, and the body is a beginning, but I'm sure there is something we can't see." Peyton tasted the bite of the brownie that Jessie handed her. "Oh wow, this is yummy."

"They always are. We need Matt and Jaxon for the crime part, and it will be up to us to discover the hidden crazy junk. That's our job."

Reba chuckled. "Jessie, my dear, I think you've enjoyed Peyton giving you a break, but I fear your little respite is almost over. You may need your cousin to rescue you at some point. Wouldn't that be an interesting twist?"

"Not as far as I'm concerned." Jessie frowned scrunching her face. "I don't like the sound of that at all."

"Why would you? Do you have a choice, or for that matter do I? We are at the mercy of the powers that be and this nifty gift of sight passed down to us." Peyton patted her hand.

"Don't fret, Jessie dear. I'm not saying this is the moment. I'm only saying you've been enjoying the sidelines in the supernatural goings-on a bit too much, and you'll be called upon again soon. You can't be too complacent. Not with your man either." Reba glanced at her. "Don't put something off so long that it passes you by. You don't want to waste life."

"What is this? Gang up on Jessie day?" Jessie asked.

Reba laughed. "No, it's a simple reminder that you're engaged to a man who loves you and may not want to wait forever while you make up your mind."

"On the subject of Matt, I'm settled." Jessie started to stand but remained seated when Reba touched her hand.

"I wanted to hear you say it. Thank you. Now back to the subject at hand. Keep your eyes and ears open. This case may have started slowly, but it is about to take off at warp speed. Be ready."

"You know, Reba, I was thinking that same thing today," Peyton said. "Jaxon is coming home for the weekend, which means it's probably going to pick up steam. I hope it doesn't ruin our weekend."

Noting the frown on Jessie's face, Reba chuckled and patted her hand. "Don't pout, Jessie dear. As my mother used to say, the wind might change, and your face could stay that way. I'm teasing, dear. I know you love your young man. I don't want you to retreat; you're still needed in the war against the unseen."

"Darn, I didn't want to hear that." Jessie stood and started to pace. "It's been peaceful and nice not having to stare down someone with a gun. I mean, I knew at some point I would be off the sidelines but, at least for now, I'm going to enjoy my downtime. I don't believe that makes me a bad person."

"Of course not, dear." Reba took a sip of her tea.

"I mean Peyton knows I'm close if she needs me. We bounce things off each other all the time. Right, cousin?"

"Yes, we do. I don't think that's what Reba is insinuating though. You've never shirked your duty, but I think we both need to understand that this is our life for the long haul. I do understand more than you know about the desire for peace and no one shooting at me. It's a strange place to be in our lives at this point. And probably the one element that makes it hard to commit to marriage."

"Yes. I love Matt, but how can I ask him to live with a woman who could be here today and gone on some strange journey tomorrow? Tell me, Reba, I would like to know."

"Girls, I'm sorry. I didn't mean for this conversation to get this far out of hand. It must be something bothering both of you."

They both replied at the same time. "Duh."

## Chapter 11

Jaxon wouldn't miss the long drive home every weekend. He didn't mind the time alone, but sharing the road with all the traffic kept him on edge. Not every person behind the wheel paid attention. He'd seen his share of near misses and a few injury accidents. An updated rail system sounded like a suitable alternative to him. He signaled his lane change.

If the last few weeks of training had taught him anything, there were lots of crimes committed every day that people knew nothing about. No knowledge might be good in some cases because folks would lose sleep at night if they heard what he had the past few weeks. Life seemed hard enough without all the extra knowledge of what people were capable of doing to each other. How Peyton and Jessie handled what they saw would make a great case study. He'd seen them in action and still found their abilities hard to understand.

One of the biggest surprises for him since moving to the cove was the great friendship he had with Matt. Besides dating cousins and working a few cases together, they liked hanging out and working on his new place whenever they got the chance. His place was starting to take shape thanks to Matt. It wouldn't be long before he could show Peyton. Jaxon had a local crew doing drywall the past couple of weeks, and he hoped to get the walls painted and the wood floors in over the next couple of weeks. Matt had hooked him up with a local contractor. His crew had done an excellent job so far.

For whatever reason, this strange connection between them as guys and as couples seemed essential. They enjoyed each other and could have each other's back. Yeah, Matt had turned out to be a great friend.

Yawning, he stretched his neck slightly and relaxed his tense shoulders. Dang, he was tired. The last few weeks had taken it out of him. He could use a break himself. Seeing Peyton was like coming home. He couldn't wait to tell her that he didn't have to go back. Thank goodness for hands-free talking. Jaxon answered his ringing phone.

"This is Jaxon. Talk to me."

"I'm talking to you." Matt chuckled. "How far out of town are you?"

"I am about an hour out." Jaxon glanced at the sign. "Closer to an hour and a half if the milage sign is right. Why?"

"Stop at the station when you get into town, would you?" Matt asked.

"I'll be there. What's up?" Jaxon passed a car slowing down to turn.

"I want to run a few things by you."

"Sounds good. I'll see you soon." Jaxon disconnected the call.

If he had to be on the road, at least this was a beautiful day to drive. It wasn't snowing, and the sky was clear. He was making good time. His mind turned to second-guessing what Matt wanted to talk to him about. It kept him alert and awake for the next hour. That and a blast of cold air hitting his face now and then when he turned on the AC.

The Blue Cove exit was a welcoming sight. He signaled and moved over to exit. After a short drive into town, he finally pulled into a parking place outside of the police station. Getting out of the car, he stretched his tired arms over his head and then walked across the slushy parking lot. As soon as the sun goes down, this would become one huge sheet of ice. A major one of the many inconveniences of living in an area with all four seasons. Along with shoveling snow and freezing his tail off. Each, a price he had to pay to live closer to his family and the woman who held his heart. No doubt he had been spoiled living in Arizona in the winter. Still, every time he saw Peyton or his family, Jaxon knew he had made the right decision.

"Hey, Jaxon. Matt said to tell you he'd see you as soon as you arrived," Kenny told him when he walked in the door. "There's a fresh pot of coffee if you want a cup, and Molly brought by some of her great cupcakes. Be sure you get one. Once the guys know they're here, they'll be gone before you can grab one."

"I'll take one for later and head back to his office." Jaxon grabbed a cupcake and started down the hall.

"Wait a minute," Kenny called after him. "Take one for Matt too. He loves my wife's treats, and they'll be gone before he gets out here." He handed Jaxon another delicious-looking cupcake to take to Matt.

"Knock, knock," Jaxon said, walking in the open door. He placed the cupcake in front of Matt. "Kenny sent this to you."

"Have a seat." Matt gestured to the open chair. "Kenny's a good man, and his wife is an exceptional cook. I'm quite fond of her desserts." He chuckled, patting his flat stomach.

"What's up? I was surprised you wanted me to stop by since I'm staying at your place, and you can talk to me whenever I'm around." Jaxon sat in the chair in front of Matt's desk.

"Official business," Matt said. "First of all, congratulations on becoming an agent. If you get overwhelmed, you can always work for me. I'd love to welcome you aboard. Maxwell will be calling you later to tell you that your first assignment will be working with me. We have a murder case involving a kidnapped victim transported across state lines. You're the agent assigned to the case." Matt leaned forward. "You can't seem to get away from the cove or me for that matter."

"If that's my assignment, then I'll be happy to work with your department." Jaxon rubbed his forehead.

"Spoken like a true agent. Now speaking friend to friend." Matt's voice grew serious. "Peyton is starting to put some things together. I've talked to her a couple of times this week. Those girls never fail to surprise me. She told me she thinks that there might be more bodies buried near where we found the murder victim. A dream had her hearing many voices coming from the ground. The victim was a young female, by the way." Matt brought Jaxon up to speed on the case and the evidence he had so far. "I've arranged to bring Frank Wagner and his dog in to go over the area. If he hits on anything, Maxwell told me you could request the ground-penetrating radar equipment."

"When do you want to start?" Jaxon asked.

"Next week. I know you have the weekend off, and I'm sure you can use it."

"That works for me. I can use the time off, but working with you on this case sounds good too. Peyton has been reading to me from Cara's journal. She believes several things are connected. I can't see how, but I know from past experience not to discount anything she tells me. Her dreams and premonitions usually pan out the way she sees it."

"What do you know about the diary? Jessie has told me a few things but not a lot. She did say that the book chose them. I figure you of all people would understand."

"I do." Jaxon went on to tell him what Peyton had told him about Cara's journal. "You realize this started because the girls wanted to know why there was so much supernatural activity at the inn and in town. You have to admit there's been a lot of crime here in the last year and a half."

"Affirmative. I'd have to be blind not to notice." Matt shook his head. "Leave it to the girls to want to know why. I assumed it was because criminals had made their way out of the big city and were looking for a place to hide while doing their dirty work. What do you think?" Matt asked.

"I would think the same way you do except for the fact that Peyton has drilled into me the past few months that there's more than what is visible. Now I admit I'm curious to see if she comes up with anything."

"Knowing them, I'd say we're about to get some unusual answers. Keep me informed, would you? Jessie has been quiet. She's taking a step back. I'm not sure how long she'll get away with it. Peyton, on the other hand, seems to have embraced the gift ever since her travel through time. I'm not sure what's going on with my girl, but eventually we're going to have a chat about what's bothering her."

"She might be worried her abilities will turn you off and she'll lose you. We have both struggled as you know, and they have too. You might need to reassure her you're not going anywhere."

"You may be right. I've never been good about talking about feelings, but it's past time to give in and give it my best shot. Jessie deserves to feel secure in my love, but I'm not sure how to pull that off."

"You, and every other man on the planet. Give me a problem to analyze, and I can do a fine job in no time, but a discussion on how I feel stumps me every time. I wonder if there's a class we could take. I'm sure there must be. Peyton helps me to think outside the box. Now all I have to do is figure out how to tell her how I feel while I'm standing outside of said box." Jaxon leaned back in the chair with a grin.

****

Peyton stood in her kitchen, preparing dinner, thinking about the strange conversation they had with Reba earlier. The one takeaway for her was that Jessie was invested in the whole gift idea but didn't want to be. Afraid maybe? Peyton understood that fear all too well. There were questions they both had that couldn't be answered upfront. Like would they ever lead a normal life? Whatever normal meant nowadays. How could she ease her cousin's fears?

Their great-great-grandmother found a way to marry, have children, and live a somewhat ordinary life, and they should be able to find a way. Helping others had to figure into the equation too. Cara had chosen them, or maybe it was like Reba said: someone else had chosen them and entrusted Cara's story to them. No one could write a news article like her cousin, and she had to be the one to write this one with her special touch. Once the idea popped into her mind, she knew she could convince her cousin to write. Writing the article might remind Jessie of all the good she was doing.

Peyton set the table with her best dishes, complete with linens, stemware, and candles. Rushing into her room, she pulled out the perfect dress to add to her surprise. She couldn't wait for Jaxon to arrive. If she knew her guy, he'd be here soon. Glancing at her reflection in the mirror, she was pleased. Her hair hung in rich waves over her shoulders, and her dress was perfect. Jessie had told her all about Sadie's comments about every girl needing a little red dress. She wasn't sure about red on her, but Jessie helped her pick out the right shade of red with cool undertones to complement her coloring. "This should do the trick." She smiled.

She checked on dinner one more time and sat down to wait for Jaxon. His knock on the locked door was her cue. "Hi, welcome home," she said as she opened the door. His eyes told her everything she needed to know.

"Wow, babe, you look great." He pulled her into his arms. "Maybe hot would be a more accurate description."

"Hot was what I was going for." She smiled. "It's that whole little-red-dress thing."

"I'm not sure what that is, but I'm grateful to whoever came up with the idea." He stepped back and looked her over another time.

"That would be my grandmother and my cousin." She chuckled.

"Remind me to thank them each personally." He

kissed her. "I've missed you. Are you ready?"

"The dress was part one of a surprise I planned for you. You've sounded so tired the last few times we talked I thought you might like a quiet dinner. Just the two of us." She took his hand and led him to the kitchen. "Does this work for you?"

"Perfect." He leaned against the wall and watched her. "It smells great, and the view couldn't get any better." He waggled his eyebrows at her.

"Sit." She turned away from him to hide the blush staining her cheeks. "Everything is ready."

"I have a surprise for you too," he said once she was seated. "I'm done with training, and I won't be gone all week anymore."

"That's great. When do you start your new assignment?" She passed him the dressing for his salad.

"I start Monday. I'm the agent assigned to help Chief Parker with the recent murder case. I'm sure you're aware of most of the details."

"I've talked to Matt about the dreams and what I've seen. Working your first case for the FBI must be exciting for you, Agent Kincaid." She smiled at him. "I had to try out the new title. Agent suits you."

"Matt's already trying to recruit me. I can see how the job can be a bit overwhelming. A lot is going on crime-wise that thankfully most folks know nothing about. Why keep everyone up every night when it's not necessary?" He took a bite of his salad. "What's for dinner? I'm starved."

"I hope you like a nice steak and baked potato. I found a recipe that sounded great, and the sauce won't disappoint." She poured some wine into his glass. "I'm happy you'll be around more." She placed the plate with his dinner in front of him.

He took a bite of his steak. "Peyton, you never stop amazing me. I didn't know you could cook like this. What did you do to this steak? The flavor is great and one of the best I've ever had. Melts in your mouth." He popped another piece of steak in his mouth.

"I'm glad you like it. Dessert will be à la Molly though. I can't improve on perfection." They chatted all through dinner, dancing around the one subject that both of them wanted to talk about.

"I'll clean up while you watch. I don't want you to ruin your dress." He removed his tie and took off his jacket. "It's your turn to sit and let me do the work."

She loved watching him clear the table and fill the dishwasher. There was something almost hypnotic about his motions. What didn't she like about him? Making dinner at home had been a good idea on her part. She liked seeing his domestic side. He talked about his day, his weeks of training, and about how happy he was to see her. She could almost see this happening every day for as long as they both should live. Almost, but not yet.

## Chapter 12

Ah, young love. She watched the couple. Her mind worked overtime, wondering how to reveal herself this time. A mere shadow from another time, a modern figure, or perhaps as herself. There were limitless possibilities. That time was fast approaching.

Mila couldn't take her eyes off the pair as they cuddled and kissed. Their love made her smile and wistful. Dreamily, she eyed the handsome man. Now she had two she needed to convince. She loved a challenge.

Truth reveals itself layer by layer. She flittered around tapping her tiny fingers to her forehead. "Think, Mila, think. You only get one first impression."

Mila had no problem with appearing to Peyton as herself, but Jaxon might be a different story. Men were a bit tougher to convince. Sometimes you simply had to work around them to work with them. Her thoughts kept her busy until she listened to what they started talking about, and then she tuned in to them. Maybe they would give her a clue as to how she should approach them.

****

Peyton leaned her head on his shoulder. "When did you find out that you'll be working here on Matt's case?" She lifted her head to glance at him.

"Matt asked me to stop at the station before I came

to see you. That's the first time that I heard I would be here starting Monday. He's giving me the weekend to study the evidence they have so far."

"Jessie said Matt hasn't told her much about the case. I wonder why."

"From what I understand there are some strange details that they don't want to get out to the public, small clues that would be known only by the killer. Matt's holding those facts tight to the chest for now not wanting any to be leaked. He also wants you and Jessie to give him any information you have without being impacted by what you hear. Matt seems to think he can use all the help he can get."

"What do you think?" she asked.

"I haven't had time to read over the case files yet, but judging from the little you've told me, I tend to agree with Matt. This has all the earmarks of being an unusual case and will need all of our input if possible." He pulled her closer to his side. "Between you and me, I think he misses Jessie's collaboration on his cases. She's there, but not, if you know what I mean. He's not sure what's up. Do you have any idea?"

"If I had to make a guess, I would say she's afraid. I feel it too at times."

"Of what?" he asked.

"It's not easy to live with the knowledge that at any time you could have a ghost or some other strange manifestation show up in your life. The truth is, she's wondering as I have whether life will ever be the same again. You and Matt must both wonder at times what living with these strange interruptions would be like. I think she is purposely trying to stay clear. It won't last. She's invested in this case already, and it won't be long before she takes another case by the horns and leaves me answering to her. Going through the book and not knowing if I could get back impacted her. It would have me, too, had the situation been reversed."

"Matt will be happy to hear this. Do you mind if I tell him?" Jaxon glanced at her.

"Not at all, as long as you tell him it's only one conclusion from a few tidbits she has shared. That and she wanted a break."

"I know you might find this hard to believe, but he misses her working with him, just like I would miss you. He loves her."

"Maybe he should tell her. It certainly couldn't hurt, and his encouragement might help her to work through her worries faster. It's nice to know that we're wanted and missed from time to time." She reached up and stroked his cheek. "I'm glad you're back. I missed you more than you know."

"Nice to hear." He kissed her. "Thank you, for tonight. I needed this. I've been eating out so much I had no idea what even sounded good. Dinner was great, and time alone with you is exactly what I wanted. I'm afraid I hadn't planned much of an evening. This was a welcoming surprise." He kissed her again. "It's been a long day. Do you mind if I call it a night?"

"Not at all." She walked with him to the door.

"Two things before I leave. I love the dress on you. You'll have to wear it on our special night out that I'm planning." He touched his finger to her lips. "It's important you know that I love collaborating with you. As soon as I get home, I'll call, and you can read me some more of the journal. I need to get up to speed on this case."

"Sounds good. I'll be waiting. Don't forget how important you are too, Agent Kincaid. It's a two-way street. I love working with you too."

"I won't. And don't you forget this." He framed her face with his hands and kissed her. One long, heated, and delicious kiss, leaving them both wanting more. He walked out the door, thankful for the chilly air that hit his face. How those girls lived with their premonitions, he couldn't understand. But one thing he knew for sure: he loved Peyton. He had almost blurted it out tonight. It was still too soon to say it to her. She would run.

**\*\*\*\***

Peyton got ready for bed and waited for his call. She opened to the place in the journal where she had left off. Her mind started processing why a federal agent would be working on a local case. She could speculate or simply ask Jaxon when he called. He might not be able to tell her, but she wouldn't know if she didn't ask. It might be as simple as Matt requested Jaxon, but he couldn't be assigned unless his superior sanctioned it. She took a sip of water from the glass on her nightstand. "Cara, something tells me your story isn't as simple as I first thought."

The only thing that could stop her racing thoughts was her ringing phone. "Hey, are you ready to read to me, sweetheart?" Jaxon's deep voice came across the line.

"I am. But before I do, I have a question. Why are you working on a local case as a federal agent?" She adjusted the pillow behind her back.

"The victim was kidnapped and brought across state lines. Maxwell assigned me to the case. This is my first one working for the agency. Thankfully, Matt and I work together well. Does that answer your question?"

"Yes, thank you." She picked up the journal. "Are you ready?"

"You bet," he said.

Peyton began reading Cara's words. Within a few minutes, she found herself lost once again in the story.

*Brenna and I felt lost. Our parents were fearful to let us go anywhere on our own. Besides the missing girls, there was an unfriendly atmosphere toward all the foreigners, as they called us. They blamed us for trying to steal their jobs. It seemed to me there were more than enough jobs for those who wanted to work hard. My parents both found work quickly. We rented a small house which sufficed as my mom would say. Still, I could see the sad yearning in her eyes whenever she talked about home. At those moments, my da would gently remind her that this was home now.*

"It must have been hard for them. Much like the movement west in our country. I've tried to imagine what a woman must have felt when she had to leave the familiar and make the arduous journey in a covered wagon. When I think of those women and how strong they were, I feel like a weakling." She reached for a tissue.

"None of that, Peyton. I doubt there are many women stronger than you. I've never met one." He paused. "All people face challenges in life. Our experiences help shape us."

"But some seem to face more obstacles than others. It doesn't always seem like a level playing field." She sniffed.

"No, it doesn't."

She read a little more and then stopped. "Listen to this."

*Being home alone with only Brenna to keep me company, I found myself growing more melancholy as the days went by. One day Da took Brenna with him to gather wood, but I opted to stay at home. I often longed to find a way back to Ireland. I missed my nana and yearned to hear her stories once again. They brought me strength and gave me a sense that everything would be all right.*

*Sitting there alone that day, overwhelming loneliness overtook me. No friends, a country that didn't want us here, and my parents saddened by what they had lost made me feel as if I had reached the end. I couldn't take the sadness anymore. I closed my eyes but sensed I wasn't alone. I opened them tentatively to see a bright light enter the room. Amid the light was an enchanting creature. Her wings fluttered on her back, as golden stardust spun around her as she waved her tiny hands. I call her a creature because I'm afraid to say, even now, that she was an Irish fairy. Alanna had promised me they would come if ever I needed one. My mother would call me emotional, and my da would say I was being fanciful, but it was the first hope I had to cling to in quite some time. She brought Ireland to my heart. She would come to me many times in that tiny house and remind me of my greater purpose in life. Little did I know at that time Alanna would also be near and remind me that I was different. Like her, I would be a traveler; it was my destiny. The next several years would reveal just how different I was.*

Peyton stopped reading. "What do you think?"

"A year ago, I would've said it was bunk or

folklore and nothing more, but now I'm not sure. It has me wondering if we've always had these folks among us and didn't know they were there. Don't quote me to anyone. I would have to deny it. Who would believe me anyway?" Jaxon chuckled. "Dang, how times have changed me."

"You and me both." She inhaled a deep breath. "We should stop here. You need to get some sleep."

"Sounds good. You might have to excuse me. I'm not sure how much more I can take. Ghosts were hard enough, but fairies. Damn, Peyton, what're next—leprechauns?"

"I have no idea. But legend says if you catch one, they have to grant you three wishes. Keep your eyes peeled. Maybe there's a pot of gold waiting for you." She laughed. "Will I see you tomorrow?" She bookmarked the journal and closed it.

"Of course. Dinner out for sure, although any restaurant will be hard to beat what you made tonight. I'll call you after I get up. Goodnight, sweetheart."

Jaxon would be easy to love. Did she love him? Maybe, but she wasn't ready to commit to love yet. When she spoke those words, she wanted to be sure. It seemed easier to think of Cara, Alanna, and ghosts than to think about falling in love and facing the ghosts of her past. One thing she knew for sure: Jaxon was proving himself to be reliable and caring the longer she knew him. She didn't want to imagine her life without him. Life didn't come with any guarantees, but he was darn close to being one.

## Chapter 13

The dream came once again. The body against the snow, the voices calling from the earth while faces, names, and dates danced in front of her. Two new elements were added that left her shaking her head when she awakened. A dark shadow hovered around the edges of the dream and seemed to creep ever closer while the only thing holding him back was a small bow of light. The darkness could not penetrate the light. And the shadow seemed more of a beast than human, reminding her of the book that Alanna had pointed out, which she bought.

Peyton pushed herself up, propping the pillows behind. She turned on the lamp, taking her notebook and pen off her nightstand. She wrote the names and dates down that she could remember. The wolf on the cover of the book seemed to stare at her as she flipped it over. Not a book she would normally read, she had placed it on her nightstand face down. Having spent most of her childhood in fear of the darkness and the snarling of her father, she went to sleep each night with a small nightlight on. Grams had given the light to her when she stayed at her grandparents' house on one of the rare moments she was allowed to. Even all these years later, the memory remained a vivid and favored part of her childhood.

A gripping nightmare had awakened her with

screams. When Grams came into the room, she brought with her the fairy nightlight. Once she plugged it into the socket, she held Peyton tightly in her arms. "Look, my little angel, how that tiny light in the fairy's hand makes it easy to see and chases away the darkness. It only takes a tiny light to make you feel safe from the shadows, and this one is yours to keep. Every time you turn on your wee fairy, you can remember her light is much stronger than the darkness." She rubbed her back until she fell asleep.

That same nightlight shone in her bathroom each night. She could see it from her bed. Many nights over the years, she would awaken and see its tiny light shining, and the memory of Grams' words brought her a sense of peace and reminded her of the love she felt in her arms that night long ago.

The names and dates were important. She knew Jaxon and Matt would need them. Only a tiny light, she mused over in her mind. Fairies, travelers, and light holding back darkness each had some significance but what? A ghost at the school, time travelers, or shadows of them in the bookstore, and a book, this book—she glanced at the ferocious beast on the cover. How does this all fit together? "Think, Peyton." She tapped the pen against the pad.

A while later, she placed the notebook on the nightstand and shut off the lamp. There was her trusty nightlight glowing from the bathroom. That's when a new thought rolled through her brain, and she was off once again chasing it in all the directions it took her. Glancing at the clock, she was thankful she didn't have to work in the morning because the morning was already here.

The next time she checked the clock, it was nine a.m. when her phone rang.

"Did you talk to Matt about me?" She rubbed the sleep from her eyes, trying to concentrate on Jessie's angry voice.

"Jessie, good morning to you too." Her voice had an edge to it. She sat up, pushing her hair out of her face. "I have no idea what you're talking about."

"Well, don't," Jessie said, "talk to him. Just don't."

"All right. What's this all about?" Peyton's voice sounded gravelly to her.

"Matt called me today all worried that something was wrong. He said he missed me working cases with him. As if I've gone somewhere."

"Don't get mad at me or him." Peyton shoved the covers off her and moved her legs over the side of the bed.

"I won't as long as you don't say anything that will make me mad," Jessie grumbled.

"Matt told Jaxon he missed bouncing things off you. You've been here but only somewhat involved. First, you needed a break after Katie's wedding, and then you said it was out of concern of turning Matt off. I think it's more than that. We battle the same feelings probably."

"Don't try to analyze me." Jessie's voice was terse.

"Hey, you're the one who called me, cousin. You haven't been the same since I went through the book. You couldn't regulate what happened to me any more than you could keep yourself from going through the mirror. We are both control freaks, and we can't control this. This gift shows up when it shows up and takes us out of our comfort zone. What can I say? Kathryn's gift will impact us until it doesn't. Jessie, you love the investigations, and you know you do. You're stronger than anyone I know. That's why you'll write the article about Cara's story and tell the world about what happened to those people. There's no doubt in my mind."

"Are you sure you didn't talk to Matt? He told me the same thing in so many words. I do love that man. If he's okay with me being who I am, then I am too." She sniffed.

A light turned on in Peyton's head. It had to be true. "Now that we've settled you're back in the game, can I ask you a question before I tell you the latest?"

"Sure, why not?" Jessie sounded hesitant.

"Was the murder victim a young female journalist?" Peyton scrunched her face as soon as the words flew out.

"Geez, how'd you know?" Jessie asked. "That detail has been kept secret along with a few more. I only know because I pried it out of him last night. It took a lot to get that much."

"That's why you're fearful. Someone got too close to the truth and was murdered. I wonder what story she was working on."

"I'm way ahead of you there. I have Jeremy trying to find out her name and the story. Still, it makes me nervous, and I don't know why other than I do want a future with Matt."

"The problem is, Jess, that truth has been entrusted into our hands. We have no choice but to find out all we can." Peyton frowned at her image staring back from the mirror.

"There's always a clause or wiggle room in any

venture. I'm still looking for mine," Jessie muttered.

"Why does it bother you? You've been stalked, kidnapped, and shot at and lived to tell about it." Peyton shook her head as she described each of Jessie's near misses. "Never mind. I understand."

"When there is love involved and others that you care about, caution seems to be a natural response. I can't see the risk, but I know it's there. For some odd reason, I'm afraid to ask too many questions because of that threat. And like I said, I want to have a future. A husband, children, the whole works, even if not yet." Jessie sniffed again. "I want those boring routines my friends complain about and kissing the same man goodnight for as long as we both shall live. Or at least I think I do."

"I can relate. Let's change the subject; this one is too depressing." Peyton sighed and went on to tell her about what she read to Jaxon last night. Recalling Reba's words to them, they chatted and then moved on to the new elements added to her dream. "What do you think we're looking at?"

"I'll have to think about it. Did you tell Matt and Jaxon about the dream?" Jessie asked.

"I will today. I wrote down some of the names and dates that I remembered. Plus, I have been doing some research. You'll never guess what I found."

"Dare I ask," Jessie said.

"Of course, you should. You're interested—you know that you are," Peyton teased her.

"Okay, I'll take the bait. Let me have the details."

"Cara's mother was a Campbell before she married. Her brother married Mary Buchannan who gave birth to three fine sons. One of those sons, Ian

Campbell, married a woman named Maggie Connor. She gave birth to Andrew Campbell who married Katie Donavon, not our Katie, of course, who became the parents of none other than Kathryn Campbell, our great-great-grandmother." Peyton's excitement grew as she shared the details.

"Are you kidding me! Cara is in our family line, along with her grandmother. No wonder we are who we are. It goes back farther than Kathryn," Jessie shouted.

"I know. I find the family connection cool. Here's another element to entice you. Cara describes a trunk with their belongings in it. We have to go back to the attic to see if there is anything like she portrays up there. It seems to me that the Cassidys, Campbells, and the Donovans are intrinsically linked." Peyton ran her fingers through her hair.

"Wow! Can I just say double wow?" Jessie yelled into the phone. "No wonder Katie and I have been besties for years."

"At least the journal choosing us makes sense now," Peyton said.

"We have to meet the guys together and talk about the case for sure now. I'll arrange a time with Matt and get back to you. Talk to you later, cousin. Oh, and thanks."

Peyton smiled. Jessie was back, thankfully. She needed her. The idea of tag-teaming on one of these cases sounded perfect. Who said only one person had to do the job?

**** 

Jaxon stretched his arms as he sat on the edge of the bed. Matt had called late last night. They had talked into the early hours of the morning. Parker wanted to talk all things Jessie, and Jaxon did his best to listen. In the end, Matt seemed to be a man on a mission. He grinned. As matter of fact, so was he. He wanted to spend time with Peyton today. He clearly understood the uncertainties Matt felt—they were probably felt by any man who wanted a relationship with the woman he loved. It's a wonder anyone ever gets together. Women could be intimidating creatures, and that was before you added all the abilities that the Reynolds girls had.

Never one to run from a challenge, Jaxon headed into the shower, whistling as he went. Peyton was a handful, but one undertaking he didn't mind getting his hands full of.

****

From where Mila watched, things were looking up. They were finding each of the clues that would be important to discover the truth. Fluttering her wings in celebration, her plan seemed to be working. Of course, she had the opportunity to observe the cousins once before, at Christmas in the background. Even her sister Elida hadn't known at the time that she was there. Celeste had sent her on a secret reconnaissance mission. Peyton and Jessie convinced her that they could see what was invisible to most and were aware of their surroundings. Filled with empathy and kindness rarely seen in the young these days made them a winning combination.

She could only continue to hold the darkness back as more light from the past got exposed. Aelfric's ability to change his form made it hard to keep him under wraps. He influenced many to do his bidding, but there was only one main power source. As of yet, Mila didn't know what human he lived as. She once had to face him as a bear and again as a raging stallion. His strange ability as a pooka was to adapt to the legends in the area in which he lived. He was legendary, and many of the nymphs feared him. He could shift from human to animal and back again. But what made him truly scary is he could settle into one person and fit into society.

The cousins' help was needed to bring the truth out of the shadows. With each piece of truth that was revealed, more light would come. Aelfric knew his power would wane too. She fluttered her wings in excitement, thinking about all the possibilities. Now all she needed to do was arrange things in the attic. She clapped her hands in glee. Discovery was such a sweet thing. She flew off to work her magic.

## Chapter 14

Peyton couldn't wait to head back to the attic to search armed with the new knowledge she had gained, but Jess asked her to wait until tomorrow. Her cousin wanted to come along too. Determined to not waste any time, she began reading the book that Alanna had pointed out. In the first couple of chapters, she could already see a connection building. The story was scary to read but enlightening.

How she had known it had been a reporter murdered was still a mystery. The thought came like someone had planted the idea in her mind. The fact that she knew the victim was a young woman and friend of Jessie's from New York added to the mystery. Peyton needed the last details confirmed before she divulged that information to anyone, especially her cousin. Unless Jessie already knew and that's why she had been acting so strange.

Per their conversation earlier, Jessie had called her with dinner plans for the evening. Now instead of a date alone with Jaxon, they would be going with Matt and Jessie. Although they needed to go through all the details of a worrisome murder, Peyton still wanted time alone with her guy. But she would go with the plan and try not to be selfish. Besides, he had just called and was on his way to pick her up now. He didn't say where they were going only that they would be spending the day together. She could live with that. Call it her reward for trying to appease everyone. The thought of being with him still gave her a thrill. That was a good sign, wasn't it? She wasn't growing tired of him; rather, she couldn't see him often enough.

Opening the closet, she reached for her jacket and draped it over the back of the sofa. The sun was out, and most of the snow from the past few days had melted. Warmer days she could live with, and not having to wear winter boots was an extra reason to be happy. Running her hand over her silky shirt, she neatly tucked the soft fabric into her slacks as she stood at the window and watched for him. What would he think if he could see her standing there waiting like a young high school girl? Did guys ever get topsy turvy over a woman? Probably not. She forced herself away from the window and went to sit in one of the chairs, careful not to mess up her blouse.

"Good grief, Peyton, anyone watching you now would think you've lost your mind," she muttered. She counted off the minutes as she watched the clock like a lovesick adolescent. She tried to take her time getting to the door when he knocked. A whole five seconds must have passed before she smiled and opened the door.

"You look happy." Jaxon grinned. "I hope it's because you're happy to see me."

"That's one way to put it. Where are we headed?" she asked.

He locked and closed the door behind her. "I thought we could take a drive to Hanover and see the new field office where I'll be working. We could grab a light lunch and hang out together. We don't have to be back here until five thirty. Does that sound okay to you?"

"Sounds great." She slid in the passenger's seat when he opened the car door. "Tom Maxwell seems like he'll be a nice guy to work for." Two unseen passengers followed her into the car.

"Yeah, he's an all-right guy." Jaxon backed the car out and passed the inn on the way to the road into town. "Matt seems to be tight with him, and that's a good enough recommendation for me."

"I'm happy you and Matt get on well. It would be tough if you didn't like each other as close as Jessie and I are." She glanced at his profile as he drove.

"Yeah. I like all the guys at the station. They're a solid group." He squeezed her hand resting on the console. "I bet this is a beautiful drive in the fall."

"Perfection in the fall and winter." Peyton already knew she liked Hanover. She had been there a few times, once for a job interview and once when Jessie took her to a great boutique off the main street that sold one-of-a-kind items. It wasn't a long drive from Blue Cove, and the town had plenty of character. The only reason she wouldn't want to live there was that the town was missing a view of the cove which in her book was hard to beat.

As they drove, she talked about her job which never failed to animate her. She loved working with the kids. Jaxon talked about the work they had done on the house over the past few months. He promised she would get to see their handiwork before long because he wanted her help decorating the place. Not one of his stronger suits, as she knew all too well from his place in Arizona. She would love to help him find a style he could live with. The one subject they steered clear of was what she wanted to talk about most, but he could use a break until tonight. Her mind was filled with emerging details of a murder that was tied to something hidden for a long time. How Cara fit into the present situation still had to be discovered. If there was any connection, she would find it.

**** 

Jaxon glanced over at Peyton. The silence in the car was deafening, and she seemed far away. "Am I boring you?"

"No. Why?" She turned to look at him.

"I've asked you several questions. You didn't answer was my first clue. The second one is you've been quiet for the last five miles." He smiled at her. "What's on your mind?"

"You know how I am once a thought gets in my head. I keep working on it. I knew we were going to talk about the case tonight and that you could use a break. I can't seem to let my thoughts go. Sorry."

"You don't need to be sorry. I want you to tell me what's on your mind. It's when you get quiet that I start to worry. Quiet with you can mean something is about to happen. Start talking, sweetheart." He moved over and signaled his turn into Hanover.

"I'm sorting through things is all, including the conversation I had with Jessie earlier. One thing I want to tell you is when I talked to Jessie earlier, I knew the murder victim was a young reporter. I have no idea where the idea came from, but Jessie told me that much was true. What I didn't tell Jessie is that the victim, a female, was a friend of hers from New York. I wasn't sure enough about the last detail to tell her. But in my heart, I'm sure." Peyton's face creased. "What I want to know is what story was she working on?"

"You're right about the woman being her friend, but Matt hasn't told Jessie. We talked last night about how he could tell her, but maybe the best way is to let you. You could drop it like you just told me. What do you think?" He glanced at her.

"I could. But it's possible she already knows. She's been acting a bit strange, trying to pull back. Even Reba noticed the problem. We talked about my concern earlier, and that's when the thought came to me about the victim. At our core, we both want a regular life. The happy ever after story. You know, marriage, kids, and the whole enchilada. We aren't super brave, don't like being shot at, and moved to the cove for a quiet life. I think you can see where I'm going here. Our lives are not working out the way we planned, but that doesn't mean we don't still want it. I can understand her reticence to be involved. I can safely say she's back in the game, as you'll see tonight." She stretched her seat belt—the darn thing had pulled tight against her neck.

"How about you? Are you doing okay?" he asked.

"I am for now. I have some positive things I've discovered along the way that have helped. Let's just say, I'm learning to live with my new life and all that comes with it." She told him about the family connection to Cara.

"I didn't see that coming." He pulled into the parking lot of a nice, newly remodeled building.

"Nor did I. I think it's awesome." She unlatched her seat belt. "Is this the new office?"

"This is the place." He opened the door for her. "I want to show you my office and introduce you to some of the guys. You Reynolds girls are a bit of a phenomenon in Tom's department." He grinned at her.

"Great." She slapped her hand to her forehead. "Not something I want to be," she muttered under her breath.

**** 

More sure than ever that they had made the right decision, the sisters got busy planning their next move. One thought here and there planted at the right moment and look how the girls connected the ideas. Add the book Alanna had indicated into the mix and Peyton would put the clues together before long. A true joy to observe even for these old pros. Mila high-fived her sister Elida with her dainty hand. Peyton and her cousin were making their job easier. Their ability to see and sense beyond the first layer was a beautiful gift to watch. Add the guys, and they might pull this job off and send Aelfric packing.

They had waited years and, in this case, waiting paid off beyond their wildest dreams. Truth is that magic could only be used sparingly to help the couples. There were rules and lots of red tape that their whole society had to abide by. The Intermediary Manual made those perfectly clear, which didn't seem fair since the dark side could do whatever they wanted. But Celeste their leader would say whenever the subject was brought up, "Might doesn't make right, and what's right wins in the end." Quite frankly there were more than a few in their group that weren't sure if that truth held up any longer. More than once a defeat had been handed to someone who played by all the rules. And the most important rule in the book was the hardest to follow at times. Mila often had to sit on her hand with the wand in it or sit on Elida's.

All parties had to feel like they were coming up with the ideas on their own. No amount of magic could be used to force their decision. Mila knew the rule by heart and repeated the words often enough. She had been sent on many cases over the past hundreds of years but none as important as this one. If things went the way she envisioned, she would be a smidge taller before she lived another hundred years. Yes, they had chosen well.

Time to get down to the important task at hand. How would she reveal herself to Peyton? How would her sister reveal herself to Jessie? This was the fun part of the job. Her dainty foot tapped against the car window as golden dust swirled through the air with the wave of her hand. Hopefully, that small dose of magic would keep Aelfric quiet for a little longer. Still, she could see his hungry eyes watching their progress as they moved along.

## Chapter 15

By the time they got to the restaurant, Matt and Jessie were already there. Matt chose the Osprey for its seaside location, and he had reserved the perfect table for a splendid view of the cove. Peyton was bursting with information begging to be revealed. As soon as the waiter took their order, she began the conversation.

"I have a few questions I need answers to, Matt. I told you about the dream, but I haven't told you what else I've sensed. The murder victim is a young woman about our age, right?" Peyton motioned at Jessie and herself.

"Yes. What else do you want to know?" he asked.

"She was a reporter working on a story." Peyton glanced at Jessie. "And she is known by Jessie from her days in New York. Correct?" She saw Jaxon nod out of the corner of her eye. "Sorry, Jess, that you had to hear it like this. If I'm correct, she worked in the same department as you."

"What?" Jessie stood up. "Were you ever going to tell me?" She looked at Matt with hurt in her eyes. "No wonder you wouldn't talk about the murder with me." She frowned at him. "You should've told me."

"Damn, Peyton, how...? Maybe I don't want to know." Matt shrugged. He coaxed Jessie gently back into her chair and reached for her hand. "You're right, I should have told you, sweetheart. But in my defense, I only found out that information a couple of days ago, and I've been trying to figure out how to tell you, Jess. Ask Jaxon. I bent his ear for hours last night." He lifted his chin, pointing at his friend.

"May I ask her name?" Jessie pulled her hand from his.

"Tamara Campbell. I've been trying to track down the story she was working on," Matt told them.

Jessie swiped at the tears forming in her eyes. "Tamara was the girl who took my place in the apartment when I moved here to be near Katie."

"Do you notice her last name, Jessie?" Peyton asked. "She's a Campbell. What are the odds of that?" Peyton knew Jessie needed time to compose herself.

"How is that important to the case?" Matt asked.

"Wait until you hear what Peyton has to tell you, and you'll understand the possible connection." Jaxon squeezed Peyton's hand. "Tell him what you told me, sweetheart."

Peyton began to tell him how the Cassidys, Campbells, and the Donovans were connected. "As you see, it's not strange that the journal was waiting for us to find it. Cara is in our family line. And I believe Tamara was getting close to the truth, whatever it is. Something bad that Cara had mentioned a few times in the journal had started many years back but may still be going on today in some form or another. I believe when you check the area where you found the victim's body, you'll find a few more. I also think there may be a mass gravesite somewhere." Peyton paused and glanced at her cousin. "Jessie can do her friend proud by finishing the story."

"What makes you think that?" Matt asked.

"I'm not sure." Peyton shook her head. "I know I need to give you more to go on than that, but we're still finding new information."

"Jess, what do you think?" Matt asked her.

"I agree with Peyton. I need to write an article." Jessie pulled out her small notebook from her purse. "With the help of Jeremy and Cara's descriptions, I've learned that immigrants haven't always been welcomed in our country, or indigenous people either. Cara mentioned something in her journal about a few women from one of the tribes in the nearby reservation being kind to her family. She also said the mothers were worried about their children being taken to boarding schools. Some of their children were never seen again."

"I haven't read that passage yet," Peyton said. "But I started the book Alanna pointed out, and it speaks of an Indian legend that comes to life."

"Wow, that's fascinating. I read ahead in the journal. The stories of Indian children being forcibly removed from their homes reminded Cara of what was happening in Ireland. She could relate to these women and became friends. Alanna liked them too. The travelers felt at home among the tribe's spiritual traditions."

"Awesome. Things are starting to connect." Peyton smiled at Jessie. "See, I told you there was no way you could stay aloof. You're needed to help."

"Yeah, yeah, so you say." Jessie laughed. "We do make a good team, don't we, dear cousin?" Jessie grinned at her.

"I should say." Peyton squeezed Jessie's hand. "All we have to do is find out who the owner of the company was where all the women worked."

"What about us?" Matt gestured at Jaxon. "Can anyone join this conversation?" Matt thanked the waiter when he put his salad in front of him.

"Feeling a bit threatened, are we?" Jessie patted Matt's hand. "You're the logical brains behind it all. You're the tough guys that wear the badge, and we're nothing without you. What would we be without you two?" Jessie picked up her fork. "I'm hungry."

As the evening progressed, they bounced ideas off one another. Peyton watched Jessie getting more involved. Her cousin had an important connection to Tamara Campbell, Neil, her old boss, for whom she still did freelance articles. He would be especially interested in the direction this story was headed. Matt and Jaxon got into the evidence side of the conversation, talking about search warrants and ballistics, which left her and Jessie to enjoy the evening their way with dessert and filling each other in on elements of Cara's story that seemed important to this point. After promises to each other to search the attic together tomorrow, Peyton had learned a lot more about the case. They were headed in the right direction.

****

"You're quiet. Is everything all right?" Jaxon asked her on the ride home.

"I was thinking about those mothers worried about what was happening to their children. It reminded me of the ghost I saw at the school. She was frantically searching among the children as if she were looking for her own. It has me wondering is all. When was the school built, and was there anything on that property before they built it or in the area? These things are never a coincidence. There is some connection, even if at the moment there are only scraps of pieces."

"You can always check the town archives and get Jeremy involved too." Jaxon smiled at her. "I like how your mind works. You'd make a great detective. You make an even better girlfriend."

"Thank you very kindly." She smiled at him, fluttering her eyelashes playfully. "You're not half bad yourself." She moved closer to him. At least as close as the car allowed. When he stopped at the light, she was close enough to kiss him.

"That's what I'm talking about." He kissed her back with one eye focused on the light about to change.

"Cara's journal is filled with the statements about how the Irish weren't received well. She talked about her dad coming home after looking for a job one day. He told them about the help wanted signs in the windows all over town. All those signs also said Irish need not apply. Cara wrote that they were being blamed for any outbreaks of disease and told they were lazy. Many of the town's folks eyed them suspiciously and blamed them for most of their problems."

"I find it strange how some ideas never change." Jaxon turned into the lane leading back to the inn. "There always has to be someone else to blame for our lot in life. Heavens knows it can't be my fault," Jaxon said, his voice holding a satirical edge.

"When you add to the prejudices at that time, and the Indian mothers whose children were taken from them, it gives me a lot to consider. I question if we will ever learn from the past and get this right as humans." She exhaled shaking her head. "One can hope." She opened the car door when he came to a stop.

"Hey, you're supposed to wait, remember. I should

open the door for you. I know you're capable, but it's one of the small things I can do for you." He grinned at her.

"Sorry, I forgot. I get in a bit of a hurry when I'm thinking about something else." She smiled sheepishly and closed the door.

He walked her to the cottage door. "Do you have the key?" He reached out his hand, and she dropped her keys into his.

"Do you want to come in for a while? I have some of Molly's desserts left over." She walked through the door he held open.

"Only if you promise to read to me. I am trying to connect what Matt told me and what we were talking about on the way home." He closed the door behind him and took off his coat.

Peyton went into the kitchen and returned with a plate of goodies. "Make yourself comfortable, and I'll get the journal."

"Do you have milk or something to go with this? Better yet, what if I put on your tea kettle?" he asked.

"Sounds perfect. I would like some tea. As Reba says, everything is better with tea."

Jaxon went into the kitchen and put fresh water in the kettle. He got cups out of the cupboard and reached for the cream in the refrigerator. When she walked back into the kitchen, the kettle had started to whistle. "What kind of tea do you want? I notice you have many."

She reached for her choice and placed the teabag in the cup. "I see you're a plain tea kind of guy."

"Yep. None of the fancy stuff for me. I drink manly tea." He flexed his muscles. "Except for the cream."

"Cream ruins the manly image." She stirred her tea.

He followed her back into the living room, enjoying the view in front of him. He sat on a chair and not next to her. She was a warm and wonderful distraction, and he needed to keep his head clear. He leaned forward in the chair, took out his notebook, and made notes as she read.

Jaxon listened to Peyton read Cara's journal, highlighting ideas they had discussed earlier. He made a mental list of topics that he wanted Jeremy to research. The murder site, the area around the school, and possibly the location of an old boarding school in the area if the building still existed. What the hell was going on? His mind raced on. Peyton was right, somehow there were connections, but she might have to help tie them together. Outside of a crime of passion, others were plotted and had roots that ran deep. This crime might be one of those that had strong correlations to the past.

"Are you listening?" she asked.

"Yes. I'm even taking notes." He waved the notebook in the air. "We should stop here for tonight. I have some things to mull over. I'll call you tomorrow." He stood and reached for his coat. He slipped his arms in and zipped up. After a quick kiss goodbye, he opened the door and was gone.

Chapter 16

Peyton stood in the open doorway until he was out of sight. "Well, that was strange," she muttered closing the door. He was definitely preoccupied. She couldn't fault him. She often was too. A longer kiss might have been nice, though. She carried the dishes into the kitchen and put them in the dishwasher.

Her phone signaled a text, which made her smile when she read his message.

—*Sorry, I left abruptly. I needed a clear head to put my thoughts together, and you, lovely lady, are the best kind of distraction. See you tomorrow.*—

Peyton smiled as she got ready for bed and was still smiling when she crawled beneath the covers. She opened her laptop and turned it on. Sorting through her emails, she found one that she was hoping for. Before she read the message, she wrote a note down to remember to talk to Sadie about her discovery of their family's connection to Cara. Besides being interested, Grams might be able to add some more helpful family information.

After reading Jeremy's email, she couldn't contain her excitement. Jessie had to hear this.

"I was about to call you," Jessie said as she answered. "Did you get an email from Jeremy?"

"You mean the one about the story that Tamara Campbell was working on?"

"Yes, of course." Peyton could almost hear her cousin's foot tapping. "Why do you think I called you? I couldn't wait to tell you. We're on the right track."

"Yes, a dangerous one. You were right about Campbell getting too close to the truth. I found out that Tamara had been asking questions about missing women as she was working on a story about boarding schools and the missing indigenous children. Somehow she was connecting the two stories, or at least trying to," Jessie replied.

"And here we are trying to do the same thing." Peyton glanced again at the details in Jeremy's email. "Does it ever make you question if we've lost our minds? I'm asking for a friend."

"Duh. Why do you think I've been holding back? Truth is, not being involved hasn't helped either. Whether I'm in all the way or trying to stay on the sideline, the gift still seems to embroil me in the case anyway."

"What are you saying?" Peyton crossed her fingers.

"I'm in. Let's go early to the inn to check the attic tomorrow. Matt has already told me we're going to spend some time together, but I have to be a part of the search. Does eight work for you? I told Katie we would be there first thing in the morning. She said anytime was okay, but we had to be quiet and not disturb the guests."

"We can do quiet. See you at eight." Peyton closed her computer and set her alarm for seven. Turning off the light, she snuggled beneath her quilt and closed her eyes. They opened quickly when her room filled with light.

\*\*\*\*

"Hello, dear." Mila fluttered her wings as the light swirled around her petite form and smiled at Peyton. "It is time for you to see me. We need to talk. There's a major problem, and your assistance is needed."

"All right, I guess. Are you Elida? The one who showed up at the inn at Christmas." Peyton rubbed her eyes.

"That would be my sister. I'm Mila. We are both here. I'm with you, and Elida is with Jessie. At least she should be."

"What are you doing here? I mean, aren't you supposed to be in Ireland?" Peyton asked timidly.

"Obviously, not. We came here long ago with the Irish who were believers who came to this country." Mila hovered in midair.

"Do you mean like Cara and Alanna?" Peyton lifted her head and leaned on her hand.

"Ah, sweet memories." She tapped her small foot on the footboard. "The journal is one of your connections to your family and the past."

"I could do the same thing tracking my ancestry. What is this really all about?" Peyton sat up.

"You're the part of the family that must break the curse that was brought upon this area by members of your family line. It must stop with you and your cousin." Mila waved her dainty hands, gesturing as she talked.

"I'm not sure what you mean." Peyton watched, pulling the covers up to her chin.

"Of course, you don't, dear girl. Most folks know very little of their ancestors and their deeds. Your father traveled the darker side. Do you know why? I daresay you don't. Why did your grandmother Sadie and your great-great-grandmother Kathryn live on the other side? What formulated their choices? You are like them, you know. The same kind heart, sense of justice, and the ability to see. But some of your ancestors ran with the beast and brought their darkness on others."

"I have only seen bits and pieces. I have no idea how any of it is connected. You can't always find that kind of information online. What beast are we talking about?" Peyton asked.

"All in good time your questions will be answered, my dear." Mila pointed her finger at Peyton. "But the right piece of knowledge can help you uncover the truth, and you will learn more in time. All people aren't good. Some only bring harm with them and to those around them. People fled the famine and their oppressors, only to find at the end of their journey those who were willing to oppress them anew. When bad things happen unseen, they can become a place where similar crimes can continue to happen. Cara's diary chose you because we chose you. You are needed."

"You're the one who planted the thoughts in my head, aren't you?" Peyton asked.

"Yes, and dreams. But to my great sorrow, my magic can only do so much." Mila shook her small head.

"Will I see you again?" Peyton gazed at the beautiful creature in front of her.

"You'll see me when you need to. Mostly, I'll be behind the scenes arranging things. The urgency of this moment can't be underestimated. If the darkness grows any stronger, it will be hard to stop its evil plan once put into action. Your young man is important too."

"Will he see you?" Peyton asked. "He wouldn't

want to. It would rock his logical world."

"It's doubtful, at least not like this. I may send him a thought or two to point him in the right direction. He might see me in human form along the way. One thing I want you to understand is that the law in the hands of a good man can make all the difference while the same laws in the hand of a bad one can do great damage. Do you understand what I'm saying?"

"Yes. Jaxon is a good man," Peyton said.

"You will understand more soon. The very laws meant to protect the victim and convict the criminal have at times been used to benefit the bad and destroy the good."

"I find that hard to accept, and yet I know your words are true from experience." Peyton laid her head back on the pillow. "How will I know what to do next?"

"Now you will sleep." She blew her a misty kiss.

"Before I sleep, may I ask you a couple of questions?" Peyton lifted her head off the pillow again.

"Of course, I'm sure you will have many." Mila landed on Peyton's arm.

"Why me after all these years?" she asked.

"Because, sweet girl, you came to the attic to search. Few people wandered up there over the years except to place more boxes or books. But you could see the possibilities and were willing to look beyond the visible. You have imagination, dear girl." Her tiny fingers tapped against Peyton's arm. "I'll answer one more, and then it's off to dreamland for you."

"Why Sally?"

"Sally was one of our special human interventions. She needed a bit of Christmas magic after all she went through. Sally handled Elida's intervention beautifully, and that's when we saw you and your cousin. Celeste sent me incognito on a reconnaissance mission. I was here only to observe. It was a lovely moment to watch Sally reborn in hope." Mila wiped the tear from her eye as she twirled into the air. "Tomorrow is a new day, and you have adventures awaiting you. It's time to rest; you'll need a clear head."

Mila watched until Peyton slept. She tapped her forehead and left her to dream.

\*\*\*\*

Jaxon worked through the notes he had written down. In light of his conversation with Matt earlier, it seemed urgent that they get Frank's tracking dog to town and let him work the grounds around the crime scene. He sent a text off to Matt. Matt sent one back telling him that a track was on for Monday. With that settled, he opened his computer and caught up on his emails. He read the one Jeremy sent to Peyton and Jessie. Nothing surprised him anymore until he read the next email. He made a note to quit saying that to himself. He was surprised constantly. Hell, nothing seemed conventional anymore. Jeremy's research on Cara and Alanna had pulled a dark character into the mix. Although, his crime spree didn't manifest itself until he relocated to America.

Jaxon read the rest of Jeremy's research. Because different cities found the influx of people hard to assimilate, the immigrants weren't welcome. The Irish were forced to fill the most dangerous and menial jobs. Local citizens formed a nativist movement in several cities that sought to deport and push the Irish out of their area. The violence against them and their families gave birth to the Irish Mafia, one of the oldest organized crime groups—a desperate response to violent persecution.

It's nuts how history tends to repeat itself. Jaxon continued to read down the page. They may be different faces and characters but the same song. Jaxon rubbed his temple. Disparities between the rich and the poor, us against them mentality, and a scapegoat to blame seemed to be at the heart of the repeated issues from one generation to the next. Hell, sometimes the human race didn't seem humane at all.

Somewhere in all this mess was the answer to a crime still going on today. On some level, there's nothing new. People blaming others and designing ways to penalize them was not new. The results weren't new either; people always ended up dead or damaged for life. There had to be a better way to make a living than to see this madness. Still, there was something to be said about getting a bad guy off the street.

He couldn't change what happened in the past, but he liked the thought of changing the future in a small way. Shutting down his computer, he stretched out on the bed. The law in the right hands was a powerful weapon, but he had studied countless examples of the same laws used unjustly. What would it take for people to change, or was it even possible? Damn, no easy task. "Knock it off, Jaxon. Don't go looking to change the world you've got a job to do." He closed his eyes.

Chapter 17

Who in their family line brought this darkness to the area with them? She couldn't let go of the thought all morning since awakening. Peyton raced through her morning ritual and in no time was headed toward the inn with her cousin.

"Good morning, you two." Katie reached for the eggs on the counter, breaking them into a bowl as she talked. "Remember to be extra quiet going upstairs. There are guests still sleeping."

"We will," Peyton said softly. Thankfully, the creaky stairs were behind the door on the second floor leading up to the attic. Each step squeaked and groaned under their feet. "Which one of us will open the door this time?" Peyton laughed. "A zing here and zip there. Who gets it this time?"

"It's all yours. Be my guest." Jessie motioned Peyton to move in front of her.

"You've lost your sense of adventure, my dear cousin." Peyton walked in front of her. "Did you happen to have a special visitor last night?"

"Yes, why?" Jessie asked. "What made you ask me that?"

"I had one too. She gave me a clearer idea of what we're up against." Peyton stopped on the top stair.

"Did Elida come to you too?" Jessie asked.

"No, but her sister Mila did. Her presence

enthralled me from her pointed ears; beautiful, sparkling, greenish eyes; down to her tiny foot tapping on my bed. Mila is beautiful." Peyton reached out to turn the doorknob and was met with the familiar tingle shooting up her arm. "Well, if there was any doubt, we have proof that we're in for another adventure." Peyton rubbed her hand and arm. She walked into the magical space followed by her cousin. The attic seemed enchanting to her every time she came here. The secrets of a time long past waited to be discovered. With each discovery, she learned more about herself in the process.

"Elida came wrapped in light, fluttering about my room with golden sparkles following wherever she went. It's the same description Sally had shared with me. I might keep the fairy details from Matt. He wouldn't get it. I could tell him I saw Holly, but I doubt he'd remember her." She chuckled. "Elida's sudden appearance makes me wonder what's in store for us today. I hope whatever it is that it won't upset Matt or Jaxon."

"I don't think we're going anywhere, but who knows. Mila told me last night that her magic could only do so much."

"Elida told me the same thing. I wonder what that means. Is it possible we will have to use our brains to solve this mystery?"

"Anything is possible. We're on a mission to find what Cara described. There are answers in this attic. I'm sure of it." Peyton moved among the boxes and furniture. Her eyes were drawn to a large trunk that appeared to have been moved recently. Peyton ran her hand across the top of it. A sense of excitement filled her, followed by a foreboding. Taking a deep breath, she slowly opened the lid and peered inside. "Jessie you've got to see this," she called over her shoulder.

Jessie knelt beside her in time to watch the first ghost fly out of the trunk followed by one after another. "What the…" Jessie never finished her question. She reached for an old, framed photo, and another ghost seemed to come from the photo. "Do you see them?"

"Yes. We've hit the jackpot. The story is somewhere in all of these treasures." Peyton pulled out a locket. She opened it, and the faces of two young girls smiled back at her. "Look, Jessie."

"Wow. I wonder who they were. These are beautiful hand-painted miniatures." Jessie handed it back to Peyton. She turned back to look through the contents of the trunk. Jessie lifted a book out and carefully turned through the pages.

"What's that?" Peyton looked over Jessie's shoulder. "It looks like another journal."

"Yes, but look at this. This one has added a family tree. How cool is this!" Jessie flipped through the pages. "I wonder what all these names mean."

There were dresses, hair combs, and personal items intermingled with photos. Between the ghosts watching them and the photos, Peyton had a feeling there was something important they might be missing. "Let me see the book." Peyton reached for the book in Jessie's hand. Peyton gasped. "I know these names," she said excitedly.

"What do you mean?" Jessie asked.

"These were the names I heard in my dream. Someone must have kept a record of the women who went missing. These must be some of their belongings.

A record of their existence. Now we need to read this book too."

"No wonder spirits are watching us. They've been waiting for generations to tell their story." Jessie continued to sort through the keepsakes in the trunk. "I'm curious if any of my possessions would be worth keeping." She lifted out a book of poetry with a rose pressed inside.

"Listen, Jess." Peyton started to read a passage.

*With each disappearance, the women's fear began to grow in our small Irish community. The first one lost to us was Brigitte. She was engaged to be married. Her wedding was only two weeks away when she didn't return from her job. Aiden, her soon-to-be husband, searched for her for weeks. Broken, he eventually gave up. He left our community. Later we heard he had joined a group of men in New York that formed a gang to fight back.*

*We loved this place when we first arrived, but who knew what heartache awaited us here. One after another of our daughters and mothers were gone, and we never knew why. Something evil was afoot, and the women knew it. This book is a record of all those that I learned about.*

The apparitions moved about frantically as she read. Peyton placed the dress and locket back into the trunk. This wasn't the trunk that Cara described. She would look for that another day. This was the one they were supposed to find today. It held secrets and part of the story that needed to be told. Peyton clutched the book in her hand and stood. That's when she saw the box that Cara described. "Strange. It's there now, but it wasn't on the treadle machine where I found Cara's journal," she muttered.

"What are you mumbling about? Did you find something else? This attic is filled with treasures." Jessie opened another trunk. "Do you remember that game we used to play? We'd say you're getting hot or cold when you were near or far away from finding something."

"I remember. I used to love that game."

"We must be getting warm. That's all there is to it. The activity level just went up a notch or two." Jessie snapped her fingers.

"I found Cara's box. What did you find?" She glanced at Jessie who had a stunned look on her face. "What?"

"You'd have to see what I've found to believe it. I don't even know how to describe to you what I'm looking at." Jessie motioned to her. "See for yourself. It's some kind of portal or window in time. Katie would freak out."

Peyton walked over and stood beside her. "Wow! This is awesome. I doubt if Katie could see anything. I might have looked inside during my search over the past few weeks, and I never saw anything. This window in time is for us now."

"Probably, but Matt will be at my house soon." Jessie glanced at her watch. "And you're not staying up here alone after the book incident, and neither of us has time to be taken somewhere else right now. Our guys would explode if one or both of us went missing. I know that look, Peyton—you're dying to explore this." Jessie closed the lid on the trunk and placed another box on the top. "Please, don't go anywhere. We'll be back tonight to check on you again." Jessie patted the top.

"Do you mean what I heard you say? You'll come back later to check it out with me?" Peyton followed Jessie to the stairs carrying the box and the other book.

Jessie reached for the knob on the door, but the handle wouldn't turn, and the door wouldn't budge. "Looks like we're here to stay at the moment. We'll be checking the trunk out sooner rather than later. This door won't open." Jessie kicked the door. "I have a feeling it won't until we see what we're supposed to see."

"First a book becomes a portal, and now an empty trunk opens to an invisible world in another time. Add an attic door that won't open, and I can't help but wonder more about the history of this inn." Peyton glanced around the attic. "Mila, the stage is all yours," Peyton muttered under her breath.

"I texted Matt to give me an hour. I told him we'd found something that might help with the case." She held up her phone. "I'm glad I brought this. We might need help getting out of here."

"I have mine too. We're supposed to see something. I bet as soon as we do, we'll be free to go." Peyton crossed her fingers behind her back.

"Let's get her done, cousin. I have a date with a hunky cop that I don't want to miss." Jessie pulled Peyton's hand to get her moving. They removed the box on top and both knelt in front of the trunk. Jessie placed Cara's box and the book beside her. "Before I open the lid, we are holding on to each other. We can't go anywhere." Jessie grabbed her cousin's arm.

"I'm not sure we could stop any trips if we wanted to." Peyton held her breath as Jessie opened the trunk.

She hadn't known what to expect, but it wasn't this. Both of their heads were sucked through the portal with their bodies left firmly in the attic. "Thank you, Mila," Peyton whispered. A scene from long ago played like a movie in front of them.

"Tell me you're seeing this." Jessie squeezed her arm.

"Yes." They held to each other tight.

The town seemed familiar. Some of the streets were made of cobblestone while some were dirt. The buildings appeared similar to those in any coastal town today, but they all had an old-world appearance. Signs were painted on the brick exteriors and in the windows of the buildings. Some signs hung from the roof of the covered walkways low enough to reach up a give them a swing. Peyton saw a laundry, a general store, a local hotel, and the old graveyard by a church she knew all too well. "This is Blue Cove," she whispered.

"I know." Jessie squeezed her hand. "Oh, wow." A carriage pulled by a smart-looking team came into view, and the driver tethered his horses to a rail in front of a restaurant.

Peyton watched mesmerized as the scene unfolded in front of them. A large man smoking a cigar got out of the carriage followed closely by two others. The man stopped to stare at the three young women who strolled by on the wooden walkway, chatting as they went. Their long, simple dresses slapped against sturdy walking boots, and their hair was hidden neatly beneath their bonnets. They paid no attention to the eyes that followed them. But unnatural chills shot down Peyton's arms. In her mind, she understood these were shadows of things that had happened in the past. Neither she nor

Jessie could change anything about what they were seeing, but she found herself yelling a warning all the same.

Suddenly, a hand reached out and snatched one of the young women as she walked by the general store. One by one the girls disappeared, and three more would take their place. The men remained the same in every scene. The town changed, as did the fashion, long dresses changed to suits and shorter dresses as time marched on, and different faces came and went. All the while the darkness hid what happened to each of the girls.

As quickly as the portal had opened, it closed, and Peyton found herself staring into an empty trunk. She dusted off her pants as she stood. "Whew, that adds more mystery to what we're looking at. Those three men might have been involved then, but who is now, and why are there always three?"

"It's obvious this has been going on for a while. We need to research missing persons. Some probably were never recorded. I bet that's what Tamara was doing when she was murdered." Jessie stood beside her cousin. "Let's see if the door will open for us now."

Peyton picked up the box and book and followed her cousin to the door. "Watching the fashion change over the years was kind of cool, don't you think? I can't imagine ever wearing some of those styles. Although Kathryn wore some funky things like a corset, I hated wearing it, but a corset was a must in her day."

"Everything is relative, isn't it? I wonder what people in the future will think about our fashion?" Jessie stopped at the door. "Or lack of it." She chuckled. "You give it try." She moved out of the way so Peyton could open the door.

"Okey dokey." Peyton turned the knob, and the door opened with no problem. "I have the magic touch."

"Yeah, right. More like we aren't needed here anymore." Jessie followed her down the stairs to the sound of the guests talking in the dining room.

"All we need to figure out is how what we saw applies now. We know women were disappearing in Cara's time from her journal, but is it still happening today? And if so, why aren't we hearing about it?" Peyton asked.

"Who were those men? Our real work begins." Jessie walked through the kitchen with Peyton by her side and out the door of the inn.

"I'm sure the first two questions will be simple to answer. But as for who the men were, that may be harder. Not impossible, but trickier." Peyton grabbed Jessie's hand. "You have to get hold of Tamara's research. Maybe you should call your old editor Neil?"

"I will. Matt's waiting at my door. We'll talk later." Jessie waved at Matt.

****

Mila smiled, quite content that the girls weren't questioning every little thing she threw their way. It would make her work here a lot easier. Elida had told her Jessie was an unusual human. She could safely say Peyton was too. Clapping her hands, she danced about in anticipation. She couldn't wait to see how these girls would go about solving the mystery set for them. It would go down in the manual as a case study for training purposes.

Darn, he would have to show up right at this

moment. Cutting her celebration short, Mila fought to push back the darkness that seemed to be getting stronger each time Aelfric showed up. The ugly beast snarled and growled at her. She waved her wand, growling back at him, a frown marring her ageless face. She shielded her eyes from the pooka. His form, this time a ferocious wolf, stood behind the shadow snarling and baring his teeth.

"Hey, sister, do you need some help?" Elida linked her arm through Mila's, and together their light pushed the shadow back.

"Thank you, sister. He is getting stronger, and he's done enough damage through the years. We had better step up the timeline, or he will simply overpower us before we can prevent him."

"Do we know what human he is appearing as yet?" Elida asked.

"It could be anyone, and there are many. We must speed things up. The beast is that of a wolf." They began to plot their next steps in hushed tones, chatting rapidly back and forth in the language of the fairies.

"We should consult the manual to refresh our memories." Mila tugged on Elida's hand to get her moving.

"Good idea, sister."

## Chapter 18

"A book that chose us and a trunk that became a portal with a moving picture show, sheesh," Peyton muttered, slapping her hand to her head. "What is next?" This had been a strange few days.

She could only imagine more of them to come. Of course, she always thought the same way each time she found herself in a similar situation. The mystery and solving the puzzle made life exciting, somewhat scary at times, but always came with an adrenaline rush. The way she looked at it, Jaxon would be lucky to have a girl like her in his life. Ghosts, fairies, and who knew what else.

The shadowy figure was what concerned her at the moment. She had no idea who they were dealing with. One major detail she knew for sure: he was getting more intense with each passing day. Who was the pooka Aelfric that Mila talked about? And who was he using to shift in and out of? She had never heard him speak—why? An added dilemma to think about. She wanted to understand why he appeared sometimes to look like a man and at other times almost like a beast with fangs and yellowish eyes. Not that she believed he was a beast but more of a man that acted like one. She would have to learn more about the pooka's abilities in folklore. It seemed almost too fanciful to her.

She glanced at the clock. Jaxon would be here in an

hour, but there was still time for her to check out a few ideas rolling around in her head. She opened her laptop and began to search. The hour moved swiftly as she chased leads through the legends of Ireland. Her research answered one or two questions but raised many more. She bookmarked a site that had a map of the Indian tribes living in the area in the eighteen-forties. She stood, stretched, and went to answer the door when Jaxon knocked.

"Did you find anything in the attic?" he asked the minute she opened the door. "A loaded question." He grinned as he walked past her.

"Let's say I've had a productive morning." She followed him. "Look at what I found." She pointed to the book and the box she had brought back from the inn. "I haven't opened the box yet. Call me overly cautious, but I don't want to open anything from the past when I'm alone."

"I, for one, am glad." He kissed her cheek. "Not that you were alone the last time. Jessie was with you and couldn't stop it from happening. But I do appreciate your caution."

"True, but I'm glad for that jaunt in time. It was scary at first because I had no idea if I would ever make it back. Plus, I had no idea where I was or why. Of course, looking back on it now, that small journey was meant to be."

"Hindsight is the best sight of all." He gazed at her. "Do you want to open the box?" Jaxon pulled her into the circle of his arms.

"Not really." She leaned her head against his chest. "If it's okay with you, I'd like us to visit my grandmother. I want to tell both of you what happened this morning. For some reason, I think it's important for Sadie to know what I've found out. Especially, the family connection. She would love to hear about our ancestors." She lifted her head to glance at his face. "After that the day is yours."

"Seeing Sadie would be nice. Your grandmother is a kick. About the rest of the day being mine, let's just say I like the sound of that. I have a few things up my sleeve, and I aim to please, sweet lady."

"Pleasing me, hmm, that has a pleasant ring to it." She kissed him and stepped out of his arms. "I'll get my coat, and we can be on our way."

****

Jaxon liked Sadie. He enjoyed watching her interact with Peyton. Proper in every way, she served them tea and was genuinely happy they had come to visit. And yet there seemed to be a mischievous side to her that he would love to get to know. Sadie loved talking about their family connections. He and Sadie were equally surprised when Peyton told them about the trunk and what she and Jessie had seen inside. Together they speculated about what could have happened to the missing women and the children. In Jaxon's mind, it added a few more pieces to the case.

Sadie took notes about the family and asked Peyton to show her where to look on the computer, which gave him time to observe them together. Sadie loved her granddaughters, and her pride was evident whenever she spoke about them. Peyton was on the receiving end of it at the moment, and she flourished under her grandmother's love. What had happened to Peyton's dad to make him the way that he was? Peyton had once told him her grandfather Max was a loving man. It seemed obvious to him they loved their sons. He waited until the right moment to ask.

"Sadie, what happened to change Peyton's dad?" he asked when Peyton stepped out of the room.

"Max and I often wondered what we did wrong. He changed from a loving son into a monster. When I think of what he did to those two girls, I get angry all over again. As far as what triggered the change, I have no idea. The truth is still coming out concerning the girls. As they remember more, we learn more. It breaks my heart. Jessie's dad is a stern and domineering man, but his love for her is evident. Max was not like either of them in that regard."

"Like what, Grams?" Peyton asked when she walked back into the room.

"We were talking about how different your grandpa was from your dad and uncle."

"Oh, heavens yes. They are nothing alike. I think I might understand why…" She paused. "But I think you might find it a bit hard to swallow."

"Try me," Jaxon said.

She told them about the visit from Mila. About the curse in the family line and how some of them went the way of Aelfric. "Others, like you, Grandma, and Kathryn went the opposite way. I know it must sound strange, but I believe her somehow. Our family line is open to magic, and the gift of sight from Cara to her grandmother Alanna, and back even farther."

"As we know, things aren't always as they seem at first sight. I might need to think about this for a minute. If I remember correctly, Max had some very colorful family members, and I'm sure the Campbells did too," Sadie told them.

"Could you write down some of their names so I can research them?" Peyton asked.

"I'll go through our old family photos and try my best to remember. You'll have to give me a few days."

"Take all the time you need, Grams." She hugged her grandmother. "You've given me a few more clues to think about. I knew you would."

"Thank you for stopping by. Your young man told me he had plans for the rest of your day. Go on and have a lovely day together."

"Before I forget, Sadie, I need to thank you." Jaxon smiled.

"For what?" she asked.

"Your suggestion to Peyton about every girl needing a little red dress."

Sadie laughed and squeezed Peyton's hand. "It works every time."

Jaxon took Peyton's hand as they left Sadie's apartment. "Your grandmother is awesome."

"Yes, she is. She's all that made my childhood tolerable."

Chapter 19

The box with Cara's belongings and the book all but forgotten, Jaxon and Peyton spent the rest of the day enjoying each other's company. He took her to see his new place.

"My house has a way to go before it's done. You'll have to use your imagination. I want your suggestions for paint colors. I have the painter coming in before the floors are laid. The drywall is finished, and the windows are in. I think you'll get the idea when you see it." Jaxon pulled into the driveway of a lovely home on a hill overlooking the cove. "What do you think so far?" He opened the car door for her.

"The garage is a great selling point. You won't have to clean the ice off your car windows in the winter," she told him as she got out of the car. "This place also has an amazing view."

"I got a great deal on the property because the house was such a mess. A real fixer-upper. Matt's the one who convinced me the house had great bones. Now that I can see how the space is taking shape, I know he was right. I'm proud of how it is turning out." He unlocked the front door and held it open for her. "We lifted the ceiling and took out a few walls to give it an open floor plan."

"This is a great space. Boy, would I love to decorate a room this size. It's perfect for entertaining.

Imagine what you could do with this open concept."

"That's the problem, I can't see it, but I want you to help me." He reached for the paint sample cards and handed them to her along with a piece of the wood he had chosen for the floors.

She suggested a slate blue or gray with white trim to go with the grays running through the wood floors. "I wish I could've seen how the house looked before."

"You can when it's all done. I took plenty of pictures during the process." He took her on a tour, describing the plans he had for each room. "I want you to help me choose all the colors and furnishings." He brought her back to the big open space. "If decorating was left up to me, there wouldn't be much to make it look like home."

"I'd love to help. This room is perfect." She went to stand by the window. "I'm glad you brought me here. I might be willing to pay you rent to park my car in your garage in the winter." She laughed.

"Sweetheart, you can park in my garage any time you want for free." He put his arm around her shoulder. "If you live in the east, a garage is a must."

"If not a garage at least a frost guard cover for my windshield, which I purchased the other day."

He locked the door as they left. The whole house was designed with her in mind, but it was too early to tell her. Jaxon could envision many nights together in those rooms. Especially cuddled up in front of the fireplace together.

"Jessie sent me a text." She scrolled through her messages. "She wants to know if we want to meet them for pizza in an hour."

"Tell her yes. It still gives us time to go for a walk

at the marina."

"Done."

**\*\*\*\***

Jaxon pulled into the lot at Angelo's and parked in the open space next to Matt. He had arrived right before them, and they were still in the car. Jessie waved and opened her door. Peyton opened hers too and wrapped Jessie in a big hug.

"Hi. I'm glad you're on time. I'm so hungry." Jessie grabbed Peyton's arm. "Let's get these guys moving. It's still too cold out here for me."

"You're cold." She slapped at Jessie's hand playfully. "I spent the past hour walking near the marina. The breeze from the water cut right through me."

"Good heavens, why would you walk outside today?" Jessie asked.

"Jaxon suggested the idea, and I thought it sounded like a good plan." She smiled at him when he walked up behind her.

"You know I like you, Kincaid. But this isn't exactly a day for a stroll outside," Jessie scolded him.

Jaxon reached for Peyton's hand. "I agree, Jessie. I have to get used to there being cold weather all over. Sunshine and blue skies doesn't necessarily mean warm." He laughed. "I lived in Arizona too long." The four of them walked toward the front door.

Out of the corner of his eye, Jaxon noticed a car idling near the back of the restaurant. Not in a parking place. Odd, and his gut told him the group needed to move faster.

"Matt, we may have a problem." The words were barely out of his mouth when the car picked up speed, rushing toward them. Jaxon pushed Peyton to safety in front of the building along with Jessie in the nick of time. Instinct told him they needed to get inside the building fast as the car sped off down Main Street before the driver came back around.

"There you go pushing me again." Peyton turned around as he practically shoved her into the people standing in line inside the door.

"It's because you seem to attract trouble like bees to honey," he whispered in her ear. "I know you attract me." He placed his hand on her back.

"Did you get the make of car? I'm calling it in," Matt told him. He was already on the phone calling Kenny.

Jaxon told him the model. "Tell him it's a black sedan with tinted windows. Something tells me they're not done and will be back around, if not today, soon."

"Make sure the patrols know what they're looking for." Matt disconnected the call. "Can't even go to dinner without some damn idiot trying to run you over."

"Proof positive that we must be on the right track," Peyton told Jessie as they followed the host to their table.

"Tamara was proof. This is a warning for us to stay out of their business." Jessie sat when Matt pulled out her chair. "Her murder makes me mad and more determined than ever to follow the trail she had uncovered. Neil sent me some of her notes and her schedule that tracked her movements right before she was murdered." Jessie placed her napkin on her lap. "Her death shook him, and he made me promise to be careful. In the light of charging cars, what does taking care mean? I paid no attention to that car. I thought he was here for takeout and trying to keep the car warm."

"I'm glad Jaxon was on his game, or both of us might have been hit. Let's hope they don't have a gun that they're itching to use the next time they see us." Peyton thanked the server for the water.

"It might not have anything to do with us." Jessie leaned her head toward her cousin. "It could be that they're after these two hunks."

"Nice try, sweetheart, but unlikely." Matt squeezed her shoulder. "You naturally attract more attention. As Gary at the stations says, the Reynolds girls know things. He said it was like you knew what was in his mail before he could even read it."

"What does that even mean?" Peyton asked.

"You scare them," Matt told them.

"That's the dumbest thing I've ever heard." Jessie slapped his arm playfully. "He's teasing us."

"No, I'm not. Jaxon heard him say it. Didn't you?" He glanced at Jaxon.

"You would have to pull me into this. The guys were talking about the bets on you girls when it came to us. I asked if he wanted to meet Madison. He wasn't interested because he wanted a normal girl. Not one that knows things." Jaxon noticed Peyton frowning at him. "Are you happy now, Matt? You couldn't leave well enough alone." He chuckled.

"All I'm saying, girls, is that your fame is growing in our small town, and it's likely to draw those unsavory types here to see if they can best you. Ouch." He rubbed the spot where Jessie pinched him.

"Now I know he's teasing us." Jessie's chin edged up. "At least he'd better be."

"Whatever." Matt motioned with his hand. "You

still need me to protect you, and that's okay with me."

Jaxon knew what was coming, and it had nothing to do with a premonition. He saw the flash as the menu caught Matt on the top of his head. Exactly what Peyton would have done to him. He was there to protect her, but he'd never tell her. Neither of the Reynolds girls liked the idea even a little bit.

Peyton changed the topic. Jessie had that look in her eye that she knew all too well. "Matt, I wasn't sure if Jessie told you or not, but we found another book in the attic. I haven't had time to read it yet, but I saw some of the names from my dream as I flipped through the pages."

"That would be a no, she didn't tell me." Matt frowned. "What else did you girls find?" He reached for Jessie's hand so she couldn't swing the menu again.

"You need to tell him about the trunk." Jaxon glanced at Peyton.

"It's your turn, Jessie," Peyton said.

Jessie told him about their morning. Peyton added the details that she had noticed.

"Damn, there's nothing normal about that. I know I should've come to expect the unusual whenever you two are involved, but I'm not there yet." Matt shook his head.

"It's your caveman mentality that keeps tripping you up," Jessie told him. "Don't even entertain the idea of moving us into your place to guard us. It's not going to happen."

"Yes, it will if I deem it necessary." Matt frowned at her. "I know you're strong, sweetheart, and you don't like a man telling you what to do. You've told me enough. I've been upfront with you too. When it comes to murder and a case I'm in charge of, then you have to play along. That's how it is if you want to stay in the game."

"So you say. I've heard this tune before." Jessie winked at Peyton.

"No, that's the bottom line, sweetheart." Matt's forehead furrowed. "My gut tells me your involvement is no longer a secret."

Peyton jumped into the conversation threatening to get out of hand if she knew her cousin. Jessie's chin had inched up twice while Matt mumbled. "Let's talk about anything else. We aren't being asked to do anything yet, Jessie. No sense in arguing over something that may not happen. Besides, here comes our server, and she doesn't need to hear our conversation."

They ordered an Angelo's Special to share, salads, and drinks. Jaxon talked about his classes at the agency, and Matt checked his phone for updates on the car every few minutes with no luck. The evening ended better than it had begun. Matt agreed with him that the case intensified the moment the car tried to run them over. Whether real or simply a scare tactic, they had to be heading in the right direction, or why would anyone bother with them at all?

Jaxon got a kick out of the girls' interaction. They kept busy chatting which freed him up to talk shop with Matt. They had a murder to solve.

****

"Hmm," she muttered as her tiny finger tapped her temple in rapid succession. Aelfric was getting restless, stronger, and taking things into his own hands. More than ever, they needed the girls to understand. More lives were at risk. What was often thought of as a legend in Ireland wasn't one at all. Men often gave over to their darker side and acted more like an animal than a human. It was time to stop him from stalking and killing again.

"Sister, do you have any ideas?" Mila asked.

"I found this story in our manual. It's often used to instruct the younger fairies when dealing with the legend of the pooka acting like a man or when he takes the form of an animal." Elida pointed to the spot on the page. "Read beginning right here. Maybe we can use this as the basis for our plan and then add more as the need arises."

"I remember reading this long ago. I used it in Cara's situation, which was similar in nature to this one. You used it with Alanna. It might work, but we will need more. We stopped his actions for a season. The curse has grown stronger over the years. Aelfric has recruited more men into his wicked ways. We are living in different times, and we must approach the subject cautiously." Mila lighted on Peyton's shoulder, listening closely to their conversation. These girls could stop the curse from impacting another generation. Aelfric might be replaced with others, but it was important to release those who had been silenced because of him.

"We will have to stand watch over our charges. And we must think, think, think." Elida twirled about Jessie.

"How we handle this could be one of the great stories added to the manual as an example of what or what not to do. Let's get it right. We need a great outcome."

The sisters huddled, whispering their ideas as they

guarded their charges, along with a few well-placed thoughts into the minds of the men who sat beside them. A good day's work to Mila's way of thinking.

Chapter 20

She read more of Cara's journal last night after Jaxon brought her home. In the pages, Cara wrote about a family curse that had brought about the separation of Alanna and her mother. Peyton wished Cara had given more details. The information she did give was quite enlightening. Peyton knew there were many superstitious beliefs during the 1800s. The whole curse idea was hard for her to figure out. What was real and what might be irrational belief left her stumped. She read the passage through several times.

*When Mama was a young girl, a powerful old sorceress came to the village where they lived. I can still remember when Alanna told me this story. Nana said she invited the woman into her home and treated her with kindness. She was often known to share what little her family had with travelers as she would call them. But others in the village weren't so kind. Many were scared of the woman and thought of her as an old hag. Her long nose and ragged clothing made her an object of childish ridicule. The women treated her cruelly, and the men paid her little attention.*

*For a few months, the woman endured the awful treatment as she lived and worked side by side with Alanna, speaking her wisdom and knowledge into Nana's life. My mother was embarrassed by the woman and angry with her mother for allowing her to live in their small home. Mama never forgave Alanna because of what happened next.*

*The old woman became displeased with what she had witnessed living among the villagers and decided to move on. As she left, she cursed the women and children for their cruelty. Her words were even harsher for the men as the providers for their households for their slothfulness and indifference to the suffering of others. She told them they all could easily right the wrong through honesty, hard work, and community. But if they chose not to, they were destined to live like the animals they had become. Some broke free and changed the course of their lives while others fulfilled her strange prophecy. Her powerful words came true for many, and my mother lived in fear because she had been unkind. But to Alanna because of her kindness, she had granted a greater mystical ability to see and heal. A quality that separated her from her daughter.*

The hair on Peyton's neck stood on end, followed by chills down her arms each time she read Cara's words. That morning at school, when she sensed someone watching her, he had seemed almost beast-like. The nights she spent in the closet with Madison were similar in intensity. She never knew when her angry father would come and find them huddled there. His angry eyes and snarling words made him more beast than human too, especially to a young girl. She shook her head to rid her of the scary memory. Curses and powerful words are what separated Alanna from her daughter. Did they ever repair their relationship? Is that what separated her father from his parents who loved him?

After the car incident earlier, Peyton understood

she needed to be on guard. Jaxon would be working with Matt this week, while students waited for her this morning. She slipped into her coat. Jaxon had made her promise last night to keep her eyes open and pay attention. She filled her travel mug with coffee and cream. Gathering her briefcase, purse, and a scone to eat on the way, she locked the door on her way out of the cottage.

Peyton waved at Jessie who was closing her door. "Right on time, I see."

"Yep, and you are too. We need to talk. I read more of the journal last night. Have you read the whole curse thing?"

"Last night," Peyton said as she opened the car door and put her things inside. "I don't know what to think."

"You and me both. I'm going to talk to Reba about it. I need to sort out things in my mind. I mean what if it's something that has passed down from one generation to the next and we need to put an end to the curse here and now? Elida said something like that to me the other night." Jessie pulled her frost guard off the windshield.

"Mila said the same thing to me. I guess we had better figure out what they mean. We'll talk later." Peyton thought it was more about personal choices and not outside curses. Beliefs and legends could be strong and force outcomes. Every family had an outcast somewhere in their family line. People could go either way. Like the preacher whose son became an infamous outlaw or a poor child who grew to be an entrepreneur who built a legacy of goodness for orphans. Maybe people could imprison themselves by the words spoken by others over them or by their own words.

She turned into the parking lot at school. Now for her favorite morning ritual of watching the kids make their way into school, followed only by her next favorite—those children leaving when her day was done. Those cheerful, happy, and sometimes naughty wiggle worms could wear a person out.

****

Jaxon stopped at the coffee shop on his way to the station. His growling stomach reminded him that he was hungry. He waved at Jessie when she opened the doors from her store into the shop. "Good morning, Jessie. Have a good day," he said as he hurried by on his way out. Tom Maxwell had kept him on the phone, going over what he needed to do as the lead agent working on the case in Blue Cove. Jaxon recalled his last words with a smile.

"Remember to work well with the locals. You don't want to give the agency a black eye." He laughed and hung up.

His first order of business was to arrive on time and, as luck would have it, the lights and traffic were on his side. He made it with a few minutes to spare.

Grabbing his laptop out of the backseat, he headed into the station with his coffee and walked right to Matt's office.

"Come in," Matt said when he saw Jaxon in the doorway. "Are you ready to get to work?"

"I am. I had to bring breakfast because Maxwell kept me on the phone for a while." Jaxon lifted the bag up in the air. "I can work while I eat. I have some emails from Jeremy I need to catch up on, and then I'm all yours."

"Sounds good. You can use the interview room." Matt tapped his pencil on the desk. "Before I forget, Frank and his dog Radar will be in town at some point today, and we'll search the property tomorrow near the murder site. I have another search area in mind too. Peyton reminded me about an area where there might have been a boarding school. I found a building several miles from here, and because you're involved, Maxwell said to go ahead with the search. Later today, I thought we might spend some time talking to a few of the elders of the tribe at the nearby reservation. They know their history better than anyone."

"I'll be ready when you are." Jaxon turned to leave and then stopped. "I remember when Peyton read to me about the missing indigenous children. I knew somehow those children would come to fit into this case somewhere. Schools should be a safe place for kids, but as we've come to see with all the school shootings, the classroom is anything but safe."

"How does Peyton feel about working at the school?" Matt asked.

"She loves the kids, but she told me the active shooter drill the first week of school shook her along with some of the kids. It's a damn shame they're even necessary," Jaxon said as he walked out of Matt's office. His coffee and breakfast burrito needed to be reheated. After a quick trip to the microwave in the lunchroom, he got down to business and read his emails.

Jeremy had found information from archived records on several missing girls and children from the nearby area. The boarding school closest to the cove recorded at least a hundred indigenous children as dead or missing over a span of a few years but didn't give any other details. The records that Jeremy had found didn't account for all the years the school had been in operation. It seemed odd to Jaxon that no cause of death was listed. The school's records should have been meticulous. That seemed suspicious to him.

In this case, mothers lost their children and had no say in the process. The more he read, he noticed troubling trends emerge. Kids were taken from their families into completely new surroundings with people who wanted to change who they were while parents wanted them to remain true to their heritage.

"You ready?" Matt popped his head in the door.

"Yep. I want to hear their side of the story. I have more questions than ever after reading what Jeremy sent me. Government officials forced those kids to go to boarding schools. I'm wondering why they didn't keep better track of them. Some of the missing kids could have simply run away back to their homes but not all of them. We're talking a span of years and many kids."

"The government did run some of the schools, but so did a lot of religious groups. I doubt they kept track of those schools' operations." Matt leaned his hip against the door frame.

"All I know is that it impacted a lot of kids. If they cared for those children the same way they honored their treaties, those kids hardly stood a chance. Not to say there weren't some great people, but there were also some bad apples." Jaxon closed his computer down, picked up his phone, and stood. He slipped on his jacket.

"I hear you." Matt pushed away from the door. "Let's find out what they have to say."

"I'm right behind you." He followed Matt out of the station to the car. Jaxon wanted answers, but he wasn't sure he wanted to know the truth. The truth often destroyed illusions. Facing how things are opposed to how you thought they were isn't always a pleasant experience. He had found that out fast when he worked as a homicide detective.

Chapter 21

Peyton's morning went from good to strange and moved on to awful in what seemed a matter of minutes. She was arranging her classroom for the day when she heard a loud commotion in the hall. Peeking out the door, she watched as an angry man got into a screaming match with one of the teachers. The fight escalated the moment the man shoved Ms. Draper, the school secretary, when she tried to intervene. She stumbled backward, hitting her head on the wall as she fell to the ground. Then the principal stepped into the fray, and the irate man punched him in the face which caused his nose to bleed profusely. Two male teachers grabbed the parent and pinned his hands behind his back to keep him from swinging at someone else. It took a third man's help to hold him until the police arrived.

More chaos ensued when the bell rang and the kids came rushing into the building. Teachers and staff tried to keep the students away from the area, which wasn't an easy task. Some of the kids were running through the halls while others kept edging nearer to the scene to watch. All the blood kept them hyped and scared. Getting the children into their classrooms and under control seemed an insurmountable job. Between sirens, police arrivals, and the paramedics, the day was a total bust.

Kip walked over to where Peyton stood. "Who

started the fight? Did you see who hit whom first?" he asked.

"I heard the shouting, but I didn't see who started it. I did see the man push Ms. Draper when she tried to intervene. I hope she'll be okay," she told him without telling him what she noticed when the two men were yelling. There was the shadow of a fierce animal that seemed to fade in and out around the man that they arrested.

"An exciting morning you could have lived without, eh?" Kip smiled at her and walked over to question another teacher.

"You've got that right," she muttered under breath.

She learned through the grapevine at the school before she left for the day that the principal's nose was broken in the ruckus. Rumors were flying that the irate man was a father who was upset with his child's teacher about the way he disciplined his students. The father was normally a quiet, unassuming man. No one seemed to see who started the fight, but there was plenty of speculation to go around. One rumor said the parent was high on meth, which would have been totally out of character for the man. And Kip told her that no drugs were involved.

Ms. Draper had a minor concussion and some sore muscles. The classrooms were filled with anxious kids who wanted to talk about nothing else. Peyton added the event to her list of concerns she had about her work environment. Maybe she didn't want to work full-time at the school after all. One bright spot in the morning was her special students didn't understand what happened and were happy to hear the story about a friendship between a big red dog and the alley cat named Sammy.

When the last child was picked up by their parents, she finally had time to think about the morning. What was the fight about? Was it a single incident, or did it fit into a bigger picture?

She straightened her room and rushed out of the school. She couldn't wait to tell her cousin about her morning. Once safely in her car, she realized that things may have calmed down inside the building but not so much outside. Someone was watching her.

Peyton wasn't surprised to see Reba in the store when she arrived. "You won't believe my morning," she said as she plopped down in a chair near Reba.

"Oh, my. You had a rough morning too, dear. So did your cousin."

"I need to hear all about it, Jessie, just as soon as I get something to eat." Peyton walked into Joe's.

"Get me something too. Tell Molly to give me whatever she thinks I'll like today."

"Okay. Would you like anything, Reba? My treat."

"I had lunch, but tell Molly I'll take my usual." She smiled at her.

"Will do." Peyton came back ten minutes later with two chicken salad sandwiches and iced teas. Molly followed with a hot tea and a lemon bar for Reba.

"Thank you, Molly dear." Reba patted her hand when she placed the tea in front of her on the table. "You know how I love your lemon bars."

Peyton took a bite of her sandwich. "Okay, Jess, don't keep me in suspense."

"Two customers got into a fight. One shoved the other into my display table, sending the books in all directions. Molly called the police, and two officers came by and arrested them. The whole affair was strange and seemed almost staged. The fight came out of nowhere. I mean nowhere. The two men came in the store together, and all of sudden one of them was on the floor with the books."

"Weird, that's plain weird. Something similar happened at the school." Peyton told about the incident. "The principal got his nose broken when he tried to intervene." Peyton paused for a moment. "The thing that makes it totally different is I saw a shadow fade in and out around the men."

"What kind of shadow?" Reba sat forward in her chair.

"A fierce wolf-looking creature, which makes no sense whatsoever," Peyton told them.

"I'm sure there's a perfectly good explanation, dear. Tell her, Jessie." Reba locked eyes with Jessie.

"Tell me what?" Peyton asked.

"I saw the same thing." Jessie pursed her lips and nodded. "What should we do?"

"I don't know. I didn't tell Kip. I wasn't sure he could handle it." Peyton sipped her tea. "Maybe we should look on the internet and see if we can find something similar."

"Not a bad idea. What else did you notice about the creature?" Jessie asked her.

"When the creature faded completely from sight, the crisis was over, and the people involved seemed more dazed than angry by what had just happened." Peyton wiped her mouth with her napkin.

"The same here. It made me doubt I had seen it at all." Jessie took a bite of her sandwich. "Thanks for this, by the way. I love Molly's chicken salad."

"Me too. It's especially good on her raisin bread." Peyton took another bite.

"May I make a suggestion?" Reba asked.

"Please do," Peyton said.

"In your search don't stray from the Irish origins of the case. It all started with the diary. Cara's journal and the other book will give the clues to lead your way forward. The guys will do the job their way." Reba took a tiny bite of her lemon bar.

"Of course, you're right." Jessie smiled at her. "It's hard to keep my mind from running away with it." She paused. "You don't suppose that car last night was a similar situation as today. Is it possible anyone could become a weapon aimed at us? That's a dumb question, isn't it?"

"No, I understand what you're asking. I was wondering the same thing. I don't like the possibility because it complicates the investigation for us. Reba is right—we have to keep the Irish aspects of the case in our mind." Peyton took another sip from her glass. "And we can't forget the indigenous tribe's traditions either. Cara mentions them several times."

"You're right. I forgot all about that." Jessie tapped her fingers on the table.

"Right now, girls, you're being warned. Who knows when or if the warning will change to an actual attack against you?" Reba licked a bit of powdered sugar off her lips. "I couldn't waste that last taste of heaven." She smiled. "You'll need each other for this one."

"Right again, Reba." Peyton squeezed Reba's hand. "Do you mind if I change the subject for a minute?"

"Please do, my head hurts from all the thinking." Jessie wiped her mouth with her napkin.

"I wanted to mention that Madi is hoping to come for a visit soon. When she does, I want to introduce her to Kip. He's such a nice guy. Is he dating anyone?" Peyton glanced at Jessie.

"He used to date a girl that worked for Katie at the inn, but she moved away. Wouldn't that be fun if Madi moved here and married Kip? All you would have to do to complete the circle is get Destiny here too. I'm sure there are enough single men here to make a good match for your friend too."

"Maybe it would be better if they didn't get too close to us. We've had enough close encounters to last a lifetime." Peyton wrapped up half of her sandwich to save for later.

"Well, girls, I need to go. Lawrence will be home before I know it. Stay safe! Use your heads and work together. I will think about what you've told me."

\*\*\*\*

"What's your gut telling you?" Jaxon asked as soon as they got in the car.

"After listening to the elders' talk, all I can say is it's a damn shame. But who do you hold accountable for what they went through?" Matt started the engine.

"A good question. How did some of their legends grab you as they talked? To me, it felt like I was listening to a conversation between Peyton and Jessie, only with ancestral beliefs and tribal customs thrown in. I'm an outsider looking in. Their exchanges were infused with visions, premonitions, and animal spirits. I found their idea of curses interesting. And how the medicine man used them against their enemies."

"Damn, if I didn't conjure of the same image of Jess and her cousin's discussions." Matt backed the car up and turned around. "There's a lot more of these folks out there than we realize. We are outsiders in their world, man."

"That field is getting more crowded, that's for damn sure." Jaxon stretched his legs as much as he could in front of him. "Who would've thought."

"Frank's dog checking the area around the boarding school is imperative after listening to the elders." Matt's forehead creased. "Let's stop for lunch at Joe's. I need to see Jessie."

"With any luck, Peyton will be there too." Jaxon turned to look out the side window. "What I've heard lately makes me wonder if I know what's going on at all." He rubbed his temple.

"I hear you." Matt signaled and moved into the turn lane heading back into town. "Frank told us a story about how a Native American man approached him and told him things that no one knew but Frank himself. The man pointed to the sky and told him to look up where a hawk circled the air above them. The old man told Frank every time you see a hawk your track will be successful. You'll have to ask him about the incident. The whole story shook my logical mind to the core, and damn if we didn't see a red-tailed hawk before we found the body we were searching for."

"Another one of those hard-to-believe incidents. I may have to rethink the stories that we heard this morning." Jaxon jotted down a few notes. "The tribal elders were deeply spiritual, and their stories fascinated me. I can see how Cara and Alanna might relate to them."

"I'm often dense, but even I could sense the deep convictions they held and dialogued about this morning."

****

"Look who is here." Peyton pointed out the window. She walked to the door to greet Jaxon and gave him a quick kiss. "How was your morning?"

"Informative, and yours?" he asked.

"Interesting would be one way to describe the day." She held his arm as they talked.

"Do I dare ask you in what way?" He pulled her close to his side.

"Yes, you should. This is a need to know, and so is Jessie's morning." Peyton glanced at his face.

"I'll get lunch and meet you there in a few." Jaxon pointed to the table in the center of the store.

"Matt, you need to hear this too," Jessie called after them.

"We have a few interesting tidbits to tell you too that fit right into your world and not in ours at all." Matt turned around and kissed Jessie. "Damn, I needed that."

"Me too," Jessie said dreamily. "Man, he manages to make me forget everything when he kisses me like that."

"Earth to Jessie, come back in for a landing. I need you to help explain what happened, since we both saw almost the same thing." Peyton sat and pointed to the chair across from her.

"I know, I know, but I love to be swept away if only for a minute." Jessie pulled the chair out.

Returning to the store with their lunch, Jaxon told them about their meeting with the tribal leaders. "We both agreed as we listened to them, the way they talked was a lot like conversations between you two." Jaxon took a bite of his sandwich.

"I'm about to bend your mind some more." Peyton told them about the school and Jessie's morning when she went to wait on a customer. "A fierce-looking dark-colored wolf faded in and out around the men as they fought. Both Jess and I saw him."

"Damn, did you hear that Jaxon?" Matt asked.

"I heard it loud and clear more than once today." Jaxon explained what they had heard from the medicine man and elders this morning. "He told us that every tribe has their version of an evil spirit that can cause bad things to happen. Like many tribes, they believe in the Great Spirit, but they also believe in multiple deities which impact their views of nature and spirit. He talked about the wolf. The white wolf is all that is good about them as a people, while the black wolf thrives on anger, fear, and hatred." Jaxon paused to look at his notes. "The fact you said the wolf was dark and angry, I find what they told us all the more fascinating."

Jessie jumped up and moved to the side of Matt's chair. "Wow!"

"My sentiments exactly." Matt pulled her onto his lap.

"You can say that again." Peyton leaned into Jaxon sitting beside her.

He wrapped his arm around her. "I wonder where this is headed, but I think we have found at least one of the links between then and now. All we need to know is how it got Tamara murdered."

Chapter 22

"We did well, sister. I think they're starting to understand." Mila smiled, giving Elida a high-five. "They haven't connected everything yet, but they're headed in the right direction."

"I agree, our plan is working." Elida landed on Jessie's shoulder. "Have you noticed that Aelfric is becoming more emboldened?"

"Yes." Mila nodded.

"I want to find out more about the white wolf they were talking about. We need all the help we can get. Maybe Celeste will know where we can find such a creature if it exists."

"All cultures have good and evil in their stories. They may depict them differently, but they are there nonetheless. Watching our subjects is a thing of beauty. They will figure it out. I'm sure of it. And we will learn alongside them. We can do our part and then watch them in action. For now, it's our job to keep Aelfric in check until they bring his deeds into the light. That much we can do," Mila said, gesturing with her tiny hand holding her wand.

****

After lunch, Jaxon and Matt returned to the station. Peyton decided to stay and help Jessie with what was left of the afternoon. The store was hopping, with people coming in and not leaving empty-handed. The mystery book club arrived for the spirited discussion of their latest book. Peyton loved listening to them. Everyone had an idea of who they thought the murderer might be, but the author had surprised them in the end. They wanted Jessie to suggest another book, and she got busy making suggestions. The leader finally chose three, and the members voted on the one they wanted. Naturally, they chose the one with the least copies which meant they needed to be ordered from the city and overnighted to the store. The noise level in the store had risen several decibels when Peyton noticed a change in the atmosphere. The three girls they had seen through the portal floated through the door. The bell above the door rang several times, adding to the chaos.

Peyton grabbed Jessie's hand as she walked past her. "Jess, we have visitors. I wonder why."

"I guess we are about to find out." Jessie squeezed her hand. "This day has been quite enlightening," she muttered under her breath as she went to the counter. "Grown men fighting like a couple of kids, and now ghosts in the store. I'd call this another normal day at Idle Time Books. This is nuts." Jessie frowned.

While her cousin checked out a customer, Peyton followed the apparitions as they moved around the store. She hoped their actions would give her a clue, any clue, as to what they wanted. Back and forth they went, weaving in and out of the book club ladies still chatting and shopping. Everything was calm and normal until it wasn't. The last customer walked out, a man walked in, and all hell broke loose. At least that's how she described it to Jaxon on the phone as she told them to get there quickly. She had no idea who the man was, but the ghosts weren't happy about him being there. The atmosphere became chilled and clammy. The spirits became agitated, and that was the calm before the storm. Like a whirlwind, they moved through the store, emptying shelves of books in the direction of the man's head. He ran out of the store, threatening a lawsuit, with the three ghosts in hot pursuit.

Slightly disheveled, Peyton stood in the middle of the room, surveying all the books that would need to be picked up. "What a mess." She pushed her hair out of her face.

"You don't think he can sue me, do you?" Jessie blew the wayward curls out of her eyes. "What just happened here?"

"I doubt that man will ever want to tangle with you or come near the store again. It would be almost funny…" Peyton bent to pick up books and stack them on the center table. She found herself smiling and then laughing. "Did you see his face?" She placed another book on the table.

"What a sight." Jessie stood in the middle of the books and laughed along with her cousin.

****

When Jaxon and Matt raced into the store a few minutes later, the sight of the two women standing amidst all the strewn books laughing hysterically greeted them. "What the hell happened here?" Jaxon stopped in his tracks. "Peyton?" Jaxon pulled her into his side.

She shook her head and continued to laugh. "Sorry," she managed to say before she started laughing again. A few snorts later, and the laughter started all over.

"Jess, help us out here. Please, sweetheart." Matt

cracked his knuckles while he waited for her to get control.

"It happened, Jaxon, just as I told you on the phone," Peyton said after gaining her composure. "Three ghosts were in the store when a man walked in, and they weren't happy to see him." She paused. "Before you ask, neither of us remember seeing him in here before. He partially shielded his face with his hand, but it was blurred anyway in the bedlam that ensued. Everything happened so fast. The ghosts cleared the shelves throwing books at him as you can see by the mess. They followed in hot pursuit when he left."

"Of course, he threatened to sue me as he yelled expletives, running from the store. I'm only laughing because I don't want to cry or get mad. But I'm this close to both." Jessie held her thumb and forefinger a small distance apart. "Look at this mess I have to clean up."

"I'll help." Peyton started rescuing books from the various locations they were tossed.

"I can help too." Jaxon walked beside Peyton as she stacked books into his arms to carry. "We'll put them on the table for now because they'll have to be sorted and put back in the right location." Peyton pointed at the table in the middle of the room.

"I've never seen anything like this. You said the ghosts tossed the books. That must've been something to see. I almost feel sorry for the guy, but he must be guilty of something." Jaxon bent to pick up three books on the floor in front of him.

"You think. The ghosts wanted to hit the man any way that they could. It was quite comical. Books were flying at him from all directions, while Jessie and I stood there with our mouths open, looking like a couple of codfish. I don't think the man was amused." She followed him to the table. "Thankfully, no one else was in the store to see it. I want to go on the record as saying this has been quite a day."

"I'm sorry, sweetheart, but there's no way you could look like a codfish. You're too pretty. I can't visualize it at all." Jaxon stroked her cheek gently and rubbed a smudge of dirt off her chin.

"Aren't you a smooth talker." She traced his mouth with her finger. "Thank you." Peyton blushed and smiled at him. "Have I told you lately how glad I am that you're in my life?" She bent over to pick up more books. "I love working with you, and I love how you make me feel about myself. Heaven knows I need all the help I can get in that area."

"Oh, yeah. That's good to know." He took the books she handed to him. "Working with you has challenged me, but you keep me on my game. Besides, you're great to look at, and I love the fringe benefits. A man can't ask for more."

"Is that all?" Her brows rose.

"Well, maybe there's more." He smiled. "A whole lot more," he muttered under his breath.

"Dare I ask what?" She glanced at him flirtatiously.

"Not if you want to get anything done. Ask me later when we're alone, and I'd be happy to show you." He met her gaze and held it.

"Come on, lover boy." Matt clapped him on the back. "We need to get back to work."

Jaxon squeezed her hand. "We'll finish this conversation later. You can count on it."

\*\*\*\*

Peyton leaned her hip against the table and fanned her face with the book in her hand. Jaxon was easy on the eyes and reliable too. What was there not to like about him? One simple look from him could turn her insides into mush. He was strong but not abusive which mystified her. Maybe that's what she liked most about him. He surprised her, and she couldn't control him. Which wasn't bad, since she had to manage everything in her life alone for as long as she could remember. Some surprises were nice. And if she took out the people trying to kill her, life had been awesome and rather exciting lately. Especially Jaxon. She fanned her face again, thinking about what he said as he left. She got to work while her mind continued to daydream.

Chapter 23

Jaxon spent the rest of the day going over emails from Jeremy and the agency. He made plans for the track in the morning with suggestions from his boss, Tom Maxwell. But maintaining his focus on the job proved next to impossible after his conversation with Peyton earlier. He loved this playful version of her. More than once his mind strayed to the ways he planned to show her exactly what he meant. It turned out to be a good thing when Matt popped in for a minute to tell him that he had arranged to take Frank and the girls out for dinner tonight. Jaxon would have to save his conversation with Peyton for another day. At least now he could concentrate on the investigation.

His gut told him they would be finding more bodies in a couple of locations which would keep him busy for the next several days. Peyton took his job and schedule in stride. He hated to miss a golden opportunity with her though. She had been so flirtatious, and he liked it. Never one to refuse a gift, he planned to seize the moment. Each day she seemed to trust him more and let down her guard a bit.

She promised to read to him tonight since their plans had changed. He looked forward to listening to her. The journal was one way to keep his head in the investigation. He kept himself thinking about the evidence they had while spending any time he could with her. Even over the phone.

Besides his earlier emails, Jeremy also sent him a list of women who had gone missing in the past few months. He wasn't sure if the list were complete but would continue to search. Jeremy also managed to get a copy of a register of Indian children and the names of a few kids who died while attending two boarding schools in the area. The incomplete lists convinced him they would find additional bodies when they searched. With any luck, they could solve a terrible crime from the past and Tamara Campbell's at the same time.

Jaxon spent time comparing the names on Jeremy's lists with those from Peyton's notes, and from the names listed in the second book found in the attic. It seemed strange that all of it surfaced, including Campbell's death, at the same point in time. When you factor in the journal and Cara's connection to the women in the tribe, it felt like the table had been set to solve this mystery. Why had it taken this long to surface?

"Did you catch those emails from Jeremy?" Matt asked as he walked into the interview room.

"I did. I cross-referenced them to the names on Peyton's list. I found quite a few listed. I put a check beside the names that are a match." Jaxon showed Matt.

"I'll make a copy. You've saved me the work." Matt leaned against the wall.

"Be my guest." Jaxon pushed the paper across the table. "What're your instincts telling you?"

"We are opening a can of worms that will make some do-gooders look bad, really bad. But it's time that truth comes out. They buried their crimes and died with their legacies intact. That's all about to change for a few folks." Matt frowned as he picked up the paper.

"Has Frank arrived yet?" Jaxon asked.

"He's already in town and at the house. The dogs have some outdoor space that way. He brought both his tracking dog and his drug dog." Matt strode toward the door. "I'll return this in a minute."

"Sounds good." The couple of times Jaxon had worked with Frank, he had found him to be an upstanding guy. He imagined Frank Wagner had some amazing stories he could tell from the cases he had worked. Jaxon leaned back in his chair. Of course, he did. Anyone who worked with the Reynolds had stories they could tell. His old boss from Arizona, Parker, and Maxwell to name a few. The last case was about as mind-bending as you could get, and this one has all the earmarks of the peculiar written on it too.

**** 

"I'll need to leave soon if I want to be ready on time." Peyton placed a stack of the sorted books back in their rightful spot on the shelf.

"Me too. The one good thing about winter is I close at five." Jessie handed her two more books that went on the same shelf. "It will be good to see Frank again. I always think when he arrives we are a couple of steps closer to solving a case. The problem is we need a suspect or two. Better yet, we need to know why the girls went missing to begin with. And how does Tamara Campbell fit into it, if at all?" Jessie pushed another book into place.

"I think she does. She was working on the same story, and from the notes Jeremy sent us, she was beginning to connect the same links we are." Peyton ran the feather duster along the rim of the shelves after she straightened the books. "Maybe we're approaching this all wrong."

"What do you mean?" Jessie asked.

"We're looking at it from the missing girls, but maybe we should start first with Tamara Campbell. We need to look into her background and see if she had any relatives in the area. A disgruntled boyfriend, perhaps." Peyton followed Jessie to the front of the store. "I admit Cara's story has hooked me, but I'm not sure where it's leading us."

"I bet it's leading us slowly toward a suspect." Jessie locked the door and turned the sign to Closed. "Don't forget the man the spirits threw these books at."

"Who could forget him? Speaking of the man, have you ever seen him in town before?" Peyton straightened the bookmarks in the basket while Jessie closed the doors into the coffeeshop and locked them. "I couldn't see his face clearly, but there was something about him that has me thinking."

"He didn't look familiar to me. But it all happened so quickly, and I didn't get a good look at his face either. I was shocked by all the flying books." Jessie laughed. "What a sight."

"The books were a total surprise. We'll never be able to complain that our lives are boring." Peyton grinned.

"We're human, complaining comes with the territory. I'm sure we'll figure out a way and a reason to have a pity party. It's what we do." Jessie reached over the counter for her keys. "Since the first man grumbled about his wife, we've been perfecting the art."

Peyton laughed. "You're right. Moaning about our lot in life is natural even when there isn't a good reason." Peyton glanced at her cousin. "In some strange way, that man seemed familiar to me." Peyton handed her cousin the last books from the table.

"How?" Jessie asked.

"I'm not sure, but it'll come to me."

"We're done. I'm wearing a dress tonight. Matt's got reservations at the Chowder House."

"Swanky. We should both wear our red dresses." Peyton flushed, thinking about the way Jaxon looked at her when she wore the dress before.

"That's not playing fair." Jessie shook her head. "But I like how you think."

"Who said we need to play fair? I want to make sure I stay in the game. There's a lot of competition out there."

"Okay, the red dress it is." Jessie locked the door behind them as they left. "See you later." She laughed as she got in the car. "Wear your red dress, and no bailing on me."

"I won't." Peyton waved as she got into her car.

\*\*\*\*

"What a day, sister. We got a bit of help. I would have loved pitching a book at the guy myself."

"What do you mean? You did, and you seemed to be enjoying yourself immensely." Elida wiggled her pointed ears.

"It was rather fun, if I do say so myself. My aim got better with each one I tossed."

"Mine did too, sister. I admit it would have been fun to zap him a few times."

"All in good time, Elida. All in good time." Mila smiled, her eyes twinkling as she did.

"I'm rather tired of being invisible." Elida waved

her wand, spinning around and around. She turned into a young man in his twenties.

"You might want to change your ears while you're at it." Mila turned into a pretty, young woman in her twenties. "We can follow them tonight, and they'll never know who we are."

"Except for your eyes, sister. Their sparkle always gives you away." She pulled a pair of glasses out of a bag. "Here, put these on." Elida waved her tiny hand. "Now you're perfect."

"We make a handsome couple." Mila chuckled. "It's not wrong to enjoy ourselves a bit even on the job. That's one of the privileges of being us." Mila smiled at her image in the glass. "We may have to stay focused, but we can have fun while we do. It's liable to get rocky over the next few days. Aelfric is pulling out all the stops and sending them out of their hiding places." Elida nodded. "We'll have to do him one better by watching over our subjects to keep them safe."

****

Peyton looked at her reflection in the mirror. She loved the dress, and she knew Jaxon did too. A dab of perfume in all the special places and she was ready to go. She put on her coat and buttoned it as she waited for him to get there. Call it her element of surprise, but she wanted to have the upper hand tonight. Keeping him off balance was important to her, and she had no idea why. Maybe she would understand her reasoning as the night progressed. Jaxon meant a lot to her, and there was no going back even though she had tried to keep her distance. She needed reassurance that he felt the same way. At times it was evident, but other times it felt like they were doing an awkward dance around each other.

She needed to know because she was falling in love with him. It was too soon, but her heart didn't seem to care. Jaxon was the love of her life, but her feelings would remain her secret for now.

Chapter 24

Jaxon walked the path to Peyton's cottage. "Am I late?" He noticed her coat was already on and buttoned tight. "Are you cold?"

"No to both questions. I wanted to be ready when you got here." She walked through the door he held open for her. She reached for his hand as they walked the path to his car. "It's been quite a day. I'm looking forward to a nice relaxing dinner."

"I'm with you. No shop talk until we are all together, and then we'll have no choice. Does that sound fair to you?" He opened the car door.

She stroked his cheek and slipped into the passenger's seat. "Perfect."

"You smell wonderful. Is that a new perfume?" He started the car and backed out of the parking space.

"It's my favorite. I save it for special occasions." She glanced at him.

"Hmmm." He smiled. "Why tonight?"

"Anytime you're with me is reason enough." She turned to look out the window with a smile.

"Lately, sweetheart, I've been wondering who you are. You're full of surprises."

"I'm the same old me." She glanced at his profile as he drove.

"I beg to differ with you. You flirt more." He moved into the turn lane.

"You have yourself to blame for that. You seem to bring out my playful side." She unlatched her seat belt when they arrived at the Chowder House.

He patted himself on the back. "Well done. I have no idea how I did it, but I'm glad I did." He reached for her hand when they walked inside. "I like you this way," he said softly.

Roger Blackman came over to greet them. "Chief Parker and his guests have arrived. May I take your coat?"

"Yes, please." She unbuttoned and slipped her arms out. Watching Jaxon's face made her little surprise worth the wait.

"This way, please." Blackman gestured. "You look lovely tonight, Peyton."

"Thank you." She followed with Jaxon.

"Lovely isn't the word I would use. I say the temperature in the room went up a notch. And you aren't playing fair, sweetheart." He leaned close and whispered.

"All is fair in love and war, isn't that what they say. Besides, I have it on good authority that you like this dress."

"You know I do. Two can play this game." He grabbed her hand and wouldn't let go until they were seated, and then he rested his arm on the back of her chair where he intermittently touched her hair and neck. It didn't take him long to notice that Jessie had on a red dress and Matt was acting as possessive of Jessie as he was of Peyton.

"Frank, it's good to see you again." Peyton extended her hand to shake his. "I'm glad you're here."

"I couldn't be more pleased. Between you two,

I've worked on some pretty exciting cases here in Blue Cove. This one sounds right up there with the others. They make my resume look quite impressive." He winked at her. His eyes crinkled at the corners. "My wife said to be sure to tell you both hi from her."

"When you talk, you can tell her the same from us." Jessie reached for the menu that the waiter handed to her.

"What sounds good, cousin?" Peyton asked.

"You can't go wrong with anything. I haven't ordered anything that I didn't like. Hmm, sounds like a shrimp scampi night to me." Jessie took a sip of her water.

"Blackened chicken salad sounds yummy to me." She motioned to Jessie while the guys were ordering. "We'll be right back." Peyton stood, and Jessie followed.

"I wondered what those two are up to." Jaxon followed their movements until they were out of sight. He saw a couple of other men doing the same thing. He couldn't fault them. The cousins were stunning.

"I'm not sure, but they conspired together. I'd stake a bet on it." Matt shook his head. "Those two are a handful."

Frank chuckled. "You're right, but I don't see you complaining. I remember you and Jessie in the beginning. It was fun watching you both trying not to notice each other."

"She still rattles me." Matt frowned.

"Peyton constantly surprises and perplexes me." Jaxon raked his hand through his hair.

"Welcome to the club." Frank laughed. "Every man has experienced the same in some way."

\*\*\*\*

Dinner was enjoyable. The conversation started low-key but turned to elements of the investigation as soon as the waiter removed their plates. Jaxon and Matt filled Frank in on what they hoped the track would accomplish. They talked about the murder of Tamara Campbell and Peyton's dream of others being buried nearby. Some of the information was new to Peyton, but it jived with what she had been thinking.

"When are you doing the track? I would like to come if I can," Peyton asked.

"What time do you get off work?" Jaxon glanced at her.

"At noon."

"I'll pick you up and take you to the one in the afternoon at the boarding school. We are doing the area around where Tamara was found in the morning."

"Works for me." Peyton leaned toward Jessie. "Can you get time off to come too?"

"I'm going to try. I love watching Radar in action. It helps in writing my articles later to see the dog at work."

"If she can work it out, I'll drive to the store, and you can pick us up there." Peyton glanced at Jaxon.

"Okay." Jaxon reached for her hand, lacing his fingers through hers.

"I have a lot of questions to get answered. At this point, we have several pieces of information, all only circumstantial at the moment. Yet I believe it will weave a sad tale of murder and neglect during a time of prejudice and anger. No one will be able to tell the story better than my cousin." Peyton pointed at Jessie. "She's the best."

"Hear, hear." Matt raised his water glass. "She did an amazing job with the bizarre story of John Ballard, leaving out the stranger facts that no one would have ever believed."

"I read that one. They're right, Jessie, you do have a way with words," Frank said as he placed his napkin on the table. "Another great meal. Thanks, Matt. I think I'm going to call it a night. I need to let the dogs out for a bit. We want to be fresh in the morning."

"I'll be there soon. Make yourself comfortable. You know the routine." Matt stood when Frank did. "I'll be right back."

While Matt was gone, Jaxon paid the bill. "We should call it a night too, sweetheart." His thumb stroked the palm of her hand.

"Jess, are you ready?" Matt walked up behind her, resting his chin on the top of her head.

"Yes." She stood. "See you tomorrow," she told Peyton.

"Roger said you paid the bill. I'll reimburse you tomorrow."

"We're good. See you in the morning." Jaxon waved him away.

Peyton and Jaxon walked hand in hand to the car. "I love you in that dress. It was a pleasant distraction all evening."

"As were your fingers running through my hair and touching my skin." She glanced at him when he opened the car door for her.

"I'd say we're even, but this isn't over yet. I have a lot to prove." Jaxon made sure her coat was out of the way before he closed the door.

"Is that a threat?" she asked when he got in the car.

She adjusted the seat belt cutting across her neck.

"No, a promise. You can count on it." He glanced at her and pulled out of the parking space. "I'm looking forward to the challenge." He grinned. "You constantly surprise me, sweetheart, and I have a few of my own."

"You sound sure of yourself." She pursed her lips.

"Not by a long shot. But you and that dress make me believe anything is possible." He chuckled. "I may be interpreting this wrong, but tonight you sent me a signal, and I'm all in."

"I'm beginning to wonder if we are talking about the same thing." Peyton fidgeted with the strap on her purse.

"Who knows, only time will tell. As far as I'm concerned, when it comes to you and me, the sky is the limit. We'll have to make it up as we go. It's new territory for both of us."

"Do you want to read more of the book tonight?" Peyton changed the subject. He was making her nervous. She might have unleashed more than she could handle with all her flirting.

"Over the phone. I know you have work in the morning, and I have a long day ahead of me." He turned off the highway onto the lane back to the inn. "I doubt we would get much reading done if I come in now."

He was right. Relief and disappointment raced through her at the same time. What was up with her anyway? She opened the door as soon as he stopped the car. "Call me when you get home." She hopped out of the car.

"Oh, no, you don't." He grabbed her from behind. "You know the rule: I walk you to the door. Besides, after somewhat behaving myself all night, I deserve a goodnight kiss, and I plan on claiming it." He pulled her into his side, his arm draped around her waist. "I've got you now."

"I can see that." She tried to pull away. This was a side of him she didn't recognize.

"Do you have your key?" He opened his hand, unlocked the door, and walked in behind her. He spun her around and pinned her up against the door. "I've been wanting to do this all night."

She gulped, never taking her eyes off his face as his lips slowly descended and took possession of hers in one long, hot, delicious kiss that left her breathless. "Wowza." She fanned her face. "Did I say that aloud?"

He grinned, brushing her cheek with the back of his hand. "Yep. Good description, by the way. I'll call you soon." He walked out into the cold night air.

Peyton locked the door and leaned against it. That kiss curled her toes. Smiling, she hummed a tune as she got ready for bed. Climbing into bed, she reached for the journal and the book underneath it and waited for his call. Tonight, she saw Jaxon unleashed, and she liked him even more.

****

Jaxon whistled all the way home. Matt was letting him stay in one of his guest rooms until his house was in better shape. Damn, he was happy. Peyton's reaction to their kiss was all the encouragement he needed. The look on her face was priceless and worth every moment of discomfort sitting beside her. What was she up to? Not important; he liked the results.

Frank was already in bed, and Matt wasn't home yet as he made his way to his room. He hopped into bed. Stacking his hands behind his head, he reached for his phone and pushed her number. "Read me to sleep," he said. "Make it interesting. I'm having a hard time concentrating thanks to you."

"Serves you right." She laughed. "All kidding aside, I found something while I was waiting for your call that you need to hear."

"I'm all ears. Read away."

Peyton opened the diary and began to read.

*I went to see my friend Kimama in the village today. I love to spend time with her. She is graceful like the meaning of her name, butterfly. Her long dark hair and expressive brown eyes make her a beauty among the other tribal women. Her life is not easy, but no one's is. In many ways, my friend reminds me of Alanna. Kimama sees everything connected and having a purpose in the circle of life. Every time I'm with her, I miss the wisdom of my grandmother.*

*She is married to the chief's youngest son. The braves of the village are helping them search for their son who was forced from the village to go to school. He was only six.*

*Kimama's eyes grew misty. "Evil people are doing bad things to your people and mine," she told me. "We must be watchful. The blue eyes at the school will not let the men see our boy. It makes me wonder why." What she said makes me also wonder.*

*Today when I was leaving I was surprised to find Alanna there visiting with an old woman at the edge of the village. I had heard that my grandparents had come to America, but I had no idea how to find them. Nana was all smiles when she spotted me and waved. I had learned in my past visits that the woman she sat with was known as the seer of the village. It didn't surprise me that they would find each other. In many ways, it gave me peace to know that Alanna was safe nearby. I had missed her since leaving Ireland. She would find me when it was time. That's how it worked with her. Alanna was elusive, a traveler that moved as she was told, and she would contact me at some point. I had grown since I last saw her, and I understood more too.*

Peyton continued to read and stopped at the end of Cara's musings about seeing her grandmother. "This is a good place to stop and to think about what we read. Get some sleep, and I'll talk to you tomorrow."

"It sounds like Cara has started to understand more. I hope she'll tell us what that knowledge is." Jaxon paused. "I'll pick you and Jessie up around twelve thirty. Sweet dreams, love."

Chapter 25

Peyton continued to read after Jaxon hung up. Cara talked about seeing a couple of the missing girls' spirits and knew they were dead. She talked about seeing a mass grave but didn't know where it was located until she talked to Kimama that day in her village. She knew the boy would not be found alive if at all. The Indian tribe didn't have many rights to challenge the government. Cara understood their dilemma after seeing how her people were treated in town. No one seemed to care about the missing girls because they were Irish after all.

How frustrating. Peyton shook her head. Things have changed and yet they haven't changed at all. The veneer of civility is quite thin. Being aware of social injustices isn't something to be ashamed of, and yet we are making those who care feel that way.

Where did these girls work? Who was responsible for their deaths? If Cara's words were correct, there hadn't been an active investigation into their disappearance. She seemed to think that no one cared, and maybe they didn't. At least, no one but Alanna. Together they searched for the truth. Peyton smiled at the thought of Cara working beside her grandmother to find answers. The gift of sight seemed to be passed from generation to generation. Finding out that the Cassidys were in her family line answered a few more questions for her. Now all she wanted to know was what had Tamara Campbell stumbled onto and what had got her killed.

She picked up her phone. "I hope I didn't wake you," she told her cousin.

"Nope. I was looking over the notes that Tamara had filed with Neil over the weeks she worked on the story. She filed them regularly because she was worried someone was tailing her. Neil told me."

"What have you found?" Peyton asked.

"The first part of the notes I didn't find much. Now I can see where she was researching a CEO of a large corporation with ties to a couple of businesses here in town. She wrote several names on the side of her notes. I don't know most of them, but I recognized a teacher's name and state rep who both have homes here."

"Did she say what she was looking at?" Peyton adjusted the pillows that had slipped.

"Human trafficking and abuse." Jessie paused. "I was just beginning to read her notes on the boarding school issues. Tamara seemed to be connecting the leader at the school and others over the next many years to the same practices. She pulled on information from the archives of the newspaper in the year the girls went missing and was beginning to sort through the business owners when she disappeared. We need to finish her work. I'm sending you, Matt, and Jaxon a copy of her files. The more eyes the better," Jessie said.

Peyton told her cousin about what she read in Cara's journal. "Whoever didn't want Tamara to uncover the truth won't like us snooping around either. Maybe the car the other night was a warning."

"Probably. Still, I'm going to make an appointment

with Rep. Holland. I want to feel him out. Do you want to come along?"

"You bet. I wouldn't think of letting you go alone. This brings my thoughts back to what happened at the school between the parent and teacher today. I wonder if he's involved. I mean the dark wolf faded in and out around him." Peyton stretched out her legs.

"I hate it when my sense of reality gets messed with. Blue Cove seemed like an idyllic town when I first moved here. Don't get me wrong—there are still a lot of wonderful people. It does make me question what goes on beneath the façade we see in a person's life," Jessie complained.

"As history has taught us, people are capable of doing some dark things and still look like normal people. They somehow believe their ideas and beliefs are the only right ones. How else could they conspire against their neighbors and turn them in to face the gas chambers? I don't get how they could live with themselves," Peyton mused.

"If the last year has taught me anything, it's that people are capable of great good and great evil. You hope you don't meet the latter on a bad day." Jessie cleared her throat.

"I hear you." Peyton glanced at the wolf on the cover of the book on her nightstand. She flipped it face down.

"Read through her files and let me know what you think. I'm going to read a few pages from Cara's diary before I go to sleep. Sweet dreams, cous."

"You too, Jess. See you tomorrow. I'm looking forward to seeing Radar at work again." Peyton clicked off her phone and put on the silent mode. She turned off her light and let her thoughts wander through the words of Cara, Kimama, and what Jessie told her. With a little magic, maybe, it would make sense. And of course, Jaxon called her love. "Pure magic." She sighed.

****

"Magic is the ideal word, my dear girl." Mila watched her from the foot of the bed. "That's my specialty. I have a few ways to help you discover the truth." She waved her wand, and the unseen sparkles danced across the room, landing around Peyton.

When Mila had first come to this country, she was sent from County Limerick, Ireland, by Felicia. Now she got her marching orders from Celeste, as did Elida. Once Cara and Alanna moved to this area, the two sisters were given authority over the cove and a few other places as well. They both knew the inn like the back of their hand.

Only on special occasions did they get to reveal their presence to a human or become actively involved. Most of the time they helped from a distance. But when they could, those moments were pure joy. They would direct the process, but the girls would help them too. Two sisters working with two cousins to right a wrong. The idea had a nice ring to it. Mila clapped her petite hands with enthusiasm.

Mila sorted her thoughts and shifted them into order pushing them Peyton's way. "Make her thoughts clear and help her to see what needs to be seen." Mila blew a misty kiss toward her and continue to wait until she slept. "Dream my dreams and learn the truth. Be the voice of those who can speak no more. Good shall triumph in the end. Let their story now begin." She waved her wand as she fluttered around Peyton's bed.

With her movements, the dream began. Mila wasn't finished with her work yet. Another location called to her, and she went to visit a sleeping figure a few miles away.

****

It was one of the strangest dreams Jaxon ever had. Crazy, disjointed, but oh, how he wished he could remember the details. Trapped inside his mind and held captive there with only bits and pieces of the images surfacing from time to time as he woke up. He pushed himself up to a sitting position and rubbed the sleep from his eyes. A white wolf, dark wolf, and words from the tribal leaders weaved themselves in pictures and words through his mind. There seemed to be a message hidden within them if only he could figure it out. Dreams were not his forte—that gift belonged to Peyton. Hopefully, she could help him make sense of what he could remember. Jaxon jotted down on paper thoughts as they came to him. He rarely dreamed or remembered any when he did. Unless, of course, they were thoughts and dreams of her. Those he had no problem remembering all the hot and bothering details.

He rushed through his a.m. routine. This morning's track with Frank's dog could break their investigation wide open. Peyton heard voices, which meant more bodies would be discovered. Someone seemed worried enough to murder the reporter for getting too close. Jaxon hurried out of the room to the smell of coffee and bacon.

"Good morning. I thought I might have to wake you from your beauty sleep." Matt glanced at Jaxon and laughed. "From the looks of it, you might need to go and try again."

"Yeah, yeah." Jaxon gestured with his hand. "Let me at the coffee, and I'll be a new man." He pulled a cup out of the cupboard and filled it with the strong brew. "Is Frank up?"

"He's outside with the dogs. They're ready to get to work, and so am I." Matt handed Jaxon a plate. "Eat up; we need to get going."

Jaxon filled his plate with eggs, bacon, and a slice of toast. The sooner he finished the sooner they could get started. Maybe getting out in the chilly air would stir his memory. Today would be successful—that was the one big takeaway from the dream he could remember. Only the next few hours would define what success meant.

Chapter 26

Peyton rushed out the door after gulping down a cup of hot tea and a piece of toast. Her schedule was packed today, and she didn't want to be late. Her dream last night still troubled her. Somehow Mila was involved. She had to be. Dreams of Ireland were not normal for her. She had never been there, and her Irish roots had never been on her radar until now.

Her excursion back in time opened up a new way to think about family and connection. Up to this point, she hadn't thought about all the different traits, environments, and circumstances that came together to make her who she was. The good and the bad were all a part of her foundation, which probably meant she needed to look at her family life in a new way. As much as she didn't want to, she probably needed to understand her parents too.

Removing the frost guard off her windshield, she tossed it in the backseat. Starting the car, she turned the heat on full blast filling the car with a rush of cold air before it turned semi-warm. She backed the car out of its space and passed the inn on the way to the street into town.

Peyton's mind was occupied with her racing thoughts, but somehow she managed to notice a car that seemed to be following her. She decided to test her theory. The dark blue SUV turned when she did and followed her on the next turn too. Darn, she didn't have time for this. She continued to lead the car into a few circles leading him to the police station where the car sped off.

Jaxon knocked at her window and motioned for her to roll it down. "What are you doing here? Aren't you supposed to be at the school?" he asked.

"Yes, but I had a tail this morning. I decided to lead him here. I was just texting you when you knocked."

"I'll follow you to the school in the patrol car. Give me a description of the vehicle."

Jaxon called it in to be on the lookout for a blue SUV as she described it to him. "Lead the way." He got into Matt's patrol car and followed her.

Relief filled her when she pulled into the school parking lot. Collecting her briefcase and papers from the backseat, she locked her car. She waved at Jaxon as she walked into the school. She had to admit it was nice having him look out for her. Not that she wanted anyone else to know. For now, she could appreciate his concern without feeling like a weakling. Not being threatened by his concern spelled growth to her, and the thought made her smile.

****

As soon as Peyton was safely in the school, Jaxon drove back to the station, watching for any sign of the vehicle that had followed her. The description was different than the vehicle that had tried to run them down the other night. Which either meant they switched cars, or they had a new player. He'd bet on the second one. Peyton had once again surprised him by letting him follow her without one of her remarks. They were making headway. He smiled and signaled his turn onto Main Street.

Matt and Frank were standing in the parking lot when he arrived. He stepped out of the car and joined them. "What's up?"

"We were planning out the day, and Frank was telling me about another case that Radar helped solve. They've seen some gruesome things over the past few years." Matt patted the dog's head. "Does your dog ever get depressed after a track?" Matt asked.

"Yes. When we find a body instead of a living person, it's as tough on him as it is me. We both need downtime after a hard case."

"I bet." Jaxon leaned his hip against the car. "Murder scenes aren't easy for any of us."

"Did you see any signs of the car following Peyton?" Matt asked. "It hasn't been spotted yet. I have Kenny at the school to keep an eye out for the car. He'll follow Peyton to the store."

"Thanks, I appreciate it," Jaxon said.

"He'll keep a low profile. I know how the girls feel about interference. But I didn't want you distracted this morning."

"That's the strange thing. Peyton didn't say anything when I said I would follow her this morning." Jaxon pushed away from the car. "It makes me wonder why."

"Maybe you'll never know. It could have been a spur-of-the-moment reaction." Matt chuckled. "At least it's that way with Jess." Matt gestured at Kip coming out the door. "Let's roll." He stood beside Frank as he loaded the dog into his crate. "I'm curious about what we'll find. Jaxon, why don't you ride with Frank, and

Kip can go with me."

"I'll follow you," Frank told him.

"If we get separated, I know the way." Jaxon closed the door and latched his seat belt.

Frank followed Matt's vehicle out of the parking lot. "Just between you and me, Peyton and Jessie for that matter aren't against being taken care of, only being told they need to be."

"You're right. Women have been lectured and told what they need most of their lives. I understand. Hopefully, I'm learning to ask her and not tell her."

"Sounds like a plan to me." Frank laughed. "The longer that lesson takes to learn the rougher times you'll have. Take it from a fella who learned it the hard way."

"Is there any other way to learn but by trial and error? Relationships are a minefield." Jaxon ran his hand through his hair. "At least most of mine have been. Peyton is a different story. She challenges me in too many ways to count, but I've always liked a good challenge."

"What you're saying is she is worth the effort. Sounds like love to me." Frank smiled. He signaled his turn and followed Matt.

The morning went off without a hitch. Radar got down to work, first finding the original murder site without an issue. As Jaxon watched, Frank knelt beside his dog. Above their heads, a hawk began to circle. The big, beautiful red-tailed hawk squawked as if on cue. His flight pattern was majestic against the backdrop of the clear blue skies.

"That's my sign Radar will be successful." Frank pointed at the bird. "Let's get to work, fella." The dog indicated on several spots near and around the original murder site.

Jaxon put a call in to Tom to request ground-penetrating radar. He also requested chemical analyses of the soil and air around the area. Radar had done his job. The rest was up to them to figure out if the hits were animal or human remains. The ground had thawed enough over the past few days for the track to be successful.

"Maxwell said the team would be here in the morning to search the area." Jaxon walked over to stand by Matt.

"Good. We'll know sooner than later what we're dealing with. I wonder if they will have more locations to check after this afternoon." Matt frowned.

"A mass gravesite, perhaps?" Kip asked.

"My gut tells me that's what we'll find." Jaxon frowned.

"It was a long time ago. What good is it to find out if no one can be charged now?" Kip folded his arms across his chest.

"Truth is important. People need to face what hatred is capable of. It might bring closure to a tribe filled with unanswered questions about their ancestors. The tribal elders heard the rumors and theories. It's past time for them to know." Jaxon moved his phone back and forth between his hands.

"Tamara's family is waiting for answers too. I hope we can give them some soon. That girl was on to something. Jess sent me her files and notes to look at. She was closing in on a crime that may have roots in the past, but it has continued into the present. I want to solve the mystery for her family too. She could be the real heroine in all of this." Matt opened the car and tossed them each a bottle of water.

"Thanks." Frank lifted his chin.

Matt nodded. "The Campbell girl was hot on the trail of someone. A living, breathing someone. I bet they're getting nervous and trying to cover their tracks. And nerves can cause people to slip up. Killing Tamara was a mistake. They'll make more. We need to keep our eyes open." Matt paused. "Especially if they know the girls are picking up where Tamara left off."

"Speaking of the girls, I need to pick them up at the store," Jaxon reminded Matt. "I could use some lunch. How about you, Frank?"

"Did you hear my stomach growling?" Frank chuckled.

"We're done here for the moment. Let's eat and get ready for part two," Matt said.

"Joe's?" Jaxon asked.

"Always." Matt smiled.

Chapter 27

The afternoon had gone about the way she had expected. It was awful to think about what might have happened to the kids staying in the boarding school. There was no doubt in Peyton's mind that the team tomorrow would find what Radar had indicated on. She and Jessie walked with Frank and Radar and watched as Frank marked every spot where Radar sat. Matt sprayed the area with bright orange paint. When they were finished, the marked areas outlined two large areas in width and length. One area was located about a quarter mile from the old boarding school and one farther out but still on the property.

Peyton tried to imagine what took place behind closed doors at the school that could lead to such a tragic outcome. While the guys finished, she walked beside her cousin to a bench still on the property. The boarding school had a nice view. Too bad the people operating it hadn't been as nice.

"Do you ever wonder what makes people do the things they do?" Jessie plopped down on the bench.

"I was thinking about the subject the whole time we walked beside Frank. I don't get it, especially when it comes to kids. Any kids." Peyton shook her head, her frustration growing.

"We've seen the same sad story often enough, and each time we find some dumb simple answer and then move on. Never dialoguing or searching for real solutions. No wonder Tamara kept searching." Jessie frowned. "People deserve that much."

"How scared those kids had to be. Separated from their families and forced into a way of life different than what they knew. When kids are afraid, they act out. It's natural. How could people not see what they were doing was wrong?" Peyton folded her hands on her lap. "It's hard to face the past. It makes us question if we are who we think we are."

"How could they simply bury these kids or anyone in a mass grave? Even if they died of natural causes, the parents should have been notified." Jessie's foot shook back and forth, picking up speed as she talked.

"Of course, they should have." Peyton shook her head. "I'm not sure that we're doing much better than they did in their day."

"The major difference is it's a lot harder to hide things from the media. News is twenty-four seven which can be bad but can also be good. It brings stories like this to light which have been hidden for generations." Jessie shrugged. "Tamara died trying to do just that."

"Are you ready to write this story and finish what Tamara began?" Peyton reached for Jessie's hand.

"You bet I am. The wheels have been turning for days. Ever since that day in the attic, what we saw has repeated over and over in my mind." Jessie's brows furrowed. "The thoughts keep coming. It almost feels like someone is putting them there. It's like…"

"Magic." Peyton completed her cousin's statement.

"Exactly. You took the word right out of my mouth. It almost feels like this is all being orchestrated."

"Agree. I understand how Sally must have felt. Speaking of your friend, does she like her new job?"

"She loves it. The last time we got together, she was happier than I'd seen her in a long time. She enjoys promoting Blue Cove, and she's doing a great job according to Chad. It wouldn't surprise me if the two of them get married at some point. Sally isn't in a hurry, though."

"Who can blame her after what she went through? Imagine being in such an abusive marriage." Peyton took a deep breath.

"I forgot to mention, she asked if she could start running with us. I said yes, of course. I hope you don't mind." Jessie glanced at Peyton.

"Not at all. The more the merrier. I never thought you could make a runner out of me. But I couldn't hold out against your pleas." Peyton laughed.

"It must be my blue eyes." Jessie fluttered her lashes.

"For Matt maybe, but not for me. It's your puppy eyes that get me every time. I need to be stronger." Peyton smiled. She told her cousin about her morning at school. The kids had been a blast today.

"Sorry to interrupt. Are you ladies ready to leave? We've finished all we can do until tomorrow." Jaxon laid his hand on Peyton's shoulder.

She reached up and squeezed his hand as it rested there. "Yes, I'm starving. I haven't eaten since this morning, and that was only toast." Peyton stood along with Jessie. "Right now, almost anything sounds good."

"I was thinking the same thing. I didn't have time to eat—the store was too busy. But I saw the guys eating at Joe's. Did they think of us? No." Jessie made a pouty face.

"That's the face I'm talking about. You and Madi are masters at it." Peyton pinched her cousin's arm.

"Sorry, ladies, we were remiss in our duties." Jaxon tugged Peyton to her feet.

"Yes, you were, and I think Matt should spring for our dinner." Jessie made sure to speak loudly as she saw Matt approach.

"Dinner sounds good to me. Why am I paying for it?" he asked, kissing her on the lips.

Jessie told him why. And Peyton watched her wrap Matt around her little finger with a silly grin on her face. "You're good, Jess." Peyton laughed.

"Don't get any ideas." Jaxon waggled his brows at her.

They made plans to meet at Patterson's after Peyton helped Jessie close the store.

\*\*\*\*

After a great meal and conversation, Peyton relaxed on the sofa at her cottage. She rested her head against Jaxon's shoulder. "This is the perfect way to end a busy day." She sighed. "I have this awful feeling the next few days aren't going to be easy. Promise me you'll be careful."

"I will." He toyed with her fingers in his hand. "I had the strangest dream last night. I wrote down the small parts I can remember. Truth is, I don't remember most of it, and it made little sense to me." He pulled the small notebook out of his pocket and explained what he had written down.

"I find the wolf in your dream interesting." Peyton explained why. "I also had a dream, although I can remember the details. The specifics fit with what I've been reading and seeing. That's what makes me think that the next few days won't be easy. We have crimes from the past intersecting with something going on now. All the names I heard in a dream can be found in this book." She handed him the second book she had found in the attic. "I told you about this book. Someone kept a record of the Irish girls who went missing. Not only are their names recorded, but what they were wearing, from their clothing to jewelry and shoes. Their height and the color of their hair and eyes are also listed. The details are meticulous. It's as if the writer wanted to have a historical record that these women existed. You'll see what I mean when you read it over. I imagine some of them are buried nearby while others may have been sold into a form of servitude and taken across the country."

"Do you mind if I take this?" he asked.

"No. But I need to return it to the attic when you're done."

"It might end up being evidence and the only original record available. I'll do my best to return it, but I can't promise you anything." He leaned his head back against the couch.

"I understand." She glanced at him. "One part of me hopes you don't find anything in the search tomorrow, but I also want justice for any victims. Every person's life matters. Their stories can encourage us to try harder at being better humans. Cara's box was filled with mementos of her life. I enjoyed going through the contents. They revealed her character and what was important to her. Her short writings encouraged me to believe in the possibility of change."

"I'd like to believe. Though I'm a bit of a doubter when it comes to people changing." He took her hand in his once again. "You've managed to surprise me as I've watched you over the last several months. Anything is possible."

"Of course, it is. Change takes time, and there will always be those who refuse to think of anyone but themselves. Still, I have to believe that most people are good and grow with their experiences in life."

"Yeah, but let's not forget there is also some really bad dudes, period." He squeezed her hand.

"Who can forget them? I've seen more than I wanted to ever see." She pursed her lips. "I carry a reminder around with me in the form of a scar as my constant reminder."

"I will never forget how close I came to losing you. That wound forced me to think about how empty my life had become. Maybe that's why I tend to feel overprotective of you now. I should have known. I was off my game." He pulled her closer.

"It wasn't your fault. It just happened. I found myself involved from the moment I saw the two ghosts at the pool, and here I am again. Dreams, visions, and yes, ghosts with a little something extra thrown in this time."

"What would you call the extra?" He lifted her fingers and kissed each one.

"Magic, pure magic. The same source of magic that Cara and Alanna knew. The one that traveled from the old country with them. They're the ones holding the darkness at bay while we sort this out."

"They?" he asked.

"Yes, there are two that I know of. One who

appeared to me and one who went to my cousin." She pulled her hand away from him. He was messing with her concentration. "Place what I've told you in the same space with all the other unexplainable things that have happened to me in the past year. At least this time I've been given more insight into my family and can understand where my great-great-grandmother came by her gift. We're not unique when you consider our ancestry. I wonder about you. Do you have others in your family history involved in law enforcement?" she asked.

"It's possible, along with a few criminals too, I imagine." He reached for her hand again and held it tightly in his. "I like holding your hand." He grinned.

"I think you like breaking my concentration."

"That too." He lifted her hand to his lips and kissed each of her fingers again. "Read to me. I love to hear your voice."

Peyton picked up the journal. "We don't have much more to read in this one. I'm curious to see if she wrote anything else. One of the sad things I found in the book I gave to you is that Cara's sister Brenna was listed among the missing. I had wondered about her when Cara mentioned it was sad that Brenna never came into her gift. This touched their family personally."

"That is sad."

"During the time they rounded up kids off the reservation under the guise of taking them to school, some were sold into slavery until they were eighteen. Many of the Irish immigrants were also sold. I wonder if that happened to some of the girls. Human trafficking has been around for more years than we want to believe. I guess it's true that there's nothing new under the sun." Peyton glanced at him.

"I remember hearing stories about the orphan train. Some of the endings for the kids were great, but others were horrific. Truth is if you can imagine it, it's probably been done I'm sad to say." Jaxon shook his head.

"I wonder if that holds true for technology and medicine. Think of all the good that could happen."

"Read." He tapped her on the shoulder to get her attention.

And she did.

\*\*\*\*

Mila loved observing the couple snuggled on the couch reading the words of one of her charges. Those days had been dark indeed, and all the magic she and Elida possessed couldn't save Brenna nor the Cassidys from the heartache they faced at her disappearance. Of course, Elida knew what happened and had followed her. They did what they could to make her life better. But the family never knew until later. Cara might have understood, but her longing for her sister overpowered her most of the time.

Not every assignment ended the way the sisters hoped. There were those among the fairies that were good and, like humans, there were some that turned bad. Aelfric was bad, and he had taken a few with him. His lust for power caused him to forsake the fairy code and turn to the dark side. As a pooka, he wreaked havoc in Ireland until he was banned. He escaped to this area on a ship with a human he had influenced for evil and had been causing trouble ever since. Celeste and her followers had been at war with him since his arrival.

How Mila wished they could put a stop to his madness permanently. That's where the Reynolds girls came in. Her job was to keep them alive and give them the tools to get the job done, if not to destroy Aelfric outright, then at least to send him packing for a season or to another region.

Aelfric at one time had been a good and compassionate leader, but something went wrong on one of his assignments. Rumors abounded at the time, but no one was sure even to this day what happened. He was demoted and later forced into exile. No amount of good magic was able to displace him up to this point. Mila was hopeful it was about to change.

Celeste said this was the time to put him in his place. Mila knew Aelfric, and he wouldn't go down without a fight. He already had humans aligned with his evil thinking and had damaged many lives over the years. Swirling her hands around the couple, she reinforced their thoughts with her strength. They would need all the help she could legitimately give them.

## Chapter 28

Last night had been perfect. Jaxon didn't stay long after they read several pages of the journal, but the time they spent together had been wonderful. He seemed to get better with time. Peyton ran a brush through her hair. The guys would be at the crime sites, and she would be hanging out with her kids. With one more quick glance in the mirror, she reached for her phone and stuffed it in her purse.

After a cup of tea and a piece of toast, she hurried out the door. One of these mornings she wanted to leave herself enough time to eat without having to rush. What happened to her punctuality? Blue Cove had upended most of her life. Though the slower pace was wonderful, slow wasn't good for her self-discipline. It might be nice to enjoy the pace without having to rush through everything to get to work on time.

"Peyton, you've become a dawdler. Shame on you. You'd never make it in the city now." She was happy to see no frost on the windows since she forgot to put the cover on the windshield. The sun was shining; what was not to like about the day? With any luck, they would be in for an early spring. That was a good reason to smile along with the feeling that answers were coming, and she would understand more soon.

Peyton greeted several teachers and students on her way into the school. Making her way into the office, she grabbed the papers from her teacher's box. She tucked them in her briefcase to look at later.

"Do you have a minute, Ms. Reynolds?" Principal Avery called to her.

"Yes, sir." She stopped to talk with him.

"I've had some teachers report some minor vandalism in their classrooms when they opened their rooms this morning. Please check yours and get back to me if there's a problem."

"I will." She rushed down the hall to check. What greeted her when she opened the door was by no means minor. Nor was the awful note left on the blackboard. She placed a call to the office, and not long afterward Principal Avery and the custodian walked in. As soon as he saw her room, Avery called the police.

"We haven't found the point of entrance as of yet. What's troubling is some rooms were left untouched and others..." His voice trailed off as he read the note. "That's disgusting. Don't touch anything. The police need to see the damage. I'll put your kids in with Jamieson's class for the morning. As soon as the police are done, you can put your room back together with help, of course. We'll need to scramble—the children will be arriving soon." Principal Avery walked out of the room.

"I think your room is the worst." The custodian whistled. "Wow, what a mess."

"Naturally," she mumbled under her breath. Taking her phone from her briefcase, she took several photos and sent them to Jaxon who would be at the crime sites by now. While she waited for the police, she began to sort through the papers she retrieved earlier—the school's monthly calendar, an announcement list of upcoming events, and the school newsletter were in the stack of papers, along with one envelope addressed to her.

The moment she held the envelope in her hand, she knew it wasn't good, and it got worse when she read the contents.

*Death awaits you and your cousin if you don't stop sticking your noses where they don't belong. If only Tamara could talk, but alas the cat's got her tongue.*

Peyton folded the paper and placed it back in the envelope. She shouldn't have touched the envelope or contents. Now her fingerprints were all over it. This was more than a simple act of vandalism or some kind of sick joke.

Kenny and Gary walked into the classroom. "Looks like you've had a bit of vandalism." Kenny shook his head. "Evan will be here soon to photograph this for Matt. I'll dust for prints."

"Only a bit," she said with her hands on her hips.

"Disgusting message, by the way." Gary picked up the chalk and put it in the evidence bag. "As soon as the photos are taken, you can erase it."

"Thanks. You'll want to see this too. I'm sorry I opened the envelope. You're sure to find my prints on both it and the note inside."

Kenny opened it carefully with his gloved hands. "Where did you get this?"

"The note was in my teacher's box with other papers from the school," Peyton told him.

When the police were wrapping up, Kenny came back to talk to her. "Whoever is involved had a key. Possibly an inside job. Keep your eyes open. If anyone threatens you, call us right away. We're sending the evidence to the lab, and maybe we'll know more before long."

"Thanks, Kenny. May I start cleaning up this mess?" She lifted one of the chairs that had been overturned.

"Have at it. Jaxon has texted several times to make sure you're okay. You might want to send him another text," Kenny told her. "I know how I would feel if it were Molly."

"I will." She walked with him to the door. "Something tells me you probably won't find any fingerprints but mine. I hope I'm wrong," she told him.

"I'll let you know, or Jaxon will, I'm sure." Kenny waved as he walked over to Gary and a couple of other officers that Peyton didn't recognize.

She got to work, erasing and cleaning the blackboard first. The message was quite clear someone knew she was taking up where Tamara left off. She filled a bucket with hot soapy water and began to scrub the marks off the walls and chairs. The custodian brought a crew in and got to work beside her.

While they continued to work, she went down to Jamieson's classroom to check on her kids. Happy chaos is how she would describe the room with both classes in the small space. Mr. Jamieson seemed to be taking the noise in stride with the help of his aides and hers too. She spent the rest of the morning replacing the colorful characters around her room. She wanted her room to be a cheery place in the morning when she welcomed back her kids. There was nothing to be done about their artwork that was ripped off the walls. The kids would get to fingerpaint or color new ones. Peyton added art to her lesson plans for the next morning.

When it came to the kids, Peyton was like a mama bear looking after her cubs. Most of them had enough obstacles and challenges in life without someone destroying the things they worked hard to achieve. The more she cleaned the madder she became.

\*\*\*\*

Jaxon's hand balled into a fist at his side when he first saw the pictures she had sent to him. The message on the blackboard made him want to put that fist in someone's face with all the force he could muster. Kenny had texted him several times, and none of them eased the tension in his shoulders. Her room had the most damage. Peyton was the only one who had been threatened. No surprise there. It wasn't about the other teachers; it was about her. What concerned him was when Kenny texted him that it was probably an inside job. He didn't want her to have to suspect her colleagues, but she would have to. It could be anybody, and that was a damn shame. Peyton loved her job at the school.

"Kenny and the guys have wrapped up at the school," Matt said. He and Frank walked up beside Jaxon. "At least now we know that someone is aware of the girls picking up where Tamara left off. Not that I was ever in any doubt."

"Yeah, but I'm not happy about it." Jaxon clenched his fist again and watched the team at work going over the murder site. "What do you think, Frank?"

"There is something buried in this area. Radar hit in several locations. Whether it is human remains or animals, we're about to find out. It's troubling about the threatening note left for Peyton."

"I'm not pleased. Seems like the girls are the bait,

even if they don't want them to be." Matt leaned his hip against his cruiser.

"If this site turns up the bodies we think are buried here, we'll have more than enough victims. We don't need any more." Jaxon watched the technicians doing chemical analysis in the marked areas.

"We'll have to prevent that from happening then, won't we?" Matt pushed away from the car as one of the agents walked toward them.

"We've found enough proof to bring in excavation equipment. It looks like there are multiple bodies buried in this area," he told them.

"Damn, I didn't want to hear that," Jaxon said.

"Hope for the best and prepare for the worst, that's how it usually goes in these kinds of cases." Matt frowned.

"Tom Maxwell said we still have another site to go to. We'll pack up the equipment and be ready in a few," the agent added.

"Sounds good," Jaxon told the agent. He turned to Matt and Frank. "I had a feeling the morning would go like this. Radar is rarely off track. I bet the boarding school site will be an even bigger find."

"We won't know until we excavate the site how old the bodies are or if there is any evidence left as to how they died. Still, it seems to all connect as Peyton told us it would. Why did they leave Tamara Campbell in the area? It seems like a dumb move to me." Matt folded his arms across his chest.

"Maybe that's where they found her snooping around and murdered her there. I'm always glad when a suspect messes up and makes a connection for us. It's one less we need to make." Jaxon walked out to talk to one of the agents waving at him.

They finished loading the equipment and drove to the next location. Jaxon had no idea what secrets the land at the boarding school would reveal. He also had in his pocket a search warrant to go through the property. Though the school had been closed for several years, he hoped they might find some old files or records left on the premises when the building was abandoned. Something was not kosher about the school or what happened to the children housed there. Whatever they might discover didn't just involve the tribe on the reservation near the cove but several other tribes too.

The search warrant in his pocket was his insurance policy that they could go through the building without local interference. They were doing it by the book, crossing the t's and dotting the i's as his boss liked to say.

"Are we ready to leave?" Matt asked.

"All ready," Jaxon told him.

"I can't image what we'll find next." Matt got in his car.

"I guess we're about to find out. After what happened at the school earlier, I think someone is nervous that we're getting close. See you at the site." Jaxon got in the car with one of the agents.

****

When they pulled into the school site, they were met by several police cars and the tribal leaders blocking the entrance. Jaxon got out of the car with the warrant in his hand.

"Who in the hell do you think you are? Can't you see we have a situation here? No trespassing, that's what the sign says, and that means you." The local sheriff stepped in front of Jaxon to stop his forward progress.

"That's where you're wrong." He showed the man his FBI badge.

"I don't give a damn who you are. You need to leave now and take these folks with you."

"Wrong again." Several of the agents and Matt came to stand with Jaxon. "I have a search warrant signed by a judge, and that means you need to get out of the way or be arrested for impeding an investigation."

"Well, hell." He motioned his guys to move after he read the warrant. "We'll be watching you."

"You can watch from here." Jaxon motioned to one of the agents. "Keep an eye on them."

"You got it. I'm calling for backup. These guys look like trouble. Maxwell told me he notified a few offices in the area and could send backup. He anticipated there could be trouble on this one," the agent said.

"Sounds like a good call." He motioned for the tribal leaders. "You are welcome to follow us in." Jaxon noticed movement out of the corner of his eye, and two of the agents had the sheriff pinned against the car.

"You wouldn't want to do that." Agent Gab disarmed the sheriff and cuffed him. "The FBI doesn't like it when one of its agents gets shot in the back." He opened the car door and helped him into the backseat. "Do any of you others want to join your sheriff?" He motioned at them with his gun aimed at the three men.

"Thanks, Gab." Jaxon nodded at him. "Don't let

any of them leave. I'm assured that help is on its way."
Who had tipped them off? Jaxon wanted to know. The
tribal elders blessed the ground before the team got
busy with the ground-penetrating radar. When their
ritual was finished, the work began. Jaxon, Frank, and
Matt went into the building. They were joined by a few
of the officers from the cove. The place had been pretty
much cleaned out on most of the levels. Windows were
broken, beds torn apart, and most of the blackboards
ripped from the walls. Graffiti filled the walls. As they
began down the stairs to the basement, Jaxon felt the
hair on his neck rise. The anger rose inside him when
he saw what was below. If this was the infirmary, like
the sign on the door said, it could have fooled him. It
felt more like a torture chamber.

"This place gives me the creeps." Matt shook his
head.

"I wish Peyton and Jessie were here to see this.
This is all wrong. I could use their perspective." He
took several pictures and texted them to Peyton. They
continued to search, taking photos as they went.

"You've got to see this," Frank called out after one
of the officers broke open a locked door.

"Bingo, this is our lucky day." Matt looked at the
boxes of files stacked five high.

Jaxon pulled one of the files out of the box. There
was a child's name, a black-and-white photo with the
date they had arrived at the school. As he continued to
flip through the pages, his ire grew. "We need to take
all of these into evidence. If what this file says is true,
this child was sold. At first glance, it appears that more
girls were sold than boys." Jaxon looked at an incoming
text. "Damn, the team found a mass gravesite."

"Some school. It makes my worst teachers seem like saints to me." Matt raked his hand through his hair. "What kind of operation was this?"

"Damned if I know. But I'm going to do everything I can to find out." Jaxon frowned.

Chapter 29

When Peyton saw the photos Jaxon sent her, she was appalled. It was like the school she once thought to work at. A mass gravesite would answer the question of what happened to some of the kids, but it would never tell the why. Most of those secrets died with the people who worked there. How could they ever get to the truth? Cara had shared Kimama's concern about her son, which gave some indication of what might have happened. She wanted to talk to Jaxon about what he sensed when he saw the room. Funny, that's what he had asked her.

—*Look at these photos, babe, and tell me what you sense. This is your gift, not mine.*—

What a day this had been. Her room vandalized, the nasty note, and now these photos. She still had a few questions to ask Matt about Tamara Campbell. Suddenly, unnatural chills ran down her spine. A tall man with slightly graying hair at his temples walked into her classroom.

"I didn't mean to startle you, but I had to see the newbie teacher whose room was vandalized the most. I wonder why that is? Hmm, it's a mess all right." He walked around the room, running his fingers over the surfaces he came in contact with. "I'm Mr. Sanders, by the way. And you are?" His brows rose in a snooty strange arch with his question.

"Peyton Reynolds." She looked the man directly in the eye when she answered him.

"You have quite a mess to clean up." His nose wrinkled.

"Not that much. You should see it when my kids are finger painting." Her chin lifted as she tried to keep the edge out of her voice. The tension in the room was almost visible. "Teaching is a noble profession, don't you think? I love it."

"Erh, noble, yes. My father was a teacher and his father before him. My great-great-great-grandfather taught when the school was only one room here in the cove. He remained until he became the principal at a mission boarding school for indigenous children. A Sanders too, he was a great man. I've taught for over twenty years. I'm proud to call myself an educator." He leaned his hip against her desk and watched her fill the bucket with more fresh water.

"That's quite a legacy. You should be proud." She placed the bucket on the floor and picked up a scrub brush. It would take a good brush and elbow grease to clean the graffiti off the walls.

"I would help, but my kids will be coming back from gym soon." He walked to the door. "I hope the rest of the school year will be uneventful for you. Good luck." As he left the room, she heard him mumble under his breath, "You'll need it."

What a pompous twit. She was thankful no one could hear her thoughts. Mr. Sanders looked down his nose at her the whole time. She had a bad feeling about the man. But he had given her a useful piece of information which she promptly sent in a text to Jeremy. If anyone could find out about the Sanders men, he could. In the meantime, she scrubbed the walls and made a lot of headway.

"You've worked hard enough for today." The custodian went to the sink and emptied his bucket. "It's way past time for you to go home, and Mr. Avery told me to send you on your way. We'll finish here. When you come back in the morning, your room will be as good as new."

"Thank you. I'll see you in the morning, Mr. Ellis." She gathered her briefcase and purse. Taking her keys out, she waved as she left the room. She couldn't wait to tell her cousin about her day. On her way out of the school, she passed the arrogant Mr. Sanders who wasn't with his students but stood in the hall with his coffee cup talking about her. She heard him say her name a couple of times. At least when he saw her he had the good sense to bc embarrassed, if she could judge from the flush on his face. Not true, she didn't think he had any good sense. "Have a nice evening, Mr. Sanders." She stopped and smiled sweetly. She waved and continued on her way.

Taking a deep breath of fresh air, she tried to make sense of the day she had, including the photos that Jaxon had sent to her. Was it possible that Mr. Sanders' relative was the principal in the school where they searched today? She could see the possibility if he was anything like the arrogant man who came into her class earlier. The man rubbed her wrong, and that was a fact. He had to fit into the puzzle somewhere.

Parking in front of Jessie's store, Peyton left the peace of her car, only to be shoved to the ground by a man rushing out of the door. Once she was upright, she walked into absolute chaos. Maybe she should go out and try coming in again. She tried, but it didn't work. "Jess, what's going on here?"

"You wouldn't believe me if I told you." Jessie righted a chair that had been pushed on its side.

"You want to bet. After the morning I've just had, I'll believe anything." She placed her purse on the counter and glanced at her frazzled cousin.

Jessie picked up another chair while blowing the hair out of her eyes with an exasperated breath. "Remember the ghosts who threw books when they saw the man the other day?" she asked. "Well, the man came in again, and so did they. Only this time they tossed whatever they could get their spectral hands on. Thankfully, no customers were hurt, but as Molly can tell you, a few were scared out of their wits. We're talking about the mystery book club. I have no idea how to explain it or to soothe their ruffled feathers."

"How about you arranged a mystery for them to solve? Will that work?" Peyton laughed. "Oh, how I wish I could have been here. We live such charmed lives. So far we've gotten away with a lot, that is until today." She laughed again and added when she saw her cousin's frown, "If I don't laugh, I would probably cry. I happen to think laughing is better."

"You're right, of course. I hope I don't lose customers over this." Jessie pouted, picking up another book from the floor.

"I wouldn't worry about that. Look." Peyton pointed to the door where the leader of the book club was coming in from the coffee shop.

"I'm sorry to have left the store abruptly earlier. Molly told us you had arranged that small exhibition to add drama to our meeting." She plopped in the chair while a few more members trickled through the open door. "All I can say is that it worked. I will never read another mystery story again without thinking about this day."

"Neither will my cousin," Peyton told them. She helped Jessie right the store as the book club settled down to talk about their latest book again.

"Another crisis averted," she whispered in her cousin's ear. "You owe Molly big time."

"You're telling me." Jessie sat down and laughed. "If only you could've seen Molly's face."

"It must have been sweet." Peyton dissolved into laughter.

"Please tell me how I will ever explain it to her." Her lips clenched together. "I'm serious," Jessie stammered between the stifled laughs.

"We'll think of something. After all, Molly did." Peyton patted Jessie's hand. "Besides, she's seen the goings-on in this store for over a year now. Nothing should surprise her." Peyton leaned back in the chair with a silly grin on her face. The only thing missing from the craziness of the day was Reba. Not seeing Reba didn't mean she didn't know what was going on. She fully expected her to pop into the store at any minute and ask them what's going on.

While the book club continued their meeting somewhat hesitantly, Peyton and Jessie restored some semblance of order to the store. Peyton chuckled to herself as the women watched the two of them warily. She couldn't imagine what was going through their minds. When the final book was back on the shelf, the last bookmark was put back in the basket, and the stapler returned to its place on the counter, Reba enter the store. "Hello, girls, I could do with some tea and a chat. I'm sure I missed something interesting, and I can't wait to hear all about it."

"Tea might have to wait until we get back, Reba," Jessie told her as she glanced at the clock. "Reba is here to watch the store while we visit Rep. Holland," she told Peyton. "You fill her in on what happened earlier. I'll check out these ladies before we leave." Jessie walked to the counter.

\*\*\*\*

Jaxon couldn't believe the records that they confiscated. They waited for the truck to arrive to take the boxes back to headquarters. He wanted to delve into the boxes right away. Tom Maxwell permitted him to take several of the boxes back to the cove and would send a few more agents to begin the process of sorting through them.

"The sheriff you had trouble with has a record, which makes me wonder if he's legit. We are checking on him and a couple of the men that were with him. My sources, at this point, say he's an impersonator. I'm trying to locate the real sheriff in that county," Tom told him.

"Sounds plausible. I wonder who hired him. Hope the real guy is okay. We messed up their operation today. He was not a happy camper." Jaxon grinned when he thought about the angry sheriff's face.

"The excavation equipment will be on both sites in the morning. I wonder what we're looking at."

"We're fairly sure there are two mass gravesites at the school. We have no idea how many bodies might be buried there. Any number at this time would be pure speculation on my part. Still, with as many kids as were reported missing from the reservation, it's easy to assume the worst. Two of Matt's officers are in the nearest town, talking to the locals. I'm sure they'll come up with some supporting rumors or hearsay." Jaxon watched as the last few boxes were taken from the school and placed in the truck.

"Put your phone on speaker." Matt walked toward him. "Hey, Maxwell. This might open a can of worms for the government to deal with."

"Probably. It might be unpleasant, but we owe the tribes at least that much," Tom said.

"Here's another kicker. I picked up one of the books that looked like a ledger and, if I'm reading it right, they sold some of those kids into slavery. If so, the government might have more than some explaining to do." Matt frowned. "I'll make sure Jaxon gets a look at it, and we'll pass the ledger on to you. This is a cold case, but the death of the investigative reporter and our welcoming committee this morning say not so cold to me."

"Get back to me as soon as you have more details, Kincaid," Tom said.

"I will, sir." Jaxon shut off the call.

"I got a strange text from Jess. It sounds like both of the girls had a chaotic day. I told her we should all have dinner at my house to talk. I'll spring for a tray of lasagna from Angelo's, and Jessie is bringing salad and dessert."

"Okay. Works for me since I'm staying at your house." Frank chuckled.

"Me too." Jaxon got into the car with Frank. "See you back in town." They followed the truck out the long dirt road back to the highway.

\*\*\*\*

"Sister, it makes my heart happy to know we are closer now than at any other time in exposing the darkness." Mila landed on one of the bookshelves beside Elida.

"I know. It's exciting to think about it, but you know, dear, Aelfric will not go quietly. He's angry and has been working this area for a long time."

"Elida, love and light always win in the end. The problem is how long it might take to bring about to its conclusion. Will this time be the demise of Aelfric or only subdue him for a season? One can hope this will end his work, but only time will tell." Mila placed her hand on her sister's equally tiny one.

"Either way will be a victory of some sort. Don't you think, Mila?"

"Yes, I do, dear. Now we have a job to do in human form. We must plan our looks. I think in this case we should be male. I know how hard this will be for your vanity, Elida, but we need to work among the men for a few days."

"I don't mind." Elida smiled, spinning around and waving her arms. "I know exactly who I want to be."

Mila laughed when she saw the buff male that tiny Elida had become. Mila chose a mature, dignified man. "I do love my job." She sang a merry song as she changed back and forth, turning in circles.

Chapter 30

After dinner, the group talked over the events of the day. "Have you seen the man in your store before? Do you know who it is?" Jaxon asked Jessie when she finished talking about her day.

"This happened when he came in before. Oh my gosh!" she cried.

"What?" Peyton asked.

"In all the chaos I forgot that I snapped a picture of him on my phone." She pulled up the photo and showed it to Matt first.

"I've never seen him. How about you?" He gave the phone to Jaxon.

"Can't say that I've ever seen him." Jaxon showed Peyton the photo.

"You're not going to believe this. I may be mistaken." Peyton pursed her lips. "What time did he come in the store?"

"He came right after lunch. He said he was on his break. Why?"

"This is too weird," Peyton said.

"Try us." Matt frowned.

Peyton took a closer look at the photo. "He looks like a teacher I met at the school earlier."

"What's the big deal? Teachers come in the store all the time." Jessie leaned forward in her chair.

"You're right, of course. But it's odd to me that he

came to see the newbie teacher and my vandalized room."

"Did he say that?" Jessie pushed her hair out of her eyes.

"Yes. I asked Jeremy to check into a Mr. Sanders who had a relative that was a boarding school principal. He made me mad. I'm sure the ghosts would react to him. I did."

"Why not." Matt shook his head with a silly grin on his face.

"All I know is he is arrogant." Peyton handed the phone back to Jessie. "I wonder." Peyton tapped her fingers against her forehead. "Why would the ghosts react to him that way? He wouldn't have been alive when they were unless, of course, they were murdered recently or he's a ghost too."

"That's way over my head." Jaxon threw up his hands, and Frank laughed.

"Or he looks like his relative. You know, like you and Kathryn." Jessie squeezed her cousin's hand.

"Stranger things have happened, I suppose." Peyton scrunched her face. "He wasn't very nice, at least, not to me. I had the feeling he was there to check up on me for some nefarious reason." Peyton paused. "Hmm, was one of the ghosts Kimama?" She stroked her chin. "I wonder."

"Any idea why?" Jaxon's chin edged up.

"It's possible he's trying to figure out what I know. You know, test the waters." Peyton placed her napkin on the table.

"A possible theory. Is that all, or is there something else we should be aware of?" Jaxon glanced first at Peyton and then at Jessie when he asked the question.

"I read something important in Cara's diary, and I wanted to read it to Peyton, but I had too many other things on my mind when you arrived." She glanced sheepishly at her cousin.

"Why don't you read it to all of us? Is that okay with the rest of you?" Matt asked.

"I'm down with it." Frank nodded.

"If there aren't any objections, you have the stage, sweetheart." Matt smiled at her, tenderly.

Jessie picked up the diary and turned to the bookmarked page.

*As I write this, Brenna hasn't been found, and my heart is broken. I walked my favorite path in the woods, thinking to go see my friend, but my heart wasn't in a visit. I found a place to sit, and there I spent myself in tears. Afterward, I roamed through the woods, keeping the path always in my sight. Ahead of me, a light shone upon a door standing between two large rocks. The green of the woods was all around the door. An unusual sight, but I couldn't help myself. I had to explore. I tried to walk around it, but there seemed to be an invisible barrier. Instead, I turned the knob and was transported through the threshold into a world I had never seen before. It reminded me of home, a place filled with magic, a doorway into another time. Beyond the door, the woods were filled with nymphs and the wee folks rushing about. Here, in these woods and not at home in Ireland. There I met Mila and her sister who would be with me whenever I needed their help to carry on.*

Jessie continued to read for a few more minutes. "Did you see the imagery of the wolf in her words, the idea of a fairy gone bad, and his ability to shift forms? A pooka in Irish folklore and as we now know in Indian legends as well. Elida has appeared as a human. She did to Chad and Sally Mansfield at the inn. I know you saw her, Matt, but may not remember who she was. Do you remember the elderly lady, Holly? That was Elida."

"I know I'll regret asking this, but are Elida and Mila in some way involved in this case now?" Jaxon shook his head.

"Yes." Peyton patted his hand. "It's a bit mind-boggling, I know, but I've met Mila, and Jessie has met Elida. I mentioned this to you before, but I know it's hard to take in. I'm sure they are orchestrating this. The truth needs to come out. As you know, Cara's friend Kimama was the chief's son's wife. They are helping us to see the connections."

"Nothing should surprise me, but hell, it still does." Jaxon rubbed his temple.

"Damn, this fact will never find its way into a police report." Matt folded his arms across his chest.

"This should be old hat to you by now, sweetie." Jessie lifted Matt's chin and looked into his eyes. "You know how to skirt around the odd details and put down the facts as you see them."

"Boy, would I like to find that door," Peyton said as she stood and cleared their plates off the table.

"Me too. We should look." Jessie reached for the basket of garlic bread.

"No, you don't." Matt grabbed her hand.

"Oh, but I do." She shook off his hand. "Who wants dessert?"

Peyton carried the dishes over to the counter and rinsed them while Jessie made coffee and placed the desserts on a plate. "I really would like to see that door. What a moment that must have been for Cara. It must have felt like a haven during the storm."

"You need to read the rest of that part tonight. I only told them a little. I didn't know how much Matt could take. Aelfric is one nasty dude and can also appear as a human."

"Great." She slapped her hand to her forehead. "It's probably good you didn't tell him everything yet." Peyton carried the desserts, and Jessie brought the coffee and cream.

For the rest of the evening, they began the process of going over a few of the files from the boarding school. What surprised Peyton the most was the astonishing number of details in each of the files. It reminded her of the book she found with each of the missing girls in it. It was as if they were helping another generation to understand what had transpired. Did that mean some of the folks involved could see that something wasn't right? Naturally, most folks were there to do their job and cared about the students. Prejudice runs deep, but not all people feel that way. There were and are many kind and caring people. What made Aelfric turn bad? The same question she asked herself with each suspect.

"I'm going to call it a night. I have to be at work early tomorrow to make sure my room is ready." Peyton stood and handed Jaxon the file she was looking at. "Somebody went to a lot of trouble to detail everything about this child. I have a theory on the reason, but I'll take some time to think about it."

"I'll walk you out." Jaxon got up and followed her to the door.

"I'm sorry they found something worth excavating, but after Radar indicated in the area, I was sure that they would."

"We'll know more soon." He held her car door open. "Are you all right after the day you've had?" He studied her face. "I worry about you." He tilted her chin up to kiss her. One kiss wasn't enough. He buried his face in her hair, his breath tickling the tip of her ear. "Do you want me to follow you home? Before you say no, I would love some time alone with you."

She felt his body shudder when she hugged him. "You're always welcome."

"You help me sort through things, and I need to do that now. The conversation tonight unsettled me."

"Get your keys. I'll wait." Peyton got in her car and waited for him to pull behind her.

\*\*\*\*

On her drive to the school the next morning, Peyton couldn't help but think of her conversation with Jaxon the night before. She didn't have any answers to his questions. She never thought that the myths and stories Sadie told her when she was little could be true. Of course, being a girl, she loved all things fairies. Besides the nightlight Sadie gave her, she still remembered dancing around in a pair of fairy wings in a school play. In her childish mind, she believed they were real. Now was a whole different story. She placed it in the same category as seeing ghosts and having premonitions—a surreal complication to her life that she hadn't expected. She would deal with this the same way she did when she found herself sucked through the pages of a book into Kathryn's life in nineteen-eighteen—one step at a time and learning as she went. There didn't seem to be any other recourse for her. If the last several months had taught her anything, it was that there are many unknowns in life. Even before all the strange things began happening, life was fraught with mysteries, unanswered questions, and its own set of problems.

As far as she could see, it was all about doing what was right or not, and the choice was up to her. If this case needed magic to finally do what was right by all the people who had been hurt, then so be it.

"Well, aren't you little Miss Goody Two shoes this morning." She glanced in her rearview mirror and signaled her turn. "It all sounds perfect in your thoughts but not easy to live it in real life. Hang in there. You'll have many chances to prove yourself if the past few months are any indication." She waved at one of the teachers when she pulled into the school lot. Hopefully, her room was ready and waiting in good condition this morning. She wondered if other drivers ever noticed how often she talked to herself.

"How are you this morning, Ms. Reynolds?" Principal Avery held the door open for her. "The custodian's crew worked late, and your room is ready for another morning of learning."

"Thank you. That's good news. I came early in case they needed help this morning."

"Other than your special touches, the room looks like nothing happened. I'm sorry about the kids' artwork that got destroyed. I know you were displaying their projects for the school's open house. Maybe you can have them do more. I know art can be a bit of a chore with your students but well worth the happy results, don't you think?" Mr. Avery smiled with every word and nodded as he did.

"I do, and that's why art is on my lesson plan for

today. I thought we might use crayons instead of finger paints, though. The children don't seem to mind either way. We can add a little glitter to make their projects sparkle, and they'll be brilliant."

When she opened the door into her classroom, she breathed a sigh of relief. It looked awesome. She needed to be sure and thank Mr. Ellis and anyone who had helped. A box of treats from the coffee shop was in order. She jotted the thought down on a sticky note to pick some up on her way home today.

After a few minor tweaks, the room was ready for her students who would be arriving soon. Taking a deep breath, she was ready for her favorite part of the morning. She went to stand in the hall and watch the students enter the school. What odd occurrence was on tap for today if any? A ghost, a wolf, or Mr. Sanders? Perhaps Aelfric the pooka. What form would he take? And that's when she saw them. Her question from a few days ago was answered. The three children she had seen were a shadow from the past. How far in the past? Her mind stopped roaming the minute her first student arrived at the classroom.

****

The excavating had begun. Matt went to the murder site, and Jaxon spent his morning at the boarding school. Jaxon kept in touch with Matt throughout the process. He knew several bodies had been discovered and were being removed. After the forensics team and the coroner were finished, they would be released to any possible relative that could be located for a proper burial.

The same painstaking work was being done by the team at the school. This wasn't a pleasant task but one that would hopefully answer the many questions left unanswered over the years.

"Tom, this is Kincaid. I wanted to give you a heads up. They've already discovered up to a hundred bodies in the first gravesite which is the farthest from the school. Some of those are already en route to the lab. Work has begun on the second site closer to the school. It's the largest of the two. They think there are even more buried there." Jaxon continued to watch the work going on.

"They've brought in extra staff from around the country to help in the lab, but it will still take time. It's amazing what they can discover even after all this time. Bones can talk," Maxwell said.

"I hope these bones do a lot of talking. The tribes want answers, and I understand. The stories they tell may make a difference between natural causes and murder. Most of the kids who died from natural causes were released to their parents at the time of their passing. It does make you wonder why not these kids. There could be legitimate reasons. But my gut tells me something else was going on here." Jaxon leaned his hip against the car. "Harsh punishments meted out over draconian rules seem to be what we're looking at."

"Damned if I know why. But one thing I do understand is that there is rarely a legitimate reason for a mass grave burial," Tom told him. "You have your hands full with this one. Someone got away with murder, and there is a price to be paid. If not in jail time at least in some form of compensation. Monetary or at least answers."

"At the very least, a rewrite of their whitewashed history. I'll keep you posted." Jaxon pushed away from the car.

"Works for me. Before I forget, that was no sheriff yesterday who tried to stop you. He was a hired thug with a long rap sheet. Right now, he's not talking, but my guys are working on him and the others."

"I didn't think the guy was legit," Jaxon told him. "We still have at least one full day of work left, if not more, but we'll talk soon." Jaxon disconnected the call and walked closer to where the first body at the second site was being prepared for transport.

He noticed how each body was placed in a pine coffin versus a body bag due to the fragility of the bones. When ready, the coffins were put into a large truck to move to the lab, a long process repeated many times over the day. Identifying each of the bodies would be tough at best because of the years that had passed. Most close relatives were no longer living. By cross-referencing the records they now had in their possession, they might be able to ID a few, but some might not ever be known. The tribes could bury them according to their traditions, which seemed right to him. No one should be thrown into a mass grave. It was way past time to address the issue.

When the last pine box was loaded into the truck, the site was closed for the day with guards posted. They would be back to work again first thing in the morning. They had only a few good weather days left to finish the job, if the weather forecasts were right.

Jaxon drove back to the cove, wanting to check out more of the files. A team of agents was doing the same back at FBI headquarters. His phone signaled a call.

"Where are you?" Matt asked.

"I'm driving back to town. How did the rest of

your day go?" Jaxon got into the turn lane.

"Productive, but there's still more work to be done tomorrow. Radar did his job again. That dog's accuracy astounds me."

"I hear you. He indicated in the right areas here too. The team recovered a lot of bodies today. We have at least another full day of work to do." Jaxon made the turn onto the highway back toward the cove.

"I'm not sure what we're dealing with or the length of time over which the murders took place. According to the preliminary analysis, a few of the remains were more recent and some from decades past. We'll talk about it later," Matt said.

"How the two sites are tied together will be interesting to discover. I believe they are because Peyton does. Like Frank's dog, Peyton is rarely wrong."

Chapter 31

After her day was finished, Peyton went to work out at the gym. Her cousin taught her she could do her best thinking as she ran. At least today had been a normal one, except for the several times the arrogant Mr. Sanders sauntered by her classroom and peered in the door. The man concerned her. Something about him seemed off to her. His standing at the school seemed impeccable, but that didn't bring her any consolation. Maybe she needed to dig into his character a little more.

Why would the ghosts flip out every time the man walked into Jessie's store? They were trying to tell them something. A man who raised the ire of ghosts and a teacher who raised hers seemed to be one and the same. Sanders had passed her open door at least four times that she noticed, and she had no idea how many times she hadn't noticed.

The regularity of her feet hitting against the track with its rhythmic almost hypnotic tempo seemed almost comforting. Her thoughts progressed with the cadence. In moments like this, she felt completely in tune with her body. The deep breathing, the sweat dripping down her back, and the euphoric feeling that came when she finished the last mile or pushed herself to go one more lap kept her coming back. She smiled at the thought that her cousin had made a runner out of her. Jessie pleaded and used guilt to convince her. But now she was a convert. Walking had been her preferred exercise. She had learned to walk fast and far. Jogging was a natural next step. *One more time* pulsed through her as she pushed herself to go for two.

Once she finished her workout, she got dressed and drove to her cousin's bookstore. Idle Time Books felt almost like her home away from home. She pulled into an open spot in front of the store and grabbed her purse on the way out of the car. The bell rang on the door as she opened it and walked into what seemed to be a quiet, normal day at the bookstore. At least right now it was unlike yesterday when she had arrived.

Waving at Jessie, she walked to the open doors into the coffee shop. "How about a late lunch or snack? I went to the gym after work, and now I'm starving. Can I get you anything?"

"Sure, I haven't had time to eat, and I have no idea when the guys will be back in town. I wouldn't mind sharing a chicken salad sandwich with you. I'm ready for a break. Better yet, surprise me. Molly always has something new to try."

"Sounds good." Peyton went into Joe's and came back several minutes later with lunch and drinks for them. She glanced at her watch. "Wow, no wonder I'm hungry. I didn't realize it was so late."

"Oh, this looks good." Jessie peered inside the container that Peyton placed in front of her. "It tastes even better than it looks." She took a bite of the chicken on her fork.

"Molly said it was her special today. Grilled chicken on a bed of greens. She promised the marinade on the chicken and the strawberry blush vinaigrette makes it extra special."

"She's right as usual. Wait until you taste it. Yum." Jessie licked her lips and took another bite of the salad.

"At least salad makes for a light late-day meal." Peyton took a bite, closing her eyes as she savored the flavors bursting in her mouth.

"Guess who came into the store this morning. It's the first time I've met her."

"I have no idea. Who? You may as well tell because I'll badger you until you do." Peyton's lips turned up at the edge, showing off her dimples.

"Mrs. Sanders. She introduced herself and then told me her husband had warned her not to come here, that something strange happened to him both times he came to buy a book. Martha Sanders laughed and told me that it made her want to come and see for herself. Of course, it was calm. I got the feeling after talking to her that she thinks her husband is a bit of a buffoon."

"She didn't say that, did she? I think you're making it up." Peyton shook her head, trying not to laugh.

"Okay, buffoon is my word. What she said was her husband can be a bit of a pompous bore and she was sorry if he had said anything that might offend me. And then she called him fastidious."

"I would agree with her one hundred percent. There's something more though." Peyton described being creeped out by Mr. Sanders strolling by her class several times. "That man bugs me, but I don't know why."

"We need to think about why that might be. Those warnings are usually for a good reason." Jessie pushed the straw into her cup.

"You're right. I tend to go into a relaxed mode

when I'm at school among my students. That's my happy place." Peyton frowned, puckering her mouth. "At least it was until the last few weeks. Now it feels more like a war zone but with less drama than your store and flying books."

"Such is our lives." Jessie gave her a sheepish smile. "I finished Cara's journal last night." Jessie took a sip of her tea. "The ending is really powerful. I cried several times."

"You cry most times."

"True, but I mean it. Cara's story spoke to me." Tears formed in Jessie's eyes as she talked.

"Tell me about it, and don't leave out any details."

"No," Jessie said softly. "You have to read it yourself. The Cassidys went through a lot, and losing Brenna was devastating for the family. I don't want to ruin it for you. The way she wrote it was powerful. I've already started writing the first part of a series of articles about Cara and Tamara. It's all rough details to be filled in as new evidence emerges."

"I'm glad. I think more than anything that's what this is about. Giving a voice to those who were silenced and telling a story about the hate and blame that cost them their lives." Peyton paused with her fork in mid-air and then took a bite.

"It's sad when you think about it. They were only trying to survive, but mistrust and fear kept them from becoming a part of the country they had migrated to." Jessie dabbed at her eyes with her napkin.

"Only look how those same people who were once blamed for society's ills are accepted contributing members of communities all over the country. We are their descendants."

"Yeah, look at how well we turned out." Jessie snorted and then laughed.

"Okay, we're strange but only in the last year at the most." Peyton shrugged her shoulders. "That doesn't do much to recommend us. But hey, we do fit in with our ancestors, don't we?"

"We sure do. I didn't tell Matt about our visit with Rep. Holland. He would come unglued. I found the good Rep's reaction to Tamara Campbell's name quite revealing." Jessie cleared the place in front of her gathering up her trash.

"I did too. He was hiding something." Peyton helped her cousin pack up what they hadn't eaten. "He knew her all right."

"Yes." Jessie turned her head when the bell above the door rang. "It's time to get back to work."

"And just like that"—Peyton snapped her fingers—"we get busy and move on. I need to get to work myself. See you later." Peyton waved and walked out the door to her car.

Jessie was always good for a laugh and putting things into perspective. Not her—she tended to overthink everything and analyze it to death.

Serious was the word she remembered being used most often to describe her. Mostly, she had been scared. She hid behind the mask of discipline, but her life needed to be balanced with joy and fun too. She still was learning to accept the fact she could enjoy herself and that it was okay. Jessie had brought laughter into her life, and for that, she would always be grateful.

"Lighten up and chill." Her fingers tapped on the steering wheel. Turning up the radio to hear her favorite song, she drove home rocking to the beat.

Once home she went to her computer and checked her emails. The one from Jeremy gave her a piece of information that got her involved in a search online. She found out that many of the young Irish women went to work for the mill when they came to the area. The owner was one of the few people in town who would hire them, which made him a key suspect in the case of the missing girls at that time. Ray Cumberland had amassed his great wealth in lumber and his gristmill. He hired men and women to work in both locations. If she remembered the story correctly, Matt was almost killed when the abandoned gristmill site was rigged to blow up with him in it—a case of revenge from his days in the terrorist division of the FBI. Jessie had told her all about it. No wonder her cousin seemed reluctant to jump headlong into any new cases. It would be easy to burn out. Too many near-death experiences would give anyone second thoughts.

Cumberland was considered by some to be a philanthropist. He had helped to build many of the businesses in town through various loans. He also took over those same businesses when people couldn't pay because of the outlandish terms he had set up. It was a win-win for him, and he rigged the system to always come out on top. From the pictures she found of him, he might be considered intimidating. A large man, seen about town with two bodyguards and smoking a cigar in every picture she saw of him. Crazy, he was the man they had seen in the portal.

One of the archived articles she read said the town was split when it came to his guilt or innocence regarding the missing girls. He was either loved or hated depending on who answered the question. There were two possible connections to their investigations now. She wanted to talk to Jaxon and Matt before she assumed anything or mentioned it to anyone else. Glancing at the clock, she realized she had procrastinated long enough and got to work on a manuscript. A few minutes later she tossed it aside and picked up Cara's journal and got swept away in time. Only the knock at her door a while later brought her back.

****

Mila watched her from the corner. It was almost time to set the next part of the sisters' plan into action. They had talked about what form they would take. Peyton might figure it was her eventually but then again maybe not. It wasn't important. What amazed Mila was that Peyton caught on quickly. She would take the idea planted in her mind and run with it until she found answers. All these new-fangled gadgets helped. Thankfully, Celeste seemed to understand how important it was to keep up with the times. When in human character they were decked out with all the equipment that kept humans connected and up to date. Both she and her sister had to learn the computer, the cell phone, and any other item that Celeste determined would help keep them in character.

Truth be told, Mila preferred waving her wand and misty kisses to cell phones and technology, but she did what was necessary to get the job done. The same rule always applied, no matter what they used. Their subject had to make their own decision. They couldn't force the outcome. That's one reason why she loved working with Peyton. She could plant a simple suggestion, and the girl would take it from there. It made her job super easy. Her sister felt the same way as she did. It should only take a few more days to wrap up this assignment and put a world of hurt on Aelfric. They could impede his dirty work for a while. As Elida loved to say, it's showtime.

**\*\*\*\***

Jaxon was left scratching his head after the two men left Matt's office. "Well, that has to be one of the strangest conversations I've ever had."

"From two of the oddest messengers I've ever seen." Matt shook his head, his pen tapping against the file on his desk.

"They were strange, but something about them resonated. Their message and warning rang true to me." Jaxon scanned over the notes he had written.

"To me too. With their warning in mind, it's time to plan. We might need to include the girls in this. I do question how those two men knew about the Reynolds. I swear the taller of the two reminds me of someone I've seen before. I know I've seen those eyes on some other face at some other time." Matt scrunched his face and added, "Maybe his mother's." Matt frowned. "All I can say, if he knows Jessie, I want to know how he does. Did you see the size of his biceps?"

"Okay, Parker, do I detect a note of jealousy?" Jaxon smiled his lopsided grin. "I know I shouldn't rag on you. I'd be jealous of that guy too. Today reminded me once again that there is real evil in this world. I'll take help from wherever I can get it no matter how unorthodox it is." Jaxon stood. "Speaking of the girls, I'm ready to see my favorite one. I'll catch you at the house later." He walked out of the station with many thoughts rolling through his mind. Having just learned that the crime was still ongoing and might include a few prominent people, he had to spend some time thinking about how it all fit together. Peyton always kept him on his toes; bouncing ideas off her was exactly what he needed right now. Did that old guy mention the word pooka? Jaxon was sure he had heard him say it. Another head-scratcher to think about.

****

Peyton opened the door with tears streaming down her face and a tissue in her hand. "Come in." She stifled the sob rising in her throat.

"Sweetheart, are you okay?" Jaxon walked into the room and pulled her into his arms.

"I'm fine." She wiped the tears rolling down her cheeks.

"You don't seem fine to me. Do you mind explaining?" Jaxon held her tight in the circle of his arms. Her body shuddered against him as she fought for control.

"You'll probably think I'm silly." She pushed back to see the response on his face.

"I doubt it. Give me the benefit of the doubt." He took her hand, closed the open door, and led her to the couch. "I'm all ears."

"I'm crying because of this." She waved the journal in front of his face. "Jessie warned me that the ending was powerful, but everyone knows Jessie cries at the drop of a hat. Let's just say she was right."

"I take it you finished reading the diary." Jaxon sat next to her.

"I finished it all. The Cassidys went through a lot to migrate to this country, and losing Brenna soon afterward devastated them. You'll have to read the passages yourself to see what I mean. Through it all, Cara managed to still believe that good could be found in people and this new country they lived in. Life to her was beautiful, filled with magic, and tinged with deep sadness at times."

"I would rather you read the pages to me. But first, we need to talk." He leaned forward on the couch. "It's been a strange day." He told her about the bodies that were discovered at the boarding school. When he told her about the two men that came to the station, her reaction surprised him. "Matt said maybe he'd seen those eyes on his mother."

She wiped the tears from her eyes. This time not from crying but laughing. "I can hear Parker saying that. OMG, that's too funny. Especially, being jealous."

"What aren't you telling me? The story isn't that funny."

"Truth is, Matt has seen the man before only when she came as a woman." Peyton found Jaxon's facial reaction hysterical and dissolved into laughter again. "Sorry. The inn's resident fairy at Christmas time was a woman named Holly. She must be a man on this visit."

"I guess we should take their warning seriously then." He held his head in his hands.

"What warning?" Peyton stopped laughing long enough to ask.

"At least I understand why their conversation sounded strange. They were talking about some dude named Aelfric who was the cause of all the problems. I remember hearing something about him being kicked out of the position as head of his organization and he'd been causing problems for hundreds of years. I admit that threw me for a loop, and I heard little after that except for the fact the time to deal with him had come. We were told to take care of you girls, and they left. The one takeaway I did catch was that this may have started many years ago, but someone is still operating today. There is a connection." Jaxon paused. "If that wasn't enough, I'm sure I heard the word pooka too."

"I can see how the conversation might have sounded strange." She patted his hand. "I've found a few connections myself. I already told you about Mr. Sanders' great-great-great-grandfather, but there is also Ray Cumberland." She showed Jaxon the photos she had found of him. She relayed what details she had discovered about him so far. "He's the man we saw in the portal."

"He sounds like a prince of a guy. A bully who led a privileged life," he said. "He's going on my list. Does he have any descendants living in the area now?"

"I don't know yet, but I'm looking into it. If he does, then we might have another possible link to connect. It's all about giving a voice to those who were cut off."

"That's what those men told us." He frowned and glanced at her when she started to correct him. "For now, we'll call them men. I can't wrap my head around pixies, elves, or leprechauns. I'm still working through ghosts."

"Fair enough. I won't press you on the subject. But, just so you know, Aelfric is a fairy gone bad, who may be a pooka taking the form of a wolf." She couldn't stop the chuckle that slipped from her mouth. "Sorry, I know all this is a bit on the unusual side for you."

"You think. I don't know how you can say any of

this with a straight face." He rubbed his temples.

"If you only knew how often I've questioned my sanity, you'd understand how I've struggled. I'm learning to live with the gift or whatever you want to call it until it goes away. I can see it would be easy to burn out over time. Maybe that's why there are two of us in the same family. Who knows, possibly three."

"Okay, I get it. But how do we approach this case? And please don't tell me to think outside of the box. I've been doing that too much lately. I like my box." He gave her a reticent smile and reached for her hand.

She handed him the journal. "Read Cara's words, and you'll understand why it's important we do this. It doesn't matter who leads us to the truth if we get there. I want to solve the crime for Brenna, for Cara, and for the families who suffered and are still suffering."

"We'll read this together later." He scooted closer and slipped his arm around her. "I have other things on my mind at the moment." He bent his head closer until his lips were mere inches from hers. Slowly and deliberately, he inched his head closer until his mouth touched her lips ever so softly. Taunting and teasing her, he explored her mouth from corner to corner until she held his face still and kissed him.

Chapter 32

Later Jaxon kissed her one more time when they stood by the door. "I'll call you. I think it might be easier to read to me if we're not sitting by each other." He toyed with the hair lying against her cheek. "You, my sweet lady, are a beautiful distraction. I can't seem to get enough of you."

"Nice to know." She fluttered her lashes playfully. "I do my best."

He lingered, acting like he wanted to say something more. His hands moved slowly up and down her arms. But the mood was abruptly broken when he turned away and opened the door. "I'll call," he said on his way out the door.

What was that all about? Peyton shrugged. Maybe it was all in her head, but she could swear he was about to tell her the words she longed to hear. She locked the door, leaning against it. He could kiss her senseless in one moment and walk out the door in the next. Did she have no impact on him? She got a glass of water, turned off the lights, and grabbed the journal on her way into the bedroom.

For the next hour, she waited, doubting if she knew how he felt at all. She heard a strange scratching sound outside her window, followed by the howling of the wind. Telling herself there was nothing to worry about, she pulled the covers up under her chin. Suddenly, the room was illuminated through the small openings in the curtain when the motion detector at the side of the cottage came on. She threw off the covers, carefully peeking out the window in time to see a shadowy figure slink around to the front of the cottage. One of the changes that Jaxon and Matt had insisted on when the cottages were remodeled was the motion detectors on the perimeter. The way the houses were situated on the property away from the inn and at the edge of the wooded area, they thought it was important to add them, along with an alarm system, which she was still reminding herself to set. Darn, she had forgotten again. A small price to pay for freedom and to stay in their cottages without Jaxon feeling the need to protect her. She tapped the numbers on the key pad, and the light told her it was activated. She had no idea what she would do if the stupid thing ever went off while she was sleeping. Hopefully, this wouldn't be the night. The light at the front was on too. The knock at the back door scared her until she heard Jessie's voice.

"Peyton, open the door."

"Just a minute. I set the alarm." Her fingers fumbled trying to deactivate the alarm. "Darn, Peyton, get a grip." She opened the door as soon as she could.

"Matt brought me home when he saw your motion detector go on. He's out there now checking it out. He saw something and took out his gun and pursued whoever it was. I hate times like this. I worry about him." Jessie plopped down on the sofa to wait.

"A good reminder about how they might feel about us when they're worried. I guess I shouldn't complain about setting the alarm." Peyton sat down beside Jessie. "I saw the lights come on and remembered I had forgotten to set the stupid thing."

Matt opened the door and walked in. "I got to the front in time to see a person run into the woods. The lights coming on were a deterrent. In the meantime, you girls need to be alert. This case is breaking opening, and you two are in danger. Keep your eyes open."

"Thanks for checking things out," Peyton told him and saw him nod.

"Don't forget to set the alarm." He turned to Jessie. "You too, sweetheart." He pointed at Jessie.

"Believe me, I won't." Peyton closed the door behind them. Her senses heightened, she reactivated the alarm. Who was outside her cottage? She couldn't see falling asleep anytime soon. What she needed right now was her handsome distraction.

****

Jaxon couldn't believe he had almost told her. He had to hightail it out of there before he messed up his whole plan. He had thought long and hard about his feelings for her, and he wanted to tell her at the right moment, not in the middle of a murder case. He should have stayed longer after what Matt told him when he called. Jaxon knew she was fine, but it didn't help. Would the guy come back? Damn, he hated her being there alone. Stretching out on the bed, he picked up the phone and called her.

"Matt told me about your company. Are you all right?" he asked.

"I'm fine. The motion lights scared him off. It's a bit daunting to think about someone prowling around outside my house. It could have been anyone and not somebody trying to scare me." She crossed her fingers as she uttered the nonsense.

"Do you believe that?" he asked.

"Not really. I'm trying to put a good spin on it. Let's just say I want to believe it." She saw her fairy nightlight in the bathroom, a comforting sight at the moment. She picked up the journal and placed it on her lap. "Can I ask you something?"

"Ask away," he said.

"Did I upset you earlier? Is that why you left abruptly?" She wished she could see his face as he answered.

"No, no, it was nothing like that." She heard him take a deep breath. "The more I'm with you, Peyton, the harder I find it to walk away. Tonight, seemed impossible. I wanted to stay, believe me. But I find it hard to concentrate on the case when I'm with you. And at the same time, I don't want the case to come between us with all its stress. Sometimes I want to be with you, and you alone."

"I get that. But we have to do the best we can with what we get. I thought we had a special thing going tonight."

"We sure did. I will explain more later, but not tonight. I promise it will be worth the wait."

"Do you remember when we read about when Cara found the door in the middle of the woods and what she found beyond the door?"

"Yes, why?"

"It plays a big part as we get to the end of her story. Keep it in mind. Remember she described it as a door into another world." Peyton opened the book and began to read. She started with Cara's summary of Ireland, and her first love as they traveled on the ship. Then she read to the last few pages where she described her life and friends.

"Now comes the hard part for me because I can relate to what she experienced. If I get emotional, you'll know why." Peyton wiped her tears.

*I am running out of pages in my book. I may start another journal at some point. I've thought in vain about how to finish this tragic year in our lives. My heart is full and yet sad at the same time. I find that words fall short of explaining all that is going on within me. How do you describe an endless hole in your life that seems to leave you limping through each day? My dilemma.*

*Alanna, my amazing nana, slipped from the mortal bonds of earth this past week, and my heart is broken. Now she will be forever with my dear Brenna. It happened so quickly my mother didn't get to tell her goodbye. Mama is an empty shell, lifeless, and broken in spirit. Gone is the twinkle from her faded green eyes. Losing both her mama and her baby girl within months of each other has left her hollow. My da says little to us, but I know he blames himself for bringing us to this country.*

*The tears threaten to spill from my eyes each time I think of the last time I was with Nana. Alanna walked with me into the woods and to the place where I first saw the door. As we sat on an old log side by side, she took my hand in hers. For a moment I could breathe without the sick feeling that accompanied every day since Brenna was lost to us. The silence of the woods swirled around us, and the rising mist was comforting in some odd way.*

*Alanna's soft voice broke the silence that hung between us as her loving arms wrapped me in their safety. "Creena, my heart, be strong. Death is like passing through this door to the unseen world beyond. You've had glimpses, my dear girl, and you know what I tell you is true. Brenna may be out of sight, but she is never far from you."*

*At the time I couldn't understand why she would talk about death. Looking back, I understand now, she knew her time was near.*

*"A traveler doesn't die, but they keep traveling on. From one place to another and one world to the next." She seemed to grow breathless as we talked.*

*"Look, Cara." Nana pointed to the door which began to slowly open.*

*On the other side, I saw a young woman waving at me, though I couldn't see her face clearly to know who she was. With a radiant smile, she pulsated with light much like the fairy did when I first saw her. I found myself desirous to run toward her but felt Alanna's hand reach out to restrain me.*

*"Is it Brenna?" I asked my grandmother. "I want to get closer to see her face."*

*"It is not your time, my dear girl. You can only glimpse what is beyond this door, but you cannot go there. Not yet. It must be enough, for now, to know that Brenna is alive and well."*

*"Does she live among the fairies then?" I asked. I remembered glimpsing their world beyond that same door.*

*"She lives—that is all you need to know. Your sister is out of sight but not lost to you." Alanna wiped the tears falling from her eyes. "Remember this door when your heart is sad. Come to this place when you need answers or when you feel lonely. Come to the door*

*when I am gone or when you need strength to carry on. I'll meet with you here."*

*In her own way, Alanna was preparing me to face my life without her near me to lean on. Telling me how to find peace with the gift that had been passed to me from her and to live a normal life in the midst of the magical and often strange world in which I found myself.*

*I miss them both. I ache with wanting to be near them one more time. The grief that I feel is my reminder that love was present with us. Though Alanna and Brenna are no longer here, the love we shared still exists, only in a different form. I can feel them close when I need them most.*

Peyton's voice trembled as she read the last few lines. "I wonder if Cara ever wrote another journal. I have so many questions."

"Wow, that was a unique perspective on death. It sounds to me like the door in the woods was a portal."

"I thought the same thing. Jaxon, there's hope for you yet to think outside the box."

"You're rubbing off on me." He chuckled. "Unlike you, I may speak about portals, but I still find it hard to believe one is possible. But you, my dear, have been there and done that and come back to tell the story. I find it fascinating at the very least."

"Alanna is the Irish version of Kathryn and Sadie. I can relate to her as a traveler."

"You're Irish too," he mentioned.

"More like I'm a part Irish, and no one knows how much. Irish with a little bit of this and that mixed in. But I've seen the fairies, and leprechauns, and ghosts. I've traveled through time and to Ireland in a dream as real as being there. Who knows what that means. Maybe the worlds were real or only a glimpse behind the door into the unseen world. No matter how I view the experiences, I think it's cool. I've learned about my family at the same time we solved a case."

"Speaking of cases, what does your instinct tell you about this one?" Jaxon asked.

"I'm beginning to connect the dots. I hope I'll know more in the next couple of days. Jeremy is helping. Ray Cumberland is the connection in the past, but how that translates to the present is where Jeremy's research will help. At least, I hope it will."

"How about Sanders?"

"Sanders. Hmm, he's another character." She proceeded to tell him about her morning and Sanders' wife's visit to Jessie's store.

"I don't like the idea of him coming by your room. It sounds like he's trying to intimidate you."

"I would imagine," she replied.

"Dinner tomorrow night, sweetheart?" he asked.

"I'd love to. Good night, Kincaid." She loved to throw in the name she called him in Phoenix from time to time. "Don't stay up too late. You need your rest."

"I think you do that on purpose."

"Of course, I do." She placed the journal on the nightstand. "It brings back fond memories. You're Jaxon, but you'll always be first in my memories as Detective Kincaid the grim-faced, hunky cop. Good night." She ended the call before he could respond. Her absolute favorite image was Jaxon the cowboy who walked the streets of Tombstone with her. She sighed and let her imagination take her back.

\*\*\*\*

"Sister, that's the most fun I've had in ages. But I say the same thing every time we interact as humans." Mila flittered about the trees. "Did you see their faces?"

"I did. Do you think Matt recognized something about me? He stared at me as if he did." Elida tapped her small fingers against her forehead as she stopped in midair. "For a moment I thought he might call me Holly even though I don't look at all like her."

"It's your eyes, sister. The twinkle is a dead giveaway if someone has seen you before. You may need a pair of these glasses too." Mila waved the eyeglasses in front of Elida's face. "I'm glad we gave them our warning about Aelfric. We also did a good job of talking nonsense. It'll make them use their logical brain, which is important to most human men."

"I agree, Mila. We must not scare them because we need them more than ever. Our enemy is getting strong again, and the aura around him is darker," Elida said as she rested on the tree branch.

"I've felt it too. Our lights combined can push him into the shadows, but he can still cause harm in the lives of too many. Jaxon and Matt can expose Aelfric's deeds through facts. It's a joy to watch them work through the clues that we give to them. In the end, they will be and must be the heroes. We've done our best work when we let them do theirs." Mila lighted beside Elida.

"I know you're right," Elida said. "I feel impatient and want to jump in and fix it."

"We've waited this long. What's a few more days?" Mila began to glow with her idea bursting inside of her. "I need to go. I think a dream is in order for a certain young man." Mila flew off into the night with Elida close behind.

Chapter 33

Jaxon went over Cara's words in his mind. Alanna was telling her something important at that moment. There was an important clue in her words. Did Peyton see it? She hadn't mentioned anything to him. He continued to go over what the facts were telling him. He didn't see his nightly visitor nor the golden sparkles floating around his head. Stretching out on the bed, he plumped the pillows behind his head. Damn, he was tired. He glanced one last time at the clock, shut off the light, and closed his eyes. The feather-light fingers tapping against his forehead went unnoticed.

He sat alone on a log in the woods in front of a door that seemed to be standing upright by itself. The woods were eerily quiet. He reached for his gun only to find it wasn't there. Not a good sign, and his training taught him to be on guard. Tension filled him from his head down to his toes. His eyes searched the woods, but the density of the trees and the mist rolling in made it next to impossible to see farther than a few feet in any direction. He waited, his hands fisted at his sides, and strained to hear any sound in the silence. Slowly the door opened.

The face that stared back at him was fierce. The beast's body was massive, much larger than any wolf Jaxon had ever seen. Baring his teeth, the creature snarled and growled at him, a sound that reverberated off the trees and echoed from deep within his large form. The black wolf's fangs were covered with blood. And when he locked his eyes on him, Jaxon knew fear. This was no ordinary wolf but an alpha male.

The wolf ran toward the open door only to be stopped in his track by some unseen force. Repeatedly the wolf tried but failed to get through until he fell weary from his effort. As quickly as the door opened it closed. The woods were filled with cheers and small lights flickering everywhere he looked. One voice rang out above all the others. "The wolf has been defeated, and the forest is safe."

Jaxon awakened with a start with his sheet twisted around his legs. "What the hell," he whispered into the darkness. Peyton and Jessie had the crazy dreams, not him. He was the logical one. What did it mean if anything?

Those strange men today messed with his thinking. They spoke gibberish as they talked about Aelfric and heavens only knows what else. He found himself zoning out more than once during their visit at the station. Maybe he should have listened. At least he had picked up on a slight element of truth in what they said, especially the warning to watch over the girls. That came through loud and clear. But still he rarely ever dreamed or remembered them if he did. Two times seemed way over the top to be coincidental. Jaxon couldn't shake the feeling there was a truth to be found in what he saw. The weird thing is he could remember every detail.

He rolled over, but sleep was the last thing he had on his mind. Jaxon went over every detail, remembering the specifics that Peyton had shared earlier and that he had written down from his previous dream. Was this the wolf she had seen in the halls of the school? His phone rang, and he had no idea with the hello he heard on the other end his life was about to change in a major way.

"Is this Jaxon Kincaid?" A man's voice came across the line.

"Yes. Who is asking?"

"My name is Joseph Kingston from the Kingston and Logan Law Firm. I'm the personal lawyer for the Dawson family. As you know EJ Dawson was the only child of Elliot and Ms. Dawson. When his son died, my client, Mr. Dawson, came to the office to change his will. You, Mr. Kincaid, were added. Elliot felt you had tried hard to save his son, and in the end, you did in some way. To get to the point of why I've called you. My client passed away suddenly this past week. His wife and some siblings were left most of the estate."

"Of course. What does this have to do with me?"

"I'm getting to that. I guess the best way to tell you is right out front. Elliot Dawson left you five million dollars. He was a very wealthy man you know. You'll have to come to Phoenix to sign the paperwork, or we can wire it to your lawyer. You, Mr. Kincaid, are a very rich man." The line was silent. "Are you still there, Mr. Kincaid?"

"I am. Are you sure about this? I don't have a lawyer." Jaxon raked his hand through his hair.

"I'm sure. But if you don't mind me suggesting, it would be wise for you to hire a good attorney and a financial consultant. I will email you my address and phone number where you can contact me for the eventual transfer of your money."

"I'm sorry, but I'm stunned. I will contact you as soon as I as hire an attorney and have time for this to sink in. I'm in the middle of an investigation right now, and it might be hard for me to get away."

"That's one of the things that Mr. Dawson admired most about you. Although he often laughed that you were a damn nuisance when it came to his son."

"Please, let his wife know how sorry I am for the loss of her husband. I count him as a good friend. Has his service already taken place?"

"No. Would you like the information? I can send it to you."

"Yes, I would like to come if I can work it out."

"I know this may be a bit of a shock to you. I'll give you a few days to digest it all, and I'll get back to you."

"Thank you." Jaxon stared at the phone when Kingston hung up. He needed to get to work. Shocked didn't begin to describe what he was feeling. He had no idea where to begin other than to try solving the current investigation. He pictured Dawson's beautiful home on Camelback Mountain, the gorgeous views over the city, and the last time he had seen his friend when he was able to give him a piece of good news after losing his son. In the end, EJ had saved a lot of lives by his actions and put away some crooks for a long time. Good grief, he was a millionaire. He didn't want it to change him. He needed to talk to Matt. He and his brothers had inherited money from their grandfather, and he had invested wisely. Parker was sitting pretty, but no one knew how well off he was. Jaxon had some thinking to do.

\*\*\*\*

Peyton had a busy day ahead of her. She arrived at the school ready to get to work. The parents' night was coming up, and she wanted her classroom in tip-top shape decorated with her special kids' work. Who could tell their progress better than them in their creations? They were an inspiration to her every day. A good reminder of how life should be lived. They found great joy in each small task they accomplished. She saw each one of them as little lights shining in their small worlds. Tiny lights shining side by side could dispel darkness.

"Peyton, where is your mind headed this morning? Focus." Honestly, she could get way too philosophical for her own good. She picked up her pace when she saw Sanders headed down the hall. She ducked into the office because she didn't want to deal with him today. His presence was like a damp blanket, and she didn't want him to rain on her parade.

The morning had a great beginning but slowly went down from there. Peyton was in the middle of reading a story when someone pulled the fire alarm. All the kids had to be evacuated. Thankfully, between her and the aides, they were able to get all the children in their coats and out of the building, including those in wheelchairs. They had to remain outside until the fire department gave the all-clear after checking the building. Then came the process of getting the children back into the classroom and getting their coats off again.

One of the kids dropped her favorite stuffed animal which went everywhere with her. She cried, and Peyton ran back outside to look for her toy. She located the small soft duck on the ground, and when she bent to pick it up, something flew by her head, just missing her.

She knew what it was—the sound of the pop had alerted her that someone was shooting at her. Principal Avery must have heard it too because he stood at the door waving at her.

"Hurry, Ms. Reynolds." He held a phone in his hand. "Stay down."

She scurried along the ground until she got to the door and rushed through it. "Ouch," she cried out. She knew what the sensation meant. This wasn't the first time a bullet hit her.

"Stay down," Avery yelled again.

She heard him tell the police that she had been shot. Peyton touched the spot where she had felt the sting. Sticky red blood clung to her fingers when she looked down at her hand. "I don't think it's bad."

"Let me have a look." Avery pulled up her pant leg and checked the wound. "Your pants have a hole in them. I think the bullet might have grazed you. I don't see an entry or exit wound. Still, it looks like you'll need stitches, but I'm not a doctor." He smiled at her. "The police are on their way. When I think about the kids out there, this could have been much worse."

Kip and Gary raced into the school, followed by several others. "I should have known you'd be involved somehow." Kip bent down to look at her leg. "The paramedics should be in soon. They were unloading their equipment when we walked in."

"I'm fine," she told Kip.

"It doesn't appear that way. Trouble seems to find you, doesn't it." He ruffled her hair. "Soon as they have you patched up, I want to talk to you."

"All right. I'm not going anywhere."

"Let's have a look," the paramedic told her as he

bent down. He pressed around the wound and began to clean it. "You're lucky, but I still want a doc to look at this. You're going need some stitches."

"I can't leave now. I have my class to finish, and I have to get my car." Peyton tried to stand.

"Don't worry about your class, Ms. Reynolds. It's taken care of. I would feel better if you were checked out," Mr. Avery said.

"I'll make sure I get you back to your car. I need to ask you a few questions." Kip turned when the door opened behind him.

"Mr. Sanders, where have you been?" The principal gave him an odd look when he walked in the door.

"I was checking the grounds." He turned his face away, checking out the chaos around him.

"Didn't you hear the gunshots?" Avery asked him.

"No, can't say that I did. I need to get to class." He started to walk away.

"I'd like to ask you some questions," Kip told him.

Peyton would have loved to stay and hear what Sanders had to say, but no, Kip patted her on the head and told the paramedic she was all his. Her leg hurt about as much as her pride did. Why couldn't she see this one coming? Ghosts she could see but not someone with a gun. She had to face the fact that she was the target. Not one shot rang out when all the kids and teachers were out there, but when she was alone, it was a different story. She hated to think what would have happened if she hadn't bent down when she did.

\*\*\*\*

Jaxon answered his phone call from Matt. "I needed to tell you there was a shooting at the school.

Kip and Gary are there now."

"How is she?" Jaxon interrupted Matt to ask.

"What makes you think Peyton was shot?"

"Come on, you and I both know they are walking targets. How is she?" he asked again.

"She'll be fine. But she definitely was the target." Matt explained the scenario to Jaxon. "The last I heard she got a couple of stitches and Kip was taking her back to her car after questioning her. It seems there is one character at the school that Kip and Gary want to run a check on. His story doesn't add up. They'll test him for gunshot residue while they're at it."

"Let me guess. A Mr. Sanders."

"You got it," Matt replied. "Are you about finished at the site?"

"We're wrapping up now. They're removing the last few bodies. At least these kids can be properly buried among their ancestors. It's a damn shame what happened here. Something tells me this scene could be multiplied many times over across the country."

"You're probably right. We are almost done over here too. There were more bodies than we thought. Radar found a quite few more. At this point, we have our work cut out for us."

"I hope you don't mind me changing the subject. I had a phone call this morning that came as a total surprise. I need some advice." Jaxon gave Matt the details about his call with Kingston.

Matt whistled. "That's a lot of money. Kingston gave you sound advice. You'll need both a good attorney and a financial adviser. I can help you there. I know both. But hey, man, that's good news."

"I'm not complaining. I never envisioned myself as

a millionaire. I'd like to keep this between us for now. I'll tell Peyton when I think the time is right."

"I hear you. Jessie and I are beginning to talk about finances now, and we're engaged. It's up to you if and when you tell anybody. It may take some getting used to. But if you're smart, you'll be set for life."

"I agree, and there is a lot of good I can do with the cash. But I don't want all the money to change me." Jaxon leaned against the building as he talked.

"It doesn't have to. I didn't inherit as much as you have, but I've made a hefty profit on what I did. You can make your money work for you with the right advice. We'll talk more about this later."

"Sounds good." The next call Jaxon made was to Peyton.

"I figured you'd be calling me at some point. I'm fine," she said the minute she answered.

"Matt just told me. I want to hear your side." Jaxon frowned as she told him the details of what happened. "You were the target."

"I know, and I'm not happy about being anyone's target. I hate to think about what would have happened if I hadn't bent down at that precise moment."

"Try not to." His fist clenched at his side. "Are you still feeling up to going out to dinner?"

"Of course. I'm taking an over-the-counter pain med for the discomfort. It's not bad."

"Go home and rest. I'll pick you up around five thirty." Jaxon relaxed his stance. She was doing all right—that's what mattered. "You might want to have your crutches or a cane for support."

"That's what the doctor said. I will rest after I stop by to see my cousin. I have to tell her in person. I would never hear the end of it if someone else tells her and she doesn't hear it from me. I think Sadie is working at the store today. I'll be able to tell them both." She chuckled. "Besides, I could use their sympathy; I've had a rough morning."

"Do what you want." He put on his sunglasses. The bright sunlight hurt his eyes. "But be sure to rest at some point."

"Before I forget, how's it going there?" she asked.

"We're almost finished at the boarding school. It's a sad deal, Peyton. All these kids. I can't help but wonder how much they suffered at the hands of people who were supposed to be caring for them." He stared off into the distance. "What's worse is it makes me wonder how many other sites there are like this across the nation. I'm angry."

"I would be too. There are probably more sites than we can imagine. The Cassidys lived decades ago, but they lost a child and knew someone whose child went to the boarding school and never came home. I guess problems haven't changed much over the years, which is sad. I'm at the store. See you later."

Hearing her voice reassured him that she was all right. The fact that she was unmistakably the target was disturbing. They had no suspect, too many bodies, and two crime scenes that left them scratching their heads. How this investigation closes would be anyone's guess. They could use a bit of luck on this one. Maybe magic. He smiled and went to work.

****

"You heard him, sister, they need our continued help." Elida buzzed around Jaxon's head as he stood there.

267

"We are right on schedule. Your nifty moves earlier, Elida, kept our dear girl from catastrophe." Mila smiled at her sister. "We'll do our best. I have a few plans up my sleeve. The Intermediary Manual gave me some helpful suggestions."

They spent the next few hours going over the ways they could help their subjects. Some ideas were embraced, and others tossed aside. They ended their session together with plans to put into action. Elida would work hers with Jessie and Matt, and Mila would work with Jaxon and Peyton. They went their separate ways with a sense of purpose.

****

Peyton arrived home in the early afternoon after spending time with Jessie and her grandmother. They had pampered her, babied her, and fed her lunch—exactly what she had hoped for. Any time she spent with Sadie was always good. When Peyton reminded her grandmother about the nightlight and how much it meant to her, Sadie just smiled. A secret, knowing smile that made her wonder what Sadie was thinking at that moment.

"I can still remember my first trip to Ireland. I have lots of memories and pictures. I need to show them to you girls someday." She reached for both of their hands. "You know, girls, we must go to Ireland together and take Madison too. I still remember the cute store where I bought that sweet little light. The shopkeeper told me a wonderful story about the fairy who lights the night to scatter the bad dreams for children. I knew it was meant for you, Peyton. Their stories and legends have seen the Irish people through many hard times in their history. That sweet fairy will see you through yours too." She squeezed her hand.

Sadie talked like she thought the stories were real. Of course, she did. There was much about her grandmother that she didn't know. It was time to learn all she could. Kathryn and Sadie were a big part of the reason why she and Jessie were who they were. Jessie had learned a lot about Sadie when she spent time in the sixties. That was something special that they could share. Peyton shared the knowledge of Kathryn with Sadie, but they had more to learn. Sadie had learned to live with her gift graciously, and they could too.

Peyton limped toward her cottage when instead she found herself headed toward the inn. A visit to the attic was now on her agenda. There was something there she needed to find.

She hobbled up the back steps and opened the door. "Hi, Katie. I hope you don't mind if I snoop around a little more."

"Be my guest. Shouldn't you be off your feet after the morning you've had?" Katie glanced at her with concern. "The tear in those pants and the blood should serve as your reminder."

"I'll only be a few minutes at the most. Besides, Jessie and Grams spoiled me before I came home. I should be good for a while."

"Be careful on the stairs. Jaxon would have my head if anything happened to you."

"Not to worry. I'm in search of something, and then I'll be on my way," Peyton told her.

"Does that mean you know what you're searching for?" Katie asked.

"I have no idea. I'm sure I'll know it when I see it." Peyton removed her coat.

"I'm giving you thirty minutes and not a minute more. You need to be resting, and I'll tie you to a chair to make sure you do it." Katie stopped chopping onions and put down the knife. "I'm serious. Jessie called right before you got here and told me they sent you home to rest." Katie walked closer to her, shaking her finger at her face. "Thirty minutes and not a minute more. You hear me?"

"Okay. I hear you." She smiled at Katie's wagging finger. Peyton was a couple of heads taller than Katie, but dynamite comes in small packages. She wouldn't push her. "Thirty minutes it is. I promise." She crossed her heart.

"You better get moving because the clock is ticking." Katie planted her hands on her hips.

Peyton took Katie at her word and limped toward the stairs. She needed another pain med to keep the pain under control. Annoyed, she wobbled up the stairs to the attic, holding onto the banister. She glanced at her watch. "You have twenty-eight minutes to find what you're looking for." She opened the door to the attic and walked in.

To her, the attic seemed like a magical place. Every time she came into the space, she could sense the charged atmosphere. From the zing when she opened the door to the books that could fly off the shelves, answers could be found between these walls. And she wanted to discover all that she could. Glancing from one corner to the next, she searched to find some sign or clue that could give a fresh perspective to an already strange investigation. Why Cara's journal? Why Tamara Campbell, and why the boarding school? There were lots of whys but not many answers. Still, she had an inkling that each one somehow built on the other, and somewhere in this attic was another piece to the puzzle.

Twenty-four minutes left. Where to start? Her sight landed on a child's rocking horse with a stuffed bear sitting on it. There was something special about the face of the bear that called to her. "Who did you belong to, you loveable teddy?" She squeezed his softness against her chest, but there was something hard in the bear's back. Taking a closer look at the bear, she noticed a tear in his back that was laced closed. She untied the laces and carefully opened the bear in a way not to tear him any more.

"What do you have hidden in you?" She stuck her hand in and pulled out another small diary. "Someone was clever to hide this inside of you, dear Mr. Bear. Are you a mister? You look like one to me. You must've been special to someone to be trusted with their deepest secrets."

She sat on a trunk near the rocking horse. Her hand trembled as she opened the journal. The minute she saw the writing, she knew who the journal belonged to. Cara had added to her story, and Peyton couldn't wait to read the pages. She couldn't stop herself and began to read. When she glanced at her watch again, she was down to ten minutes. Putting the bear back on the horse, she went over to the bookshelf. One book stood out to her. Literally, it jumped from the shelf into her hand. She had to take it with her too.

"Peyton, your time is up, and you need to go home. Don't make me come up there."

"I'm coming." She hobbled to the door, her leg stiffer than when she arrived. Closing the door behind her, she worked her way slowly down the first set of stairs to the landing where Katie was waiting.

"Did you find what you were looking for?" Katie asked.

"I did. I'm ready to go home, and don't worry—I'll put my leg up and rest," she promised and lifted her pinky in the air.

"I should hope so." Katie handed her a cane. "Use this until you get home and get your crutches. I don't want you to fall and sue me." She laughed. "Jessie and you are both so stubborn when it comes to being strong and independent. I would be lying in my bed milking it for everything I can get."

"I'm not much different than you." Peyton smiled at Katie. She wasn't sure if she smiled at what Katie said or the fact that she made it down the stairs without falling on her face.

Happy to be in her cottage after limping down the path, she elevated her leg, took a pain med, and began to read a book of the early days of Blue Cove. Her trip to the attic was worth every twinge of pain in her leg.

Chapter 34

Once Jaxon finished the day by talking to Matt and Maxwell, he went home to shower. Somebody would have to answer for what went on at that boarding school. Too many children suffered over who knew how many years. They found over two hundred bodies between the two gravesites. In the record books he read through, he had counted at least three hundred children sold over a period of several years. It was a damn shame what happened to the kids. How many tribes were impacted, and would they ever be able to figure out what tribe to which the children belonged? DNA might make it possible.

By the time he made it to Peyton's house, he was coming to terms with a case that continued to surprise him and with his new status as a multi-millionaire. What a day this had been.

He walked in after he knocked to find Peyton looking like an angel sitting on the sofa, her leg up, and a book in her hand. "You should have locked the door."

"I know, but then I would have had to get up if you knocked." She patted the space beside her. "Truthfully, I was so happy to be home and off my leg that I forgot to lock the door. I'm sorry."

He placed her feet in his lap. "I would ask how your day went, but I already know it could have been better."

"The day turned out to be great despite this inconvenience." She pointed out her leg. "Grams and Jessie pampered me, and then I found this in the attic." She waved the diary at him. "I couldn't ask for more. I've already learned a lot about the cove in the early days. The main bonus is this." She showed him the other journal and told him how she came to have both of the books in her possession.

"Do you feel like going out?" Jaxon took off her shoe and rubbed her foot.

"Oh my, that's lovely. Yes. I may hobble a bit, but I want to spend time with you. It frustrates me that I got hit at all. Thankfully, I was the target because the shooter could have wreaked havoc with all the kids and teachers standing outside."

"Why was everyone outside? It's a little cold for a fire drill." He lifted her feet off his lap and stood.

"It wasn't a drill. Someone pulled the fire alarm. Everyone must exit the building. It's hard enough moving my kids when you know it's a drill. I have to arrange for help and get them in their coats. This came out of the blue. We managed to get everyone out, but then we had to remain outside until the fire department checked the entire school."

"What were you doing outside alone?" he asked.

"One of the girls dropped her favorite stuffed animal. She keeps it with her day and night. I had to run back out to find the little critter. Who knew someone was watching and waiting. Usually, I would know or at least have an idea. Not today. One of the many things I find strange. When I came home, I knew I needed to go to the attic. It makes me wonder." Her finger tapped on her forehead.

"What sounds good for dinner?" Jaxon asked, changing the subject.

"Somewhere quiet, with food. I want to hear all about your day." She glanced at him and placed the diary on the table.

"I had an interesting day." He watched her swing her legs off the couch and stand. He was ready to catch her so she wouldn't fall. "Be careful."

"I'm good. Thankfully, I still have my trusty crutches from Arizona." She pointed at them. "The doctor said there were no bullet fragments or major muscle or nerve damage. I knew the minute I felt the sharp pain that I got hit. I got six stitches to repair the tear. He said it was a small-caliber weapon, which saved me from greater injury. It makes me wonder if it was another warning rather than a shot to maim." She leaned on the crutches he handed to her.

"I'm not sure. I do know if it would have hit you in the head or a vital organ, tonight would be different." He helped her put on her coat. "They found more bodies where Tamara was murdered. This investigation is growing by the day."

"It seems to go that way." She wrapped her scarf around her neck and put on her gloves.

"Heck, I even had a dream last night. What's up with that?" He tucked her scarf into her coat.

"Well, that piqued my interest. I can't wait to hear the details." She hobbled out the door he held. "I will have to get the hang of these things again." She stopped walking to adjust the crutches under her arm. "Do you remember the dream?" she asked.

"The funny part is I remember the details, which is rare." He held her loosely about the waist until they got to his car. "No falling on my watch." He opened the door for her and then put her crutches on the backseat.

"Tell me all about your dream," she said as soon as he started the car. "I want specifics, please."

As soon as he pulled onto the roadway, he began to relay his dream to her. "The cheers of celebration at the wolf's defeat brought a smile to my face after the fear of seeing him to begin with. What fascinates me is that I could sense my emotions in the dream. I don't often pinpoint those emotions in my real life."

"Dreams can often be life-like. But dreams of this nature are beyond that. I hope that makes sense." She turned to look at him.

"Not until now. I've never had a dream quite like this in my life. Almost prophetic in nature, for lack of a better description." He stopped at the red light. "I know you understand."

"Yes. I've found myself sucked into a dream or premonition more than once. Speaking of premonitions, I could use one about now. I see many pieces but no links to connect them." She glanced at him. "I mean why shoot me? I don't get it."

"Someone sees you as a threat." He started driving again when the light changed.

"Okay, but I don't see why. I've been too busy to get into trouble." She adjusted the purse in her lap. "Between teaching at the school, helping Jessie at the store, and editing a manuscript, I have less time than ever to nose around."

"But you still do, and someone is aware of it. Aren't you the same girl who made a mission out of finding the reason for all the supernatural activity in Blue Cove?" He glanced at her with a grin on his face.

"As I'm finding out, yours is a strange world, my dear. Unusual knowledge seems to run in the circles you're involved in. You must have challenged the powers that be." He chuckled to cover the unnatural chill that ran down his back when he said the words.

"That is probably closer to the truth than we both know," she said. "Let's change the subject if you don't mind. I may have pressed my luck taking on this challenge. Where are going for dinner? We seem to be driving around in circles."

He laughed. "That's because we are. I've been waiting for you to notice. I need your help on the place tonight."

"How about the new place that opened up in Seaside Village? I've heard it's great if you like Chinese food."

"Lead on." He flipped on his turn signal.

****

Sipping her green tea, Peyton observed Jaxon. He seemed preoccupied tonight, with her in body but far away in his mind. "Is everything all right?"

"I'm sorry, I have a lot on my mind is all." He reached across the table for her hand. "I've been debating how much to tell you."

"Is this about your investigation? I understand you have to be careful how much you reveal." She squeezed his hand.

"You know I tell you what I can in that regard. I like talking over the facts with you."

"I'm open to listen, or to simply hang out. Being with you, even when you're quiet, is better than not seeing you at all." She placed her fork on her plate and let the server take her plate.

"I like that about you because I feel the same way. I also like that you're not demanding. You go with the flow." He placed his napkin on the table.

"I'm sure I can be challenging at times, but I'm also patient. You'll talk to me when you're ready." She studied his changing facial expressions and knew the moment he made up his mind. He may be ready to tell her. The question is, did she what to hear it?

"Do you remember meeting Elliot Dawson? I introduced you to him at the trial."

"EJ's father?" she asked.

He nodded. "I got a call this morning that he passed away. We became friends over the years. I arrested EJ on more than one occasion, and Elliot would get him off. Ours was an unlikely friendship, but it worked somehow."

"Oh, Jaxon, I'm so sorry. I know you were good friends." She reached for his hand.

"They're having a memorial service next weekend for him, and I want to go. Would you consider going with me? It would have to be a quick trip, but I'd appreciate it if you came along."

"I can arrange my schedule. The weekends I usually save for you anyway. I'd love to go with you."

"There's more to the story, but I'm still trying to wrap my head around the details. I'll tell you when I'm ready, if you don't mind."

"I can wait. Truthfully, I'm relieved that you didn't tell me we were through. That's where my mind traveled to." She sighed.

"No danger there, sweetheart. I only wish we could tie up some of the loose ends with this case and head into next weekend free of the investigation. I know that's asking a lot."

"Well now, anything is possible with a little magic working on our side." She sipped her tea watching the golden sparkles floating around them. *Mila, work your charms.* "I get the impression you may get what you wish for." She smiled at him, knowing things would be rough over the next few days and they had better buckle up for a bumpy ride.

The rest of the evening, they spent sitting on the sofa watching TV. Cuddled up in his side whether he talked or not seemed to be her favorite spot. She liked how his hand randomly stroked her cheek or squeezed her shoulder. She loved these moments with him.

"You're probably aware, the next few days could be hard. I appreciate these quiet times with you." She turned her face toward him.

"My thoughts, exactly. We should enjoy every minute." He laced his fingers through hers and kissed her hand.

"You read my mind." She watched him inch his head toward her until their lips touched in one long delicious kiss sealed with a promise of more to come. Later, after a TV show and several more kisses, he left, locking the door behind him and exacting a promise that she would set the alarm.

The evening had turned out to be a relaxing, wonderful time. Preoccupied, yet he still managed to make her feel cherished. How was that even possible? Jaxon never failed to surprise her. All her concerns of whether she could trust him had melted away the past few months. A weekend trip to be there for him seemed to be coming at the perfect time. He had done the heavy lifting in their relationship. Her time had come to invest in him.

Pulling back the covers on her bed, she stretched out, plumping the pillows behind her. She reached for the new journal and began to read. Lost in Cara's world she found the book hard to put down. Then she came to the place where Ray Cumberland showed up. She read and reread Cara's description of him. She mentioned his size and his "infernal stinky cigars." Those were Cara's exact words. She suspected him and followed him more than once. Sadly, she never found any evidence to support her belief in his connection to the missing girls. He had a reputation for being a womanizer. More than one of the women who worked for him said they had fought off his unwanted advances. Cara concluded her thoughts about Cumberland with these words:

*I will go to my grave believing he is guilty but without proof.*

Two observations about Cara's second journal stood out to her. First, Cara seemed stronger, more sure in her writing and word choices, and second, she never gave up the search for her sister and her friend's son. She closed the journal, marking the place where she stopped. There were truths to be found in the pages, words that could help uncover answers today. She forced herself to turn off the light and not to pick the journal up and continue reading.

Tomorrow she would read more of the beginnings of Blue Cove. Both were historical perspectives. Sleep didn't come quickly. Her mind went over each event of her day. Mr. Sanders came into the school after she had been shot. He tried to act as if nothing had happened. She didn't trust him. At this point, she had more questions than answers. But the answers were there at the edge of her mind like a name or word she couldn't remember. "Think, Peyton," she whispered into the dark room. "Alanna, Cara, Ireland," she spoke aloud. "Cumberland, Sanders, Campbell." Somehow they all fit. How? She stretched out her legs and winced. "The Old Grist Mill, the boarding school, mass gravesites. You can find the link." Around and around her mind went until her phone rang, bringing her back.

"You'll never believe what happened to me." Jessie's voice came across the line. "I hope I didn't wake you, but this is too important not to tell you."

"I can't sleep. I found another journal written by Cara." Peyton told how she found the two books in the attic. "I'm sorry. I got carried away. What happened?" she asked.

"I met the great-great-great-grandson of Ray Cumberland."

"What? Are you kidding me!" Peyton almost jumped out of bed.

"I'm serious. I nearly fell over when he introduced himself to me at the store. Richard Cumberland lives in Rocky Pointe but oversees his family's trust and business interests in town." Jessie went on to tell her about their conversation.

"Do you think he has anything to do with the missing girls?" Peyton asked.

"Honestly, I do. The guy gave me the creeps. He couldn't leave fast enough when I asked him if he knew Tamara Campbell."

"Oh, Jess, you didn't." Peyton shook her head. Of course, she would.

"I did. Someone has been getting away with

murder. I primed the pump so to say. It's past time."

"I know you're right, but be careful. Did you tell Matt?" Peyton asked.

"Of course. He reacted like I thought he would." Jessie sighed.

"How's that?" Peyton sat up.

"He's sleeping on my couch right now, and he'll probably hang out at my store tomorrow if I know him." She laughed.

"I for one am glad that he's at your house." Peyton frowned. "I don't want anything to happen to you."

"Neither does he. Besides, look who's talking. I didn't get shot today."

"I need to be more careful too. What do you think this means? Why did he show up in your store? They must suspect we are snooping around." Peyton turned on the light and propped the pillows behind her. "Rep. Holland possibly, do you think?"

"Could be. The way he questioned me, I'm sure he knows. He seemed too sweet and syrupy if you know what I mean."

"I do. He and Sanders could be twins. Hmm, I wonder." Peyton pushed her hair out of her face.

"What?" Jessie asked.

"Are they connected? I have lots to think about. I'll talk to you tomorrow. Stay safe." Peyton pulled her blanket tight to ward off the chills running down her arms.

"I could say the same thing to you. Stop by the store tomorrow. It's supposed to be nice tomorrow, and we could have run outside but not with your leg."

"I will. As for running outside, I can't, and neither should you. We might be sitting ducks for someone's target practice." Peyton pursed her lips.

"You're right, but I hate to give up one ounce of my freedom to these creeps."

"Love you, cous. No running alone. Maybe Matt will run with you."

"He will, but he'll grumble." Jessie laughed. "He's not fond of running even though he can outrun me."

"Impressive. I for one will sleep better knowing Matt's close by. You're something, Jess."

"That's what Matt always says. Nighty, night."

****

Jaxon lay awake in the dark. Matt had called earlier to tell him about staying at Jessie's and why. Wasn't he the one who hoped things would speed up? He got part of his wish anyway.

Peyton shot and a Cumberland showing up in Jessie's store on the same day—what were the odds of that? A high probability when it came to those two. The excavations at the gravesites must be pushing their response. People like Cumberland rarely did the dirty work. There had to be more people than him involved.

Peyton had told him that Reba said some prominent people might be involved. He sent a text to Peyton. She responded:

—*I'm awake*—

"I take it your cousin told you what happened?" he said when she answered his call.

"Yes, she called earlier," Peyton told him.

"How did you react to what she told you?" He stacked his arms behind his head.

"I'm still thinking about it. The timing seems strange considering the shooting earlier. I can't help but wonder if the two are connected."

"They have to be. Let's go through the evidence we've got so far." Jaxon told her about the boarding school and what he knew. She went back over her dreams, the notes left in her vandalized classroom, and the ghosts at both the school and Jessie's store, as well as in Katie's attic. They talked about Ray Cumberland, the tribal elders, and Cara's new journal.

"The answers are staring us in the face. We'll meet tomorrow and go over them one by one. If you think of anything else pertinent to the investigation, be sure to let me know. I'm meeting with Matt and Tom in the morning to compare notes." He rubbed his eyes. "See you tomorrow, sweetheart."

Matt gave him the number for an attorney and his financial advisor. One more job for his to-do list. He would call his parents in the morning. Maybe they would have a few suggestions too. *Five million dollars, wow, that's a lot of money.* What a crazy time to find out. "Elliot, I don't know what to say. Thank you seems small in comparison to your generosity. I'll miss talking to you, my friend." He had talked to him several times in the past few months. Jaxon knew EJ's death had devastated both his parents.

He checked up on them regularly to make sure they were doing okay. Dawson's death wasn't something he saw coming. Peyton being with him would take some of the sting out of losing his friend. He laid his head back on the pillows. Life comes fast and furious, and before you know what happens, time slips away. He smiled. Damn, but he sounded like Peyton. He could live with that. She had a philosophical approach to life and astounded him with the wisdom that came out of her mouth. She could hold her own with Sadie, Reba, and his mother. Alone with his thoughts, he made a monumental decision. His body instantly relaxed, and sleep followed quickly.

****

"Sister, I flew home to meet with Celeste. We have a part to fulfill in defeating Aelfric." Mila landed on a branch beside Elida.

"I must know what she said. The atmosphere is charged, and I know he's getting ready to act. I've seen him prowling about, fading in and out among the residents of this town. He has caused more than one fight," Elida told her sister.

"Our subjects are doing all they can, but they can't fight what they don't see. It's our job to help them see the invisible world," Mila said. "I have a plan; Celeste helped me put it together. Each of the next few days, we will need to open their eyes to the possibilities that exist beyond what they can see."

"The two girls will be easy, but the men I'm not too sure of." Elida shook her head.

"I said the same thing to Celeste, but she told me not to sell them short. They have been with the girls and have learned to appreciate their abilities. They will never embrace the gift for themselves, but they are more open than we might believe." Mila repositioned herself on the branch—the needles of the pine were uncomfortable.

"Celeste is wise and right. Of course, they'll be open. Those girls have helped the men out of a few sticky situations with their gifts."

"You catch on fast, sister. I can see the ideas formulating in you already. I have them too. Celeste reminded me we must expose Aelfric every chance we get. They know him as the dark wolf." Mila waved her wand, and for a moment the light from her magic exposed Aelfric. "And they are beginning to know those whom he has influenced, but they have yet to know the man as he appears in town."

"I'm ready to get busy. Don't wait for me." Elida flittered about her sister. "I will see you soon. Jessie is waiting."

## Chapter 35

Mila sat on the foot of Peyton's bed. The dear girl had certainly known her share of sadness in her life. Despite it all, she had come to trust her heart to a good man. Mila knew as far as humans went, Jaxon Kincaid seemed to be good to his core. Having lived hundreds of years, she had seen her share of people. Some were capable of great good and others of great evil. Some operated between both.

This girl had the gift like many of her ancestors before her. Although she accepted what was happening in her life, she had yet to understand the possibilities of the good that can be accomplished through her. With only minimal time to convince her, Mila hoped she could perform the task and help Peyton understand. Cara learned over time, as did Kathryn. Sadie embraced some but not all. What would Peyton do? Mila sighed. Only time would tell the story. With her musing done, she waved her wand three times, swirling golden sparkles all around the room, and left for her next destination.

Peyton awakened refreshed and ready to face another day. She glanced at herself in the mirror before leaving the bedroom. The bright color in her face made her appear as rested as she felt. She ran her hand over the silky material of her blouse. She smiled. Jaxon would like this one. Glancing at the clock, she noted she even had time to make a cup of coffee.

If time permitted, she wanted to do a bit of shopping before next weekend. She needed a few items for the trip. Which reminded her of the real reason for going to Arizona. Elliot Dawson's service. He seemed like such a nice man. Jaxon liked him, which told her everything she needed to know. Elliot never missed a day at court during the trial. He seemed to accept that EJ had saved many lives as a way to make sense of his death.

Grabbing the crutches, she walked into the kitchen with a bit of help. Leaning on them took some of the pressure off her leg, and she was glad that she had kept them. A sunny morning gave her a beautiful view out the window while she sipped her coffee and ate her scone. Funerals were never easy. But she wanted to be there for Elliot's wife and Jaxon. He had supported her through the many ups and downs of her crazy life. Her choice to stop running and let Jaxon be the man to catch her happened to be the best decision she had ever made. She sighed. It was hard to believe how much her feelings toward him had changed since their meeting in Arizona.

The sun felt wonderful against her skin as she walked to her car. Putting her crutches on the backseat, she got in and started the engine. Jaxon had a hand in the choice of her car too, and she loved it. He was right when he said it suited her completely. A lot like he did.

The school appeared normal a few minutes later when she hobbled through the door being held open for her by Mr. Avery. Luckily, she had listened to the doctor instead of being her normal muleheaded self. There were moments when the word stubborn suited her perfectly.

"I wasn't sure we would see you this morning. I waited for the call that didn't come." The principal smiled at her. "You're one of my dedicated teachers. Let me carry this for you." He reached for her briefcase.

She thanked him. "You have many great teachers and staff too. It's a pleasure to work here."

"Yes, we do. We have a great school, and I'm proud to be a key part of it." He walked the hall with her. "How are you feeling?" he asked.

"I'm fine. These seem to help me get around easier." She lifted one of the crutches.

"I have a bit of news. The police found where the shooter waited, but there is still no suspect. I don't envy their job."

"Their investigations can take time, but it's amazing how successful they can be."

"If you need extra help in your class today, let me know." He took the key from her hand and unlocked the door. "I'll leave you to get ready for your day."

Normal changed to a heightened sense of abnormal the minute the principal left. Glancing around the room, nothing seemed out of place or accounted for the unnatural chills like spiders crawling up her arms. Once at her desk, she found an envelope addressed to her. The minute her hand touched the edge, she knew. Careful not to touch the casing, she slipped the paper out of the inside. After reading the contents, she called the station and asked the dispatcher to send an officer over. Maybe they could get a print off the envelope. While she waited, she read the note again.

A ferocious black wolf, his fangs covered with blood, glared from the page with a simple caption.

*Death is coming for you.*

Not a pleasant way to start her workday.

When the officer came into the classroom, she handed him a plastic bag with the envelope and the note. "My kids should be coming soon, and I don't want to worry them. I doubt you'll find prints, but one can hope."

"We'll see." He fingered the bag in his hand. "I hope your day improves."

"I'm sure it will." She smiled at him as he left.

Why, oh why, hadn't she kept her mouth shut? No, she had to speak the words out into the universe, a challenge to the powers that be any day of the week. Her day went downhill from there. Mr. Sanders walked past her and purposely kicked her crutch, making her leg give out. He swore it was an accident, but she had witnessed his action. Her leg hurt, and she hoped the fall hadn't torn a stitch in the process. A ghost looking for whatever a ghost searches for kept popping in and out of her class. The students grew agitated, and she did too. Glancing at the clock, she noted the day still had twenty minutes left. Would this day never end? While the children ate their snack, she sent a quick text off to her cousin.

—*I hope your day is better than mine.*—

A swift reply came back.

—*You must be kidding.*—

She would be stopping at the bookstore to hear her cousin's story. As soon as the last of her kids left for the day, she grabbed her briefcase and locked her classroom. A lot of good the locked door did. Someone still planted an envelope, which meant they had a key. As she made her way down the hall to the door, she heard the snarling sound of a wolf. The sound seemed too real and menacing to be only her imagination. She waved at Mr. Avery standing outside the office as he sent a sixth grader running over to open the door for her.

She couldn't be happier to leave a place than at this moment. Mr. Sanders looked guiltily at her. Maybe she wasn't being fair to him, but her aching leg made her think he was to blame.

****

When Jaxon arrived at the station he went into Matt's office. He called Maxwell for their morning meeting on the speaker. "Hey, Tom. Are you ready to meet?"

"I'm here. How's it going, Kincaid?"

"Not bad. We finished up at the boarding school yesterday." Jaxon went on to explain to them what he had learned in the files he had read so far. "I don't understand how this could happen."

"Every generation seems to have their own set of prejudices," Tom replied. "The lawsuits are guaranteed to pile up. Only time will tell if we do what's right by the tribes." Tom went on to describe what the bodies had revealed so far.

"The coroner here is in the process of identifying the victims at the site in Blue Cove," Matt said. "We've also requested a search warrant and sent a letter ordering the Cumberland business conglomerate to keep all records even if the business is no longer in operation. Hopefully, we'll get the warrant before they receive the letter. We want the element of surprise on our side. Because of a fingerprint found on Tamara Campbell, we have the name of our first suspect. The man, hired by Cumberland and Associates, serves as a bodyguard for the company." Matt gave them the name and thanked Kenny when he brought a note in and handed it to Matt.

"When will you search the offices of Cumberland?" Tom asked.

"Tomorrow. I just got word that the warrant is approved. We'll be searching recent records and looking for those going back many years."

"I'll want to tag along with some extra agents," Tom told them. "Tamara Campbell is considered part of a federal case since she was taken across state lines. I'll be there bright and early." Tom disconnected the call.

Gary stood in the open doorway and knocked. "Come in," Matt called out. "What's up?"

"Jessie had some guy come into the store who caused some trouble. He was gone by the time we got there," he said.

"What kind of trouble?" Matt frowned.

"He threw a few books around and threatened her. The guy left when Molly came into the store yelling with a phone in her hand calling us." Gary gave them the details he knew.

He handed them the plastic bag. "Peyton found this on her desk this morning."

"Did you find any prints?" Jaxon reached for the bag.

"Not a one. Clean as a whistle." Gary leaned against the wall.

"Damn. Look at this." Jaxon read the note and gave it to Matt.

"We must be getting close." Matt glanced at the photo.

As soon as Gary left, Jaxon went into the conference room and started going through more files. The teleconference with Tom Maxwell confirmed what his gut had already told him. Examinations on several of the exhumed bodies had shown they hadn't died from natural causes. Skull fractures and broken bones told the story. Reading through the files the past couple of days, Jaxon had noticed the principal at the time called the kids savages or heathens, and he used the word several times in his entries. Appropriate punishments he listed were spanking with a wooden paddle, use of restraints on hands or feet, and going without meals. In the worst cases, isolation and whipping were suggested. Any or all forms could be used when the children didn't obey, spoke in their native language, or tried to run away. They were not to practice their "heathen ways." The more Jaxon read the angrier he became. Many of the children were sold into labor for pennies on the dollar. It seemed a damn shame that no one living at the time paid for what they did.

An hour later Matt stuck his head in the conference room where Jaxon sat. "I'm headed to Jessie's store and to get some lunch. Do you want to come along?"

"Yeah. I need to step aside before I put my fist through the wall." He stood.

"Not light reading I guess." Matt's brows rose.

"You could say that." They walked out of the station together.

\*\*\*\*

Peyton pulled into the space in front of Jessie's store. Reaching for her crutches, she hobbled on them to the front door. Darn, her leg hurt after the fall. She wasn't sure what hurt more—her wound or her knee.

293

She fell wrong, landing on her knee awkwardly. Maybe she should trip Sanders the next time she saw him. Two wrongs might not make a right, but she would feel a whole lot better. She walked in the door.

"Why the crutches?" Jessie asked walking toward her.

"The doctor suggested I use them to take the pressure off the wound, and they helped when I went out last night with Jaxon. They're helpful to lean on when I stand, but now I need them for real." She sat in the chair, leaning the crutches beside her.

"What happened?" Jessie sat across from her.

"Sanders kicked the crutch on my weak side, and I fell on my knee. Hopefully, it's only sore and not injured."

"You've had a couple of rough days, haven't you? How about lunch, my treat?" Jessie asked.

"Sounds good. I can for pay mine." She reached for the money in her pocket.

"Nope, this one is on me. Besides, we'll both need extra fuel because Reba is on her way in."

"I'm not surprised." Peyton leaned her head on her arms.

"Me either." Jessie walked toward the open doors into Joe's. "I'll bring you something good."

"Hi, Peyton dear. Where's Jessie?" Reba entered the shop and took off her coat, folding it neatly over an empty chair.

"She's in the coffee shop getting lunch," Peyton told her.

"As soon as she comes back, I'll get myself a little something." She sat at the table across from Peyton.

Molly walked in, carrying a tray with Peyton's

lunch, and Jessie had her own and something for Reba.

"Thank you, Jessie dear. You never forget me," Reba said. "The salad is perfect, and you always remember the lemon bar. My favorite."

"I keep trying to entice you with other treats, but you're faithful to those lemon bars." Molly squeezed Reba's shoulder.

"I like all your desserts, sweet girl. But these lemon bars are light, flakey, and lemony delicious. Perfect for an afternoon tea or dessert when nothing heavy will do." Reba stuck a five-dollar bill in Molly's hand.

"I'm glad you like them." Molly thanked her. "I'll be right back."

"Yum, this salad is good. The dressing tastes wonderful. According to the description in the menu, it's a light apple cider vinaigrette. All I know is that the flavor pairs perfectly with the chicken and the crunch of cashews. I marvel about how she keeps the new recipes coming." Peyton took another bite of her salad.

"You're right, this is perfect." Jessie adjusted the napkin on her lap. "Have you noticed how often the three of us eat at this table?"

"Yes, it's one of my favorite places to hang out." Peyton took another bite of her salad.

"Here you go, Reba." Molly returned and handed her a box. "A few desserts for you and Lawrence. You ladies have brought lots of business my way, and I'm appreciative."

"It's your food that brings in your business, Molly. Look, here come two more customers." Jessie pointed to the door.

Molly laughed when she saw Matt and Jaxon. "Matt's only here every day because your store is next to mine and he can see you. It's true, and you know it."

"Probably, but they would go somewhere else to eat if they didn't like the food." Jessie took a sip of her iced tea. "Remember a way to a man's heart is through his stomach."

"I still think you're the ticket, and now Peyton is too. I have a box for each of you. Enjoy!"

"Hello, ladies." Matt walked into the store before Jaxon. He bent down to kiss Jessie's cheek. "I want to hear details. I'll be back after lunch."

"How's your leg, Peyton?" Jaxon leaned close to her and asked.

"I'll tell you later. Enjoy your lunch." She watched him follow Matt into the coffee shop.

"Okay, girls, I want to hear what's been happening." Reba placed her napkin across her lap. "I know trouble is rearing its head once again, and you girls are involved as usual."

Peyton described her day and the note left on her desk. "I love working at the school, but since the ghost first appeared at the school and the fight between the parent and teacher, trouble seems to be escalating. I know there is a link to the case, but I haven't wrapped my mind around the clues yet." She shook her head. "From your reply to my text I take it your day wasn't stellar either, cousin."

Jessie told her story about the man in her store. "When Molly came to my rescue, she was a glorious sight. Between the ghosts and this jerk today, I'm tired of picking up books." Jessie scrunched her face. "Does no one respect books anymore?"

"I would've loved to see that. We owe her our gratitude." Reba patted Jessie's hand.

"She stood in the doorway like my avenging angel with her phone in her hand, talking to the police and yelling at the man at the same time. She was something else."

"Did you recognize the man?" Peyton asked.

"Richard Cumberland stood by his car. I could see him. This goon I've never seen before. Thought he could rough me up." She snickered. "I managed to get off a kick or two and a knee strategically placed."

"Only you would think to do that. Did you drop him?" Peyton and Reba both laughed.

"No, but he was a soprano when he ran out." Jessie joined in the laughter.

"My dear girl, you manage to make the scary funny. I salute you. We all need to laugh occasionally."

****

"It beats me what ladies find to laugh about. Look at them," Jaxon told Matt who had a huge grin on his face. "Why the smile?"

"Jessie's laugh gets me every time. I love seeing her happy especially with all the junk going on in her life."

"I never picked you as a romantic." Jaxon took a bite of his sandwich.

"I'm rough around the edges but not when it comes to her. Love does make a mess out of you, man. If this relationship kills me, at least I'll die a happy man." Matt put his hand to his heart.

"I would have called you odd a few months ago, but not now." Jaxon smiled. "I suffer from the same condition."

"Have you told her about the money yet?" Matt asked.

"No, I'll tell her next weekend. She's going with me to Elliot Dawson's memorial service. I wanted all my ducks in a row with the attorney and financial adviser before I told her." He paused. "I guess I want to know how she feels about me before she knows I'm rich." Jaxon frowned. "Does that sound as bad as I think it does?"

"You sound cautious, and I get that. For what it's worth, I don't know two people any more suited for each other than you and Peyton. Well, except for me and Jessie."

"I agree. Not to change the subject, but keeping them safe the next few days may be a challenge considering their morning." Jaxon's gaze strayed toward Peyton. "She's damn capable of taking care of herself, but with her leg, she might need help."

"I know Jessie is. She reminds me often enough. Did you hear what she did to the guy earlier?" Matt laughed as he told the story that Gary had told him.

"Those two are something," Jaxon said.

"I think the number is three." Matt flashed three fingers.

Jaxon had to agree with him. Reba and the Reynolds girls were changing Blue Cove for the better. They didn't have any idea how much, but after his dream the other night, he had a small inkling of what went on in the world not visible to most. Thankfully, some could see what others couldn't and fight to do something about the evil around them. Jaxon shook his head. Damn, Peyton made him a better man, and he liked it.

## Chapter 36

Jaxon kept watching her during lunch, and Peyton wished she knew what he had been thinking. Reba had given them one of her strange exhortations, which she had heard only half of. Darn, why hadn't she paid closer attention?

"This case involves good and evil, light and darkness, and fear, which only love can destroy. Fear is the real enemy here; guard against it," Reba said with a warning tone in her voice.

"Fear of what?" Jessie asked.

"Find the answer to that, and you'll free many tortured souls." Reba stood. "I must be going." Jessie held her coat for her to slip on. "I love you girls. I think I'll stop by Sadie's and bring her a treat." She pointed at the box of desserts. "You're in my thoughts. Be strong and don't be afraid. Oh, and keep in mind the Irish roots. That's where the story begins and ends."

Peyton stood by her cousin at the front of the store. "There are times I don't get her at all. She says what she needs to and then moves on like we've had a normal conversation."

"It's who she is, and you get used to it after a while," Jessie told her.

"Look, there's Pastor John. He's such a kind man." Peyton pointed across the street at the church.

"How can you not be afraid when someone is

trying to intimidate you?" Jessie mused while she followed Pastor John's movements to his car.

"You make him a soprano." Peyton glanced at her cousin with a straight face, and they both dissolved into laughter.

Although she could laugh about it, Peyton understood the words that Reba had told them were important. Once Reba left and the guys followed a while later, the store was quiet enough to think.

"I'll dust the shelves for you." Peyton took the feather duster and got to work.

The first shelves were filled with fantasy novels—stories filled with demons, angels, and magical creatures. On the cover of one of the books she reached for was a door standing alone in the woods. As she opened the book, she stood before the door which opened slowly to reveal what was beyond. Reba's words danced through her mind. Good, evil, light, and darkness. Scenes rolled through her mind, depicting each word. With the word fear came the wolf snarling, growling, and chasing his prey, but when she thought of love, the light came and exposed the fear for what it was—merely a shadow of the wolf. She had no idea how long she stood there, but when she finally closed the book, she understood.

Those who intimidate and control others by fear are bound by fear themselves. On some level, everyone was impacted by fear. Only love could break the cycle. *Reba, you are wise, my friend.* Peyton knew she had to be on the right track when Alanna and Cara appeared in front of her. Arm in arm, they stood before her like guardians. Cara extended her hand and touched hers. A strange warm sensation rushed up her arm, filling her with peace. Alanna touched her other hand, sending a zing of energy coursing through her. The strength that filled her started at her toes and flowed up her legs. What was happening to her? Suddenly, she could see the whole picture while heat flowed around her wound, easing her discomfort.

"Peyton, hello, are you in there?" Jessie lightly tapped her back.

"What?" She shook her head to dispel the images in her mind.

"You've been staring at that book for at least ten minutes. What's going on?" Jessie led her to a chair. "Sit."

"I'm not sure how to explain what happened, but I'll try." She gave her cousin her best description. "At least I can see why I had to find the journal, why we saw what we did in the trunk, and the importance of the victims' story being told. Once truth reveals what has been hidden in time, the practice is exposed and stopped. One crime at a time. Not gone forever, of course, only until someone else comes along and takes up where they ended. But it is stopped for now."

"Why fairies?" Jessie asked.

"Why dragons, or angels, for that matter? Our beliefs sustain us in tough times, but if we let them, they can turn to hate and trap us in our anger and fear. Some people take their fears a step farther by trying to influence others to do the same. Remember Reba said not to forget the Irish roots of the case. That is why there are fairies and a pooka. This comes from Cara and Alanna's belief."

"What can we do?" Jessie scrunched her face.

"We can only do our part." Peyton leaned forward

in the chair. "Whatever that is."

Jessie nodded. "I guess that's what Kathryn and Cara did in their lifetimes. They changed their world the best they could."

"When I consider our predicament and the characters involved, fear is a big part of what motivates them. Sanders and Cumberland are afraid of the truth revealing who they are. Their actions and those of their ancestors have been hidden for a long time. We have to find a way to take this magical abstract idea of the way we see this case and bring it into reality. We can't make them all sopranos." Peyton smiled.

"We could try." Jessie stood when the bell above the door rang. "It's back to work for me."

"I'll finish dusting." Peyton got to work with the feather duster again, relieved that this case made more sense, even if she didn't know how to explain why. She finished the task before long and headed home. She had some reading to do.

****

Jaxon knew the numbers that showed most of the children suffered some kind of trauma would be high, but not at the rate the figures were already coming in. Whether that's what killed most of them might never be known. But the bones didn't lie—many had suffered at the hands of those meant to care for them. These facts left Jaxon feeling a bit sad and depressed as he read over the reports. The perpetrators were already dead and couldn't be tried for their crimes.

The second crime site near town was a different scenario. Secrets from the past and present had been buried in that wooded area. A lone fingerprint gave them at least one suspect. Tomorrow's search would hopefully give them more clarity.

Tamara's cause of death was blunt force trauma. She also had several stab wounds. Her murderer had lost control and made it personal. When agents searched her apartment, they found several notes like the one sent to Peyton, an interesting piece of evidence which connected both Tamara, Jessie, and Peyton to the same possible suspect. Another crucial link showed two other bodies identified had gone missing recently. When their parents and friends were interviewed, the same theme emerged. Both girls had received threatening notes and felt like they were being stalked at work. The women worked in the office of Cumberland Lumber. Jeremy's research turned up a link between the principal at the boarding school and Ray Cumberland. Kids from the boarding school were sold to Ray to work in his mills.

With all the technology at their disposal today, they were able to follow the evidence, but back then those who searched for the missing had little to aid them. Rumors, gossip, and possibly the law, if they were on their side, were their only recourse. He understood what Peyton meant by their stories needing to be told. If not, they would simply fade away as if they never existed.

The same with the Native American children. The crime still existed today in the form of young indigenous women missing and murdered being found all over the country. The foundation of the crime was clear; now all he had to do was find any living responsible characters.

"Hey, do you have a minute?" Matt pulled out a chair across from him. "I've been thinking over the evidence we've got so far." He tapped his fingers on the table. "I can't believe I'm going to say this, but I'm starting to see a connection between the two." He made a motion to stop Jaxon before he said anything. "I know I'm sounding like the girls, but I can see a connection."

"I've been thinking along the same lines." Jaxon pointed to one of the files and went on to explain where his thoughts had taken him. "We have the name of the bodyguard and the names of two men from the past plus their descendants today. I think there are more involved because of the money on the spreadsheet that Jeremy sent. What they're doing is lucrative."

"Let's begin by peeling the layers back," Matt said.

"I've set up an appointment for tomorrow afternoon with Principal Avery. I want to see if the school has had any complaints filed against Sanders." Jaxon glanced at his watch. "I'll be at Cumberland and Associates when the search warrant is issued in the morning too."

"Good because that is one of the layers. We need to start from the past and come forward. I'm hoping we'll find the names of other folks involved. Jeremy sent us a few already, but we've had no proof. I'm guessing that changes tomorrow. I'll see you back at the house later."

"Sounds good. The painters should be finishing up at my place. I'm going to stop in and check on their progress." Jaxon put his files in his briefcase.

"Let's meet the girls for Italian. I'll arrange it. Does six at Angelo's work?"

"Works for me." Jaxon stood when Matt did. "I've been hungry for Angelo's lasagna. See you in a few." Jaxon headed out to his car.

The painters were done, and the wood floors were in. Peyton had suggested perfect colors. Jaxon was pleased. The place was starting to take shape. With all the money Elliot Dawson had left him, he could do a few extra touches that he hadn't figured into the costs of the remodel. Landscaping for one, and an upgrade on the kitchen. He needed a designer to help him with both. The ideas were there but not the knowledge of how to bring them to life. Matt could help him with a person. His place seemed perfect although it needed a few feminine touches to balance the heavy masculine ones. Jaxon had opted for the large windows and more modern exterior versus the kitchen. Now he could have both and pay off the loan he had to take out for the work.

Watching a sailboat skip across the cove, he knew he would never tire of the view. The house sat perfectly on the property. The only add-on that would make the place perfect would be for Peyton to live there with him. And at some point, for a few little Reynolds-Kincaids to join the party. He glanced at his watch and headed for the door. At times life seemed to run by the watch on his arm. Damn, he was late.

****

At the restaurant, Peyton tried to concentrate on Jessie and Matt's conversation, but she kept watching the door for Jaxon to arrive. She couldn't remember him ever being late before. Her mind tended to conjure up the worst-case scenarios even if she knew better.

"Are you listening to me, cous? I've asked you the same question twice." Jessie blew out her breath in frustration.

"Sorry. I confess I wasn't." Peyton shrugged. "I wonder where Jaxon is. He's never late."

"He's not that late; give him a break. Someone

might have stopped him to talk for all you know. He'll be here." Jessie shook her head. "Sheesh."

"I probably should've mentioned," Matt said guiltily, "he stopped by his place after work. He wanted to see the progress."

"What were you asking?" Peyton glanced at her cousin.

"Darned if I can remember, although I'm sure it seemed important at the time." Jessie's brows furrowed.

"You can always ask again when you remember." Relief filled her when a flustered-looking Jaxon raced in the door.

He sat in the open chair beside her. "I had a tail a block from my place. I drove around trying to shake him. Not easy to do in a smaller town. I eventually managed, and that's why I'm late."

"Did you call in the make and model?" Matt asked.

"Sure did. The SUV got close enough a couple of times to see numbers on the plates. They're running it now."

"I guess you had a good reason to be worried," Jessie told Peyton.

"You were worried?" Jaxon reached for her hand.

"You're never late, and I was concerned." She laced her fingers through his. "With what happened at the store and school today, we can't be too careful."

"I was about to give you the same warning." He tightened his hold on her hand and leaned close to her. "Thank you for your concern."

Peyton gazed into his gorgeous honey-brown eyes. "My pleasure."

"Let's order, I'm starving." Matt passed the menus around the table. "It's spaghetti for me with their homemade Italian sausage and meatballs. Some of the best I've had."

After they ordered and finished a great meal, Peyton nudged Jessie's foot under the table. "We have company," she mouthed.

Jessie turned to see who. "Well, what do you know." She turned to Matt. "Don't look now, but Sanders and Cumberland came in together. They haven't seen us yet, and hopefully, they won't."

"At least we've answered another question. They know each other, which makes connecting them a whole lot easier." Jaxon handed the server his credit card. "Tonight is on me."

"Thanks, man." Matt's chin lifted. "We'll leave first." Matt stood and pulled Jessie's chair out for her. "We'll be in the parking lot."

Jaxon nodded. He placed his card back in his wallet. "Let's make our escape." They stood and walked out of Angelo's with Jaxon guarding her back.

"I don't think they saw us, but you never know." Peyton reached for his hand when they were out of the restaurant. She had left her crutches in the car, and her leg had started to ache.

"Seeing those two socializing confirms one of my theories. Tomorrow we should know more," Jaxon told her.

"I wish I could tag along tomorrow." Peyton glanced nervously about as they rounded the corner of the building to the parking area. "We should go."

"Okay. I'll tell Matt we're leaving." He called as he started to walk and slowed down for her to catch up.

"No. We need to leave. Now!" she yelled and hobbled toward her car. She felt herself lifted off the ground and carried to the car.

"I'll come back for mine." Jaxon helped her into the car. "Latch your seat belt and hold on," he yelled. He started the car and pulled onto Main Street, followed by Matt and Jessie as a car raced into the parking area where they had been standing. "That's the same SUV," he told Matt.

"I don't think he recognized your car, Peyton." Matt was on speaker. "Drive around for a few minutes. Kip is on his way to the restaurant with backup. We need to join him."

"Sounds good." Jaxon pointed at the police cruisers with lights on that passed them. "I'll turn around in the grocery store parking area so Peyton can drive. She can drop me off at the front of Angelo's and go home and wait for me," Jaxon said.

"Okay, we're right behind you. She can take Jessie with her."

Peyton got out of the car when they stopped and switched places with Jaxon. "You lead, Matt, and I'll follow you," she told him as she started driving. As she drove past Angelo's parking lot, she stopped when Matt did. She noticed the police had the SUV blocked. Jaxon exited her car and joined Matt. Jessie got in with her. As much as she wanted to stay and watch, she would go home and wait.

"Times like this, I worry about Matt. His job is dangerous," Jessie said. They had arrived without incident and walked from the car down the familiar path.

"I'm beginning to understand that for myself. I also understand their need to protect us. I feel the same way toward Jaxon. Good night. If you get bored call me."

Peyton waved at her cousin as they parted on the path.

Peyton changed her clothes into something more comfortable. She made a cup of hot tea, reached for the throw on the sofa, and settle in to read a few more pages from Cara's second journal.

****

Jaxon knocked at her door, and a glance at his watch told him the time was later than he thought. He should've called her, but he wanted to see her. Knocking again, he started to second-guess his decision. Maybe she was in bed.

"Are you okay?" She opened the door, sounding a bit groggy.

"I hope I didn't wake you." Even with her hair tousled and rubbing the sleep out of her eyes, she looked gorgeous to him. He walked through the door she held open.

"I must've fallen asleep." She closed the door and followed him to the living room. "What happened?" She rubbed his shoulders as he sat in the chair.

"We spent the last few hours questioning the two men in custody. They were heavily armed and had a cache of weapons in the back along with a few explosives. We were lucky we took them by surprise and they didn't have time to offer resistance. A lot of people could have been caught in the crossfire." Jaxon sat forward in the chair. "I'm glad your warning radar worked." He smiled at her. "Those two seemed to have big plans but are tight-lipped at the moment. The longer they stew in jail the more likely they will talk. They already have a weapons charge against them and more charges pending. Matt has his team running a background check. My gut tells me they are hired guns

309

and we'll find ties to Cumberland's organization at some point. Jeremy and Gary are working on that part together."

"Jeremy's good at what he does, and so is Gary. They'll make a talented team. I wonder why the men were tailing you."

"Who knows. It could have been a warning. I tend to think they were hired to get rid of me."

"I thought you might say something like that." She frowned.

"I'm being realistic is all. People don't carry the kind of weapons they had on them unless they plan on using them. We confiscated several Glocks, AR-15s, and two high-powered, long-range scoped rifles along with several boxes of ammo and high clip magazines. We're talking about the kind of weapons used in hired hits. Assassinations. This leaves me wondering who hired them and who the main target or targets might be."

"A lot to think about. It sounds like more than a boarding school and employee issue. To me, it sounds like something more lucrative."

"I agree. Matt said they shut down a group operating in the area last year. Their cover was a children's store. It seems when one operation closes down, demands open another one."

"It's sad how that works."

"I've been wanting to ask you something for a while." He glanced at her as she moved to the sofa and sat. "Do you believe in the whole magic stuff?"

"Funny you should ask. I read something tonight that Alanna told Cara when she asked her the same question. Let me read it to you."

*"For some, it's fairies and nymphs, and for others, it is angels or ghosts. I would say, my dear girl, believe what it takes to get you through. You may or may not see them with your eyes; you might only hear them in your heart. Belief is what matters. The invisible world exists whether you see it or not."*

*Of course. Alanna is right. Whether we believe what we can't see or not doesn't change that it is.*

Peyton closed the journal.

"I can live with that. I don't need to see it. I fight the effects of the evil of that world every day on my job." He stood and pulled her up into his arms. "I'm sorry I awakened you. It was selfish of me. I wanted to see you. You make the world seem right again for me." He kissed her. "Goodnight, sweetheart. I'll call you tomorrow when we're done." He kissed her again and left.

\*\*\*\*

Sometimes she wondered if they were slightly nuts to think they could make a difference in the world. She stretched out on the bed. It scared her to consider that someone might want to hurt Jaxon. Guns and explosives, being driven around in the trunk of the car. What were people thinking? She needed to see the bigger picture.

Whether it was a bad fairy, or a devil as described by some, she did not doubt that evil seemed present in the world. She wanted to understand.

"If only…"

She shut off the light, closed her eyes, and reminded herself she needed to visit her grandmother tomorrow.

\*\*\*\*

311

Mila watched her subject and heard her request to see the bigger picture. The time had come for the girl's eyes to be open. This wasn't only about today. Crimes sometimes happen in a moment of passion, it's true. But many have been nurtured in darkness over many generations. Passed down like an inheritance to an unsuspecting heir. Once the web is discovered it's too late, they are ensnared.

Mila began to weave the story as a picture in Peyton's dreams. Spanning several generations of one deception built on another until it exploded, causing harm only to recede and surface again at another time.

Flittering about the room as Peyton tossed and turned upon the bed, it saddened Mila to show her such things. *Dream on, my dear. You asked for understanding.* With the wave of her hand, the misty fog swirled around the girl upon her bed.

****

The dark mist swirled at her feet as she stood in the middle of an open field. The landscape changed constantly before her eyes as people came and went. One generation was born, and another died while life continued to move forward. Travelers and the ghosts of the restless, those with kind hearts, and those who seemed to have no heart at all passed in front of her, all with a story to tell. Where she stood made no difference; the story seemed to be the same. The fear that caused others to control another found its way from one group of people to another, bringing a blight of their own making upon the humans. The fear that they wielded ate at their lives as well as destroyed their dreams. Bright stars of human potential rose among the throngs, shining their light into the darkness, impacting a small circle around them, and then they faded away. One voice would call out a warning while another told men what they wanted to hear, but those listening found no relief in their words.

Once again, she stood outside Cara's home. She followed the path of her journey with a new understanding. From Ireland to America, from hope to great loss, Cara found solace in the world beyond the door. She did what she could, with what she had, and made a difference in the small world in which she lived. She fought back the darkness all around her with the light of hope she aspired to every day. Hope in a better tomorrow, hope that one day she could find her sister, and hope that like Alanna she could be a healer and not a destroyer like Aelfric.

The dream raced on with wolves at war and lives healed or destroyed. Light and darkness fought each other over the people who marched in front of her. In the end, she recognized that those who loved and showed kindness flourished, while a small amount of hate could overtake a human heart and destroy their lives along with those they hated. They became trapped within a prison of their own making.

Peyton awakened with a start, drenched in her sweat. The dream had left her shaken. Turning on the light, she picked up her pen and begin to write in her notebook. All the dreams and all the words she read seemed to come together in this dream. They were dealing with something that had been going on for years, passed down from one generation to the next like a curse descending and continuing until it subsided and took root again. There were many ways to fight. The law for one, but also with optimism and kindness.

Without greed, there would be no famine. Without fear, there would be no discrimination and no need for mass graves or Irish gangs. The actions of some produced the reactions in others.

Mila told her in one of their conversations that she could use magic to create possibilities, but each person had to make their own decision. People invested in the ideas that they took ownership of. Her magic created the atmosphere, but change came from within them.

Is that what happened to her? Events in Arizona transformed her from a closed and unhappy person. Circumstances thrown at her caused her to dig deep and find a strength that she never knew she had. Whatever pushed her there—destiny, fate, or magic—she was grateful.

## Chapter 37

With the search warrant in hand, agents served and swarmed the Cumberland facility, boxing current files and taking out boxes of archived files. Employees stood by in shock. One of them had called Richard Cumberland because he showed up quickly, ready to do battle, along with two of his goons or bodyguards as he liked to call them. Two of the officers and agents made quick work of sidelining them. Tom had driven into town to be a part of serving the subpoenas.

Jaxon smiled when Cumberland got in Matt's face. Matt appeared patient until Richard took a swing at him. The raging man went down faster than he knew what hit him.

"That's one way to shut the guy up," Jaxon told Matt as he stopped to talk to him.

"I'm a patient man, but he punched and missed. Mine didn't." Matt folded his arms across his chest. "We got the jump on them, which means they didn't have time to destroy records. Especially since the letter advising them not to destroy records that we sent hasn't had time to arrive yet."

"I flipped through the calendar on Cumberland's desk, and you might be interested in this entry." Jaxon showed Matt a name written next to a time.

"Tamara Campbell—that's an interesting turn of events. She comes to see him and winds up dead in a few days. We might need to take him in for questioning along with his goons. Troy, the man over there"—Matt pointed him out—"his prints ended up on a couple of pieces of evidence, including on Tamara. I find that noteworthy. Don't you?"

"Yes, attention-grabbing like Sanders and Cumberland having dinner together. It could be an innocent coincidence, but I have my doubts. I think we're about to find a few connections between them that might surprise us." Jaxon frowned, his fist clenching at his side. "I want to know which one shot at Peyton."

"Steady, old boy. Remember, they have to swing at you first." Matt grinned, walking away when Kip called him.

"Jaxon and Tom," Matt called to them. "You need to hear this. I had Frank lead his dog through the lumber mill with some of my officers. Go ahead, Gary. The phone is on speaker, and Kincaid and Maxwell are with me."

"Frank's dog hit on a couple of places. Radar's first hit was several wooden crates they were getting ready to ship out from the warehouse at the mill. Imagine our surprise when we found a couple of kids in two of them that we opened. We're checking them all as we speak. A few of the crates had several pounds of cocaine hidden among the merchandise. I have no idea about the exact amount by eyeballing it, but street value has to be high. Based on the discovery, we decided to search the boxcars with lumber orders ready to ship. To our surprise, we found more people. They spoke little English and were terrified. One boxcar was filled with laborers holding their sales receipts among their papers.

I doubt they even knew they had been sold. The lumber mill seems to be a front for drug and human trafficking."

"Thanks, Gary," said Jaxon's boss, Tom Maxwell.

"Jaxon and Tom are heading your way. I'll wrap up here. Keep me updated. Looks to me like Richard Cumberland and his associates have some questions to answer. I can't wait to hear what they have to say. I want to see them squirm."

Once they arrived at Cumberland's office, Gary took Jaxon and Maxwell on a tour of what they had found. They had confiscated records from the office. Cumberland's operation had gone undetected for years. Why now? Peyton's quest for answers began an escalation of events. Her dreams about the murder victim, the ghost at the school, and the missing girls built the tension. Cara's connection to the Indian reservation opened a whole new direction. Who knew that a journal written at the time of the potato famine in Ireland could be a part of solving a case in the present. Once again Jaxon had to face the idea of policing on a different level.

At least he had found evidence today, and the law could take over from here. He and Peyton made a good team. She could see the big picture, and he could reason out the facts in a way that the law could understand. People would be going to jail, and others' legacies would be rewritten. He was cool with that.

"I love this part of a case," Jaxon said as he stood beside Frank and Gary. "Evidence starts to come together and tell a story of what happened."

"Matt says the same thing." Gary leaned his hip against the corner of the receptionist's desk. "For a while, you feel like you're flying blind, and then bingo, then you can connect the dots, and you can see."

"Unless of course you have Jessie or Peyton working with you. They see the big picture, and then you have to prove it." Frank chuckled. "Radar is helpful at that point."

"He sure is." Jaxon patted the dog's head. "I can't wait to see which suspect sings first. I'll catch you back at the station. I have an appointment at the school after lunch."

"Sounds good. We'll be finished here soon and head back to town. Later, man." Frank nodded at him.

Jaxon walked out to the car. He saw a couple of agents and police talking to a few of the employees. For now, the mill would be closed. They had to be worried about their jobs or more if they knew what was taking place and didn't report it. One person's actions tended to affect others.

\*\*\*\*

There seemed to be a strange atmosphere at the school today. Nothing had happened yet, but Peyton sensed an undercurrent. Tension had been building all morning, and she found herself constantly looking over her shoulder. At least the kids were being good. Aides were working with a few of the younger kids with their projects for the walls. The beauty of teaching these kids was she never knew how any art project would go, but the children loved creating their masterpieces. In their eyes, they were perfect and often would praise each other's projects in their own unique way. The world could learn a lot about kindness and acceptance from these special children.

She would be content to work here all the time if

only she could figure out the negative vibes. Mr. Avery seemed to be a good man along with most of the staff. She didn't care for Mr. Sanders' attitude, but she had no beef with him.

Suddenly, Mr. Avery announced over the speaker, "We have a Code Red. I repeat, a Code Red."

Peyton jumped into action, locking the doors, and, with the help of the aides, pushed several chairs in front of the door. They rounded up students, wheeling or walking with them into a small storage room away from the windows and door. Code Red meant an active shooter in the school, and this incidence didn't seem to be a drill. Even now she could hear the awful popping sound that seemed to be repeating quickly for what seemed an eternity.

Sirens filled the air. Peyton had no idea what was happening in the halls of the school. In her mind, she saw the dark wolf running down the hall, snarling as he went. She heard someone try to turn the door handle, followed by yelling and more gunshots. Knowing the drill, the school had to be in lockdown, but the police could always get in. The doors held so far, thankfully.

When several shots hit the classroom door, Peyton relived in her mind the feel of the bullet tearing through her side. She shook herself when some of the kids whined, sensing something wasn't right. Bless her aides—they worked in tandem with her to reassure them the best that they could. She had no idea how long they had been hiding, but she knew the moment the shooting stopped. It became quiet. Eerily silent. The smell of sulfur whiffed under the door. Peyton stood up to stretch her legs. Her nerves on edge, shoulders tense, she strained to hear any sounds coming from the hallway.

From where she stood, she could observe the wall clock as the hands ticked off the seconds, then minutes, not daring to move from their hiding place. She wanted to know what had happened, and at the same time, she didn't.

"Remain in place," the principal said over the intercom. "Police are clearing the building room by room."

"I wonder if everyone is okay." Betsy, one of the aides, stretched her arms behind her. "I've never been more scared in my life."

Peyton heard the key turn in the door. "Is everyone all right?" Kenny asked when he pushed the door open, clearing the chairs as he went.

"Back here." Peyton waved at him. "We're good. Shook, but doing fine."

"You can get your kids ready for the bus. I'll let you know when you can move them. We have a couple more rooms left to check."

She walked over to him. "Are all the kids okay?" Her body tensed. She was afraid to hear the answer.

"Rooms are still being cleared, but I can safely say that Principal Avery's quick action saved lives."

Kenny leaned close to her. "The biggest loser today seems to be the building and a lot of people's nerves. Units are still checking in, and we have a few people unaccounted for. Right now, that's all I know." Kenny walked out of the room.

"Thanks," Peyton called after him, then got to work gathering the kids' belongings and settling them. They would be ready when they could move them to the bus.

Kenny checked back in about ten minutes later. "Hey, Peyton, I thought you should know all the children are fine and accounted for. The only casualties were a teacher and a parent. Their status is unknown, but they are en route to the hospital. We have two deceased suspects."

"Thank God, the students are all safe." Tears filled her eyes. She began moving her kids as soon as the all-clear sounded. She rode on the bus with them to their parents, crying every time a child was reunited with their parents. After witnessing moments like this on the news, how strange it seemed to be living one.

****

Jaxon's heart was in his throat when he saw the damage at the school. He heard the calls on the radio on his way back into town and rushed right over. Two ambulances were pulling out of the school parking lot when he raced in. When he got into the building, he saw two bodies in the hallway and more bullet holes and casings than he had ever seen. Two automatic weapons and high-capacity magazines were close by the victims. The crime scene would take time to process.

"Jaxon, she's okay." Kenny came and stood beside him. "I'm amazed that none of the students were injured." Kenny went on to explain what he knew at this point. "The front doors are locked once school is in session, and everyone including parents must buzz in. When one of the office personnel saw on the camera two men approach the school, the principal alerted staff and students to a Code Red, and the school went into their practiced lockdown. Many lives were saved."

"How'd they get in?" Jaxon glanced at him.

"They shot their way, as you see from the doors. The two victims in surgery are a teacher and a parent. They were in the teacher lounge talking and were caught off guard. I guess feuding would be a better description. Neither one of them had guns. Although, from what I understand, there is no love lost between them."

"Have any of them been identified yet?" Jaxon asked.

"Not yet. We're working on that now," Kenny told him.

"Thanks, I'm going to take a look around." Jaxon walked into the office.

After stopping to talk with Mr. Avery, he had a better idea of what they were looking at. He continued to walk down the hall until he reached Peyton's classroom. The door had several bullet holes. Imagining all the memories the gunfire must have triggered in her, he shuddered and stood in the middle of the room quietly and still. The kids must have been in the middle of art when plans had to be changed. He tried to visualize their morning.

The principal and staff needed to be commended for the plan they had devised and practiced. The safety policy worked, and today was proof positive.

He couldn't take his eyes off Peyton when she walked in the door. Assessing her face, making sure for himself that she was okay, he opened his arms.

She rushed into his waiting arms and hugged him tightly and sighed.

He could breathe again. "Are you okay?" He rubbed his hand up and down her back.

She gulped, and tears began to flow. "Yes," she

whispered against his chest.

"You've had a rough morning." He brushed her hair from her cheek with his hand.

"It was awful." She sniffed and swatted at the tears rolling down her face.

He shuddered and pulled her tightly against his chest. "I think I aged a few years when the call came over the radio."

"You and me both. I need to leave." She lifted her head and glanced at him. "They want us to clear the building. The authorities want to process the scene."

"Do you want me to drive you home?"

She shook her head. "No, you need to do your job." She gazed into his eyes. "Thank you, for being here. I wanted to see you."

"It's hard to let you out of my sight. I'll call you at some point, sweetheart." He walked with her to her car.

"Are you going home?" He opened the car door for her.

"I'll stop by the store. Jessie has probably heard, and I need to show her I'm okay."

He pulled her into his arms. "I'm thankful you're safe." He kissed her and watched until her car was out of sight.

****

"Well, sister, we did what we needed to do. Aelfric is crippled but not defeated yet. We have more work to do before we can say it's over."

"I know I shouldn't feel this way, but when all the bullets were flying, making sure they didn't injure children was quite exhilarating. Each one robbed Aelfric of a victory and exposed him to more light." Elida flittered about, darting in and out of the classrooms.

"We have another stop, sister. Hurry!"

\*\*\*\*

Peyton pulled into an open space in front of the store. Jessie came running out of the store when she saw her. "Are you all right? It's all anyone can talk about today." She wrapped Peyton in a hug.

"I'm better now. Honestly, after walking through the halls and seeing all the bullet holes, I have no idea how no one was killed." She shook her head and walked into the store. "I don't think I'll ever forget the sound of the bullets hitting my classroom door. I lived through memories and tried to calm my kids at the same time. My aides were amazing."

"I've had a quiet morning for the most part, but the phone has been ringing off the hook. People need to talk, I guess." Jessie hugged her cousin again, swiping at the tears forming in her eyes.

"I can understand. Once the shock wears off, you have to try to make sense of a senseless act." Peyton stood at the counter and straightened the bookmarks in the basket. She noticed Jessie give her an odd look. "I need to keep my hands busy. I cried every time a parent hugged their child when they were reunited."

"I would've too. Busy works for me, but you're putting them in upside down, and I'll be fixing them later." Jessie smiled at her.

"Sorry. I may be a bit distracted. Frankly, I don't know how the door remained closed much less standing. You should see where the bullets riddled the wood. Amazingly, we kept the kids safe, and that is all that matters."

"Yes, to both." Jessie smiled and patted her hand.

"Distracted and amazed. I would be acting the same way. Worrying about your students took the incident up to a whole other level. I'm glad you and your kids are all okay." Jessie wiped the tears spilling freely from her eyes and hugged Peyton. "Call Grams and tell her you're okay. She's called several times."

Peyton sat in one of the cushy chairs and called Sadie. She heard the concern in her voice. "I'm okay, Grams, don't worry," Peyton told her.

"Even though you had to be scared, I'm thankful you're fine. Someone was looking out for you, dear." Sadie sniffed.

"Yes, they were. I will stop to see you tomorrow. Love you."

"I love you too. You girls be careful. Promise me."

"We'll do our best." Peyton disconnected the call. "Thank you," she whispered to Mila who had to be somewhere nearby.

"How is Grams?" Jessie asked while walking over to where Peyton sat. She squeezed Peyton's shoulders.

"Worried. I think the two of us give her more stress than she needs."

"I hear you. I could live with less myself." Jessie sat across from her in the small reading nook.

"One can wish." Peyton smiled at her. An hour later the quiet was interrupted when a bullet hit the front window, spraying shards of glass on the book table, followed by the bell above the door ringing. When Peyton turned to look, she knew this wasn't one of the moments. Stress was the least of their worries. Survival was the word that came to mind. "Jess, follow my lead." She called the station, putting the phone on the chair when she stood and picked up one of the crutches. "Hi," she whispered when Joe answered. "Listen." She put the phone on speaker.

"May, I help you?" Jessie walked toward the man.

"There's a dumb question. It doesn't deserve an answer." The man waved a gun around, shooting the gun in the air. He grabbed her arm and began to twist until she screamed.

"Put down your gun, and let's talk this out." Jessie winced when he struck her cheek.

"You had to stick your damn nose where it didn't belong. I've been told to deal with you and shut you up permanently, if you know what I mean. Consider yourself warned." He turned the sign on the door to closed. "Backroom, both of you." He poked Jessie in the back with the gun. "You're going with us," he yelled, poking her harder this time. "You too, missy." He waved the gun in Peyton's face.

"Ouch. We're moving." Jessie cried out.

"Lady, if you think that hurt, wait until I'm done with you. I'm sorry to have to kill you both. It's a damn waste of beauty." He snarled. "It'll be a pleasure for the trouble you've both caused."

Peyton leaned on her crutches and limped with a bit of added drama to slow their progress. She glanced at her cousin and mouthed the number one. When she got to three, she leaned her weight on one crutch and spun around on her good leg. She kicked the gun out of his hand, knocking it to the floor and under a chair. Wincing, she lifted the crutch and whacked him on the head. Jessie used his distraction to pull his hand behind his back and up. The man's curses fill the air.

Joe and Kip raced in the door in time to see it all. "Nothing left to do here." Joe cuffed the man while grinning at Jessie. "You'd both better be ready for a lecture on taking unnecessary chances."

"You may be good at this, but I know two guys who get stressed about it. Still, we may need to call for you as a backup when there's trouble." Kip chuckled. "Jaxon warned me to stay clear of your lethal leg. I see why. I can add a crutch to that list too."

"Another window has to be replaced. My insurance company is going to get upset about one more window shattered, which means my premium will be going up again. Darn." Jessie frowned at the broken window and the glass on the book table.

"Matt said not to worry about the window, Jessie. He already has a guy on the way," Joe told her. "He made a calculated guess your window was a victim."

"Speaking of Jaxon, where is he?" Peyton asked. "I thought he was at the school."

"Several agencies are working the school which freed him up to interview suspects. We have another one to add to the mix. I hope this is the last of them and their surprises."

"The thugs maybe but not the surprises," Peyton muttered under her breath.

"We'll get this scum out of here for you when the officers arrive to take him to jail. Don't touch the glass yet. Joe and I will process the scene, and then the store's all yours."

"We appreciate it." Peyton walked to the front of the store and watched Kip take the suspect out to the waiting patrol car.

This had been a day for the record books. She could go a lifetime without another day like this. The next case would belong to Jessie. She wouldn't say it out loud since she didn't want to jinx anything. Hey, it worked for Jessie when she said the next case was all hers. For now, she would keep her thoughts under wraps, simply between her and the powers that be.

Chapter 38

Peyton didn't see Jaxon for the next few days. He kept busy putting together the evidence and interviewing suspects. The school had to close while the crime scene was processed. After the shooting both the teachers and students needed the time off. The teacher was indeed Mr. Sanders. Both he and the parent were recovering from their wounds, but it would take their minds longer as she knew all too well. The days off gave her a chance to help Jessie at the store, catch up on her editing, and get ready for her trip to Arizona with Jaxon. He kept telling her he had something important to tell her, but it had to be in person and not over the phone.

She had gone to the doctor yesterday, and today she wanted to finish Cara's second journal. Cara seemed to finally be finding happiness, and each page Peyton read built a ray of hope in her heart. People can survive through challenging times and even thrive. Her family found new life again with Cara's marriage and children. Cara's mother embraced the gift her daughter had been given because eventually one of her dreams brought Brenna home to them again. Not literally at first, but it gave them a glimmer of hope that she was still alive.

A few months later they weren't completely taken by surprise when Brenna walked in the door. Sold into slavery and taken out West, Brenna eventually escaped and made her way home to them. Traumatized by all that had happened to her, she was alive but in need of her family's love. It would take her a while to be herself again. Other Irish girls weren't as lucky.

She had only the last few pages to read. Life seemed to be a crazy mixed bag of emotions at times. Peyton reached for her ringing phone.

"What did the doctor say?" Jessie asked.

"My leg is healing fine with no muscle or tissue damage. And thankfully, there's no infection either. My knee is bruised and will heal fine. Yay!" Peyton answered.

"That's good. Are you getting excited about your trip?"

"Yes. I found a pretty dress yesterday to wear to the service." Peyton's eyes lit up as she described the dress to her cousin.

"I'm bored. Matt's been busy, and I haven't seen him since the day my window was shot out. He calls, but he is working all the time. We should go to dinner."

"Sounds good. Jaxon is busy too. He calls and tells me a few things every night but not much. He's always this way when he's trying to wrap up a case. Last night he said that they are presenting Tamara's case to the DA. The state representative we visited that day hired the hit on us. He told me that Jeremy had been accurate when it came to who was on the list. Many were investors in Cumberland and were named associates."

"Matt said the same thing. I guess we stirred him to anger on our little visit. Matt wasn't happy that I never told him about our meeting."

"Jaxon lectured me about our harebrained idea."

Peyton chuckled. "Who do you think Aelfric shifted into as a human?"

"I have no idea. Who?"

"I'm not sure yet, but I'm working on it." Peyton leaned back in her chair.

"Why Blue Cove?" Jessie asked.

"This may sound odd, but my guess is it's the age-old battle of good versus evil, only with an Irish twist. Mila and Elida versus Aelfric."

"You won't find that in the police report," Jessie muttered.

"No, but real, just the same. Who is to say what's behind a crime that goes unseen. We've seen enough to understand that. What's in a person's mind when they kill someone? Not light or love, that's for sure." Peyton stood and wandered to the window, looking at the cove. "I can't help but wonder where the next adventure will take you."

"You think there will be another adventure? Why me?" Jessie sputtered.

"It's your turn, that's why." Peyton laughed.

Peyton and Jessie decided to go to the inn for dinner when Katie told Jessie that Matt was keeping her new husband way too busy. She hadn't laughed this much in weeks. It was the perfect end to a quiet day, until the three of them opted to go to the attic and return Cara's first journal.

Peyton opened the door and went in first, followed by Jessie. Before Katie could get in, the door slammed in her face, and the doorknob wouldn't budge.

"Quit goofing around and let me in," Katie yelled, knocking on the door.

"I can't get it opened." Jessie yanked on the knob

only to fall to the ground.

Peyton extended her hand to help her cousin up. "Looks like there is something only we're supposed to see. I wonder what it could be." She still heard Katie complaining on the other side of the door.

"Let's find out fast. Katie will break down the door if she has to." Jessie grinned at her. "I'm looking for a screwdriver. Hold your horses," Jessie called through the door.

"Well, hurry up, or I'll break it down," Katie yelled at them.

"See, I told you so," Jessie declared.

Peyton went one way, and Jessie went another, and they met at the armoire in the middle of the room. The doors were opening and closing at a rapid rate. Feather boas, hats, and vintage clothes fluttered in the winds created by the swinging doors. "Not very subtle, is it?"

"Remember when I couldn't get the drawer to budge?" Jessie's jaw dropped, and her eyes opened wide. "Look at it now." She pointed at the drawer that slowly opened before them.

On one corner of the drawer sat Elida, and on the other Mila smiled at them. "You have seen the space, dear girls." Mila waved her wand. "The place where the veil between the worlds opens. Most only see it when they leave this one behind."

"Take a deep breath, my dears. Give yourself time to adjust to the events that make little sense to you now but are pictures of what is beyond the door. A battle for light versus darkness, and love over hate. Look and take your fill. The invisible is only a breath away."

The scene they watched in the drawer took them from Ireland through the events of the past several days and ended when light filled the room with faces of thousands whose voices could be heard.

"Write their stories. Their light is not extinguished even though they are no longer visible. They journey on beyond the veil and are only out of sight." The drawer slowly closed, and the light retreated inside.

"We will be leaving you. Aelfric is banished for a season," Mila called.

"Will he return?" Peyton's voice softened.

"If hatred and darkness return, he might find a breeding ground again. But the roots are cut, and it is doubtful he can build his kingdom the same way again. His power has diminished. He's a forsaken fairy with no place to call home."

"I know he took the form of a wolf, but what human did he shift to?" Peyton asked.

"Think about it, dear. The answer will come to you. Ta, ta, for now." Mila fluttered in circles, followed by Elida weaving a trail of golden dust and sparkles. "We'll be back if ever we're needed."

"Darn, I wished they would've told us who it was." Jessie walked to the door and turned the knob. It opened on the first try.

"It's about time." Katie stood tapping her foot. "I'll check the attic out with you another day. Dylan texted, and my hunky husband is on his way home." She walked down the stairs. "I'm going to have him look at that stupid door," she muttered under her breath.

"Another day sounds perfect." Peyton closed the door behind her but not before she saw Mila blow her a kiss.

Later Peyton would dwell on the events of the night. At the moment, she wanted fresh air and Jaxon.

At least fresh air could be found easily enough. She put on her jacket and followed Jessie out the door.

"For once I'm speechless, but that doesn't mean wordless. I'm going home to write. Love you, cous." She hugged Peyton tightly. "We'll talk tomorrow."

"Good night." Peyton followed the path to her cottage.

\*\*\*\*

Jaxon rubbed his temple after another long day and evening. He had to race to get his end of the case wrapped up before his trip. Indictments were finished. Suspects were in jail and had their arraignment dates. Finally, he would have the weekend off because of the trip, but it would all begin again next week. There was one major surprise that no one had seen coming. One that wouldn't be written in any of the reports, and one that he wouldn't have believed if he hadn't seen it himself. He wondered if Peyton knew.

He had missed seeing Peyton and holding her in his arms. Talking on the phone wasn't the same. He would have loved to have seen her face when she told him about the scene in the attic. Placing the finished paperwork on Matt's desk, he walked out to the car.

"Hey, sweetheart, I'm giving you fair warning. I'm on my way over, and I won't take no for answer," he said the minute she answered the phone.

"I'll be waiting." She ran a brush through her hair as she talked.

"We have a lot to talk about. See you in a few," he told her.

He pulled into the space beside her car. If he weren't so damn tired, he would have run to her door. She held it open, watching him all the way. Damn, she looked good. He pulled her into his arms, kissing her face and burying his hand in her air. "I've missed this most of all," he whispered in her ear.

He took her hand, closed the door behind him, and led her over to the sofa, pulling her into his lap. "Tonight, we talk about the case because tomorrow we have other news to discuss."

"All right. First, I wanted to tell you about a dream I had." She told him how she saw everything fitting together.

"You're spot on, babe." He tightened his hold on her.

"Did you find out who shot at me?" she asked.

"I did, and I promise I'll get to it. Let's start with Cumberland and Associates. Richard Cumberland's lumber business was a front for drug and human trafficking, as you already know. The associates listed are none other than Mr. Sanders, a town council member, a state representative, and a senator to name a few of the high-profile folks. Of course, you already know how I feel about your visit to the congressman. Sanders, according to Principal Avery, had several complaints lodged against him by the parents of students in the past few months. A few of the kids came home sporting bruises from where he grabbed them. Sounds a bit like the boarding school practices, doesn't it? The school board was investigating him and was about ready to issue a ruling. Nerves were getting the best of him. He could see his dreams of taking over for Avery one day going up in smoke." His hand rubbed up and down her back.

"Did he shoot at me or vandalize my room?"

"No. That would be beneath him. He told

Cumberland who had one of his men mess up your room and leave the notes for you to find. His thugs tried to run you over, shot at you, and followed me. Of course, someone killed Tamara Campbell when she started connecting the links of the missing girls and the boarding school. One of his goons meant to kill you and Jessie that day at the store.

"Ray Cumberland and Sanders' great-great-great-grandfather were connected, and it seems that connection has been kept generationally—a bit like a mafia family. I'm amazed how long the corruption went on. How many years it spanned and how many lives were destroyed because of the Cumberland legacy we are only beginning to find out."

"Hmm. A dynasty of darkness surrounding a family." She toyed with the collar on his shirt. "What happened to the missing girls?"

"Some were murdered, and many were sold into slavery and sent to other countries. The FBI is trying to trace the whereabouts of the girls from the records of sales. The same was true with the Indian children at the boarding schools. The people found in the boxcar were destined to other states and Canada. One good thing that has come from it is the tribes can bury the children on the reservations when the bodies are released, and talk about restitution has begun."

"Oh, that's good. Cara would like that." Peyton smiled.

"We'll never know how many girls were murdered, but they found several bodies buried where Tamara was found. Some of the corpses were in better condition than others. We have staff that is willing to testify against Richard. It's such a big case, spanning so many years, that the DA has convened a grand jury."

"Why did they murder Tamara Campbell?" Peyton asked. "Mila showed us, but I want to know what you found out."

"Tamara had relatives that came over during the famine. She was tracing her ancestry when she learned about Brigette Campbell who went missing. This was about the time when Cara's sister went missing. We found that bit of truth in one of her notes. What she learned sparked her curiosity, and off she went. Her appointment with Rep. Holland was the catalyst for her murder. Ray Cumberland was told, and he wanted to put a hit on her, but someone else did the job first. Cumberland's family had suffered its own loss due to the Irish mafia, led by a man named Aiden. Remember Aiden was Brigette's fiancé at the time she went missing. Ray had taken Brigette, and Aiden found out. Ray Cumberland's daughter was abducted by the Irish gang and never seen again. In an eye for an eye scenario, Aiden forced her into a loveless marriage. Ray's only son was filled with hatred."

"Let me guess. His son is where Aelfric began his reign using whoever he could get to do his bidding. He appeared as a wolf in dreams and faded in and out where his actions were directed by people. But in our time Aelfric took the human form of Rep. Holland. Am I right?" she asked.

"Yes, I didn't see that one coming. How did you guess?"

"The way Tamara was killed suggested it was up close and personal. Not like a normal hit. The fact she was stabbed suggested anger directed toward her. The fingerprint belonged to the thug who had to bury her and cover up his mess. Representative Holland's ancestry can be traced back to Aiden and a child he never loved. You can see how anger and hatred opened the door to a generational crime spree." She shook her head. "My father was influenced by the hatred, and my grandmother wasn't."

"Peyton, it's still hard to believe. But I knew the minute that Holland was merely a man. He had no idea what had happened to him. Aelfric faded into the background in defeat."

"How do you charge him with murder when it was a pooka that did it?"

"That's the main question, isn't it?" Jaxon held her hand. "He was a member of the group that benefited monetarily from the drug and human trafficking. He's guilty in my book. After all, he opened himself up to the crime, and Aelfric took over from there. Holland has been angry for a long time. The town council member and one of the officers in Matt's department covered up for them over the years. This has gone on for over a hundred years. Generationally, passed from father to children in a pact of hatred and anger."

"Another strange one, if not for the record books at least for our own." Peyton squeezed his hand. "Reba kept saying we had to stay true to the Irish roots of the case, and I can see why. It wouldn't make sense without them."

"I find it hard to make sense of it all. Oh, I get the generational hatred, we've seen it often enough in history, but a fairy turned bad, who became a pooka that could shift between man and a wolf is too much for my brain. I will say the tribal leaders helped a bit with that."

"You won't miss any of the trials, will you? This should be a feather in your cap at the Bureau." She ruffled his hair and pulled away to glance at his face.

"No feathers. Only doing my job." Heat tinged his face.

"I think you're blushing," she teased him, fluttering her lashes at him. "Seriously, you're good at your job."

"How about you?" he asked.

"*Moi*?" She placed her hand on his chest.

"Did you find the answer you were looking for?" He grinned at her, pulling her hand into his. "I know you're doing that on purpose."

She rolled her eyes at him. "I found some of the answers, and I'm satisfied for now. How long my curiosity is mollified only time will tell. I found out Cara worked here as a cook when the inn was a smaller version. She and her husband became the owners eventually. That's why her diaries were in the attic."

"That's cool and shows her connection to the inn." He hugged her. "What's next?"

"I have no idea. I do know I'm going to Arizona with my handsome guy tomorrow who keeps telling me he has something important to tell me, and I can't stop thinking about what it might be." She played with his shirt collar and ran her hand through his hair.

"It's all good. At least, I hope you think it is. I'm still in shock."

"Now you have me worried." She scrunched her face.

"Don't be." Her hand was driving him nuts.

"Well, that's easier said than done. Are you sure you don't want to tell me now?"

"I have something else I've wanted to do for over a

week." He took the time to show and tell her exactly what had been on his mind.

She sighed, giggled, and sighed again between the nibbles, kisses, and sexy words whispered in her ear.

Chapter 39

Peyton's suitcase stood by the front door. She couldn't wait for Jaxon to get there. Most of the night she couldn't stop the thoughts racing through her mind. She was more than ready to hear what was so important that he wanted to wait until today to tell her. She carried Cara's second journal to read to him the last few paragraphs. She wanted him to feel the hope that normal life was possible because Cara had found one.

Honesty made her admit that this past case seemed stranger than the one before, and yet she had learned about the family she did not know of. Her heritage took center stage—beliefs, legends, and mysticism. After talking with Sadie, she filled in some information. She understood that when Sadie gave her the fairy nightlight, she was giving her hope.

Jaxon's car pulled in beside hers. She opened the door to watch him walk up the path. All the strange new experiences in her life, starting with EJ Dawson's ghost, had brought this man into her life. She found the whole probability of ever meeting him next to impossible if it hadn't been for a trip to Arizona during a heatwave. Call it Destiny, her friend, fate, or magic, everything aligned to make it happen, and she had no regrets.

"Hi," she said.

"Hi, yourself. Are you ready?" he asked.

"Yes." She slipped on her coat and grabbed her purse.

He lifted the handle on her suitcase and pulled it out the door. "A perfect day for flying. I want to take you to my favorite place in the city for lunch before we catch our flight."

"I'm happy to get away for a few days. Too much has happened. I have to go back to work next week at another school until the building is repaired. I'm not sure I'll ever see the school as a safe place to work again. That gunfire shattered more than windows. The bullets had shattered the happy place for lots of children. I can't imagine what I'll feel when I walk through the doors again." She placed her hand on his shoulder. "At least, I'll have the next few days to sort it out."

The drive to the city seemed longer than normal. Jaxon seemed preoccupied, and she was left with too much time to think. Another one of her flaws: once her mind got going, there seemed to be no stopping her mind from various rabbit holes.

"You're quiet. Is everything all right?" He glanced at her.

"Yes." She opened her purse and took out the journal. "Do you mind if I read this to you?"

"Have at it. I like when you read to me." He checked his side mirror and moved over into the left lane to pass a car.

Peyton read a few pages talking about Cara's marriage to a man she had met on the ship a few years before.

*He loves me for who I am with all my oddities and flaws. I'm not sure if this ability will pass to one of my girls, but if I had to venture a guess, I would say most likely. I tell them stories about my homeland and of the magic that lives there. They love to hear about the little people and the fairies who live under the mounds of earth. Their auntie Brenna, who has the gift too, visits them often. She loves to play with the girls which at times seems sad. She would be such a great mother, but I doubt she will ever marry. She suffered greatly at the hands of the man who bought her. Still, she seems content to be home, and we are so glad she is.*

*To any of my family who reads this one day, I want to say, stay true to who you are. Alanna taught me believing in something bigger than yourself is important for survival. I understand why now. That belief has encouraged me to be a better person. I refuse to let hate fill my heart, even if at times it would be easier. I have managed to live a normal life and find myself to be quite content.*

"Her story gives me hope." She closed the journal and put the book back in her purse.

"I can see why. Not only are there more folks like you, but she managed to live a regular life despite it all. I'm happy Brenna made it home. I can't imagine what she went through."

"Sometimes life seems harder for some. You wonder how they manage to survive all that is thrown at them." She glanced out the passenger window at a car they passed as they entered the city.

"I hear you." He smiled. "Wow, a parking place. This rarely happens. Must be my lucky day." He got out and opened her door.

Peyton loved the restaurant's atmosphere, an impeccable blend of old world and urban charm. A perfect fit with the city. Holding hands, they followed the host to their table.

****

Jaxon's fingers tapped on the table until their waiter finished taking their order. He reached across the table for her hands. "I have something I've wanted to tell you. It's still new to me. You're such a big part of my life, and I want to know what you think."

"I'm listening."

"I got a call from a Joseph Kingston from the Logan and Kingston Law Firm. It seems that Elliot Dawson changed his will after EJ died. Kingston told me that Elliot thought of me as a son. I never knew that. To make a long story short, he left me five million dollars." He studied her face as she responded to what he told her. "I want to know how you feel about it."

"Truthfully, it's a lot to wrap my head around. You're an instant millionaire." She smiled at him. "It seems you found the pot of gold at the end of the rainbow after all." Her voice softened. "The question is how do you feel about it?"

"I'm shocked, to say the least, but I'm warming to the idea. I have to sign the paperwork when we are in Arizona. I hired an attorney and a financial advisor. I don't want the money to change who I am, and I don't plan to let it. Can I count on you to keep me in check?" He saw her nod. "I know having the money can make life easier in some regards."

"Does your family know?"

"Yes. I wanted my dad's advice on what to do." His hand stroked hers. "How you feel is important to me. Can you live with the idea of us being wealthy?"

"Us?" she asked.

"Yes, us. I can't see my future without you being with me. I love you, Peyton. I hope it's not too soon to tell you how I feel." He lifted her hand to his lips. "Everything I've done since moving here, including buying the house, is with you in mind. I want to fall asleep at night with you in my arms and wake up next to you in the morning. I love you."

She touched his cheek. "I've hoped and dreamed that you would say those words to me. And now that you have, they are sweeter than I could have ever imagined." She gazed into his eyes. "I love you too, Jaxon. I'll take you rich or poor as long as you want me."

"Wanting is the easy part. I've wanted you from the first moment I saw you." Her brows shot up in question. "Well, almost from the first glance. I love you, sweetheart. Our happy ever after is only beginning." He leaned across the table and kissed her.

## A word about the author...

I am a multi-published, award-winning, Amazon best-selling author who writes romantic suspense with a touch of the paranormal. I enjoy writing fiction. The character development, their stories, and the twists and turns in the plot intrigue me. Once I let the characters loose, I can't wait to see where they take me. I'm hooked from the first words on the paper, and I have to keep writing to see how the story ends. Layer by layer I build it until I come to the happy conclusion.

I live in Colorado with my husband and family. I am a member of the RMFWPAL (Rocky Mountain Fiction Writers Published Authors League) and have enjoyed becoming involved in my community as one of the many authors living in Colorado. I invite you to read one of my Blue Cove Mysteries and see for yourself why Blue Cove is a special and unusual place. http://www.ionamorrison.com